Sister Mary Baruch

Read All of the Sister Mary Baruch novels from TAN Books

Volume 1: The Early Years
Volume 2: The Middle Ages
Volume 3: Vespers
Volume 4: Compline
Volume 5: Wintertime

Sister Mary Baruch

Volume 3

Vespers

Fr. Jacob Restrick, O.P.

TAN Books
Charlotte, North Carolina

Cover design by Caroline K. Green

ISBN: 978-1-5051-1484-3

Published in the United States by
TAN Books
PO Box 269
Gastonia, NC 28053
www.TANBooks.com

Printed in India

To Sr. Maria Slein of the Holy Eucharist, O.P., in thanksgiving for her 75th Jubilee as a Dominican cloistered nun on the Solemnity of the Assumption, 2017

Preface

Love songs, both contemporary and classic, are usually not addressed to Roman Catholic nuns, especially ones living within the silence and mystique of a cloistered monastery. But Sr. Mary Baruch has struck a chord with many people, and on her sixtieth birthday she received a musical card which featured a recording of this love song first recorded by Jimmy Dorsey and His Orchestra in New York City in 1941, but here sung to her:

> In this world of ordinary people Extraordinary people
> I'm glad there is you

In our world and the popular culture of our day, the life of a cloistered nun is indeed extraordinary. Most people never get to visit a monastery of nuns or get to know a cloistered nun in person. And then they met Sr. Mary Baruch.

Sr. Mary Baruch was known as Rebecca Feinstein in the world. She grew up in a close Jewish family in New York City's Upper West Side. Becky came out of the turbulent years of the 1960s not like most people did, but to the surprise and chagrin of her family, she became a Roman

Catholic. We met her in these "early years" and followed her through the circumstances of her conversion and entrance into a Dominican cloistered monastery in Brooklyn Heights, New York.

Becky became Sr. Mary Baruch of the Advent Heart in 1970. In the early years and later in the middle years of her daily cloistered life, we see in her an abundance of grace given in times of crisis, death, and reconciliation with her family.

Her community at Mary, Queen of Hope Monastery is ordinary in many regards, living the spiritual life in its daily repetitious round of prayer, work, study, and community life. Because she and her monastic community are totally fictitious, they experience together some unusual happenings within and outside the regular common life of a contemporary monastic community. One meets the panoply of Sisters in her community, many of whom are quite extraordinary women!

The joys and sorrows, emotions and exuberances of these Sisters are the same human struggles we all experience. But, because of the unique circumstances of the cloistered life, perhaps they are lived more intensely.

Many thanks to the fine editors of this new volume: Sr. Mary Dominic, O.P., of the Monastery of Our Lady of the Rosary in Buffalo, New York, and my two Dominican Brothers, Reginald Hoefer, O.P., and Nicolas Schneider, O.P. Their untiring help and expertise make it all possible! Special thanks to all who have contributed their support, suggestions, and fondness for the "life and times" of Sr. Mary Baruch and the Sisters at Mary, Queen of Hope Monastery.

In this third volume Sr. Mary Baruch finds herself again in the heart of her Jewish experience of Passover as a fulfillment of her union with Christ. The trials we all experience become something "blessed" because it is all God's doing—His Paschal Mystery being lived out in our lives. In your living the life of faith, may you find a companion in Sr. Mary Baruch and hear God say to *you*: "In this world of ordinary people, extraordinary people, I'm glad there is you."

Fr. Jacob Restrick, O.P.
Solemnity of All Saints, 2017 Dominican House of Studies

Part One

In the cloister the nuns devote themselves totally to God and perpetuate that singular gift which the blessed Father [St. Dominic] had of bearing sinners, the downtrodden and the afflicted in the inmost sanctuary of his compassion. (Constitutions of the Nuns, 35)

Overture

The third act of the Sister Mary Baruch story is set in late 2005. But our narrative opens years earlier, before the new millennium, when Pope John Paul II would lead the Church across the threshold of hope. In her prayers and avid journaling, Sister remembers those years in all their joy and sorrow. Like the theater masks of Comedy and Tragedy that hung on her childhood bedroom wall, they speak loudly of the tragic death of her younger sister, Ruthie, and the exalting joy of reconciliation with her mother and older sister. That leaves only her older brother, David, with whom she is still alienated and for whom she prays.

As the new millennium approaches, Sr. Mary Baruch prays to find in herself the faith, hope, and charity which will carry her into the first decade of the twenty-first century. Looking back, she realizes that despite the stability of her monastic life, there are lots of changes, new people, and new experiences that have filled these years with grace. There will continue to be lots of "pass-overs" from old to new. Is she able to hold it all together? Or does her life come crashing down like the Seder plate in the haunting dream of her childhood?

As the curtain rises, Sr. Mary Baruch is enwrapped in the Lord's arms: in other words, she is sound asleep in her choir stall in the chapel . . . it is 10:30 p.m.

One

Chametz: Leaven

Clean out the old leaven so that you may be a new lump, just as you are in fact unleavened. For Christ our Passover also has been sacrificed. (1 Cor 5:7)

"Good afternoon, Miss Rebecca," came the polite and friendly greeting of Eli, our daytime doorman. His big white teeth spread across his round face as he opened the door and half bowed to us like Mama and I were royalty. He wore spotless white gloves, and his shoes were big and shiny.

"Good afternoon, Mr. Eli," I returned with a likewise broad smile for a six-year-old. "Tonight's my night," I blurted out, as if he and the rest of the whole world knew that.

"Tonight's your night, is it? Do you have a date?" Eli's smile got even bigger than big. His front white tooth had a gold tip on it which sparkled when he smiled. I had never seen anyone with a gold tooth; right in front too.

"No, Mr. Eli," I blushed three shades of red. "Tonight is Pesach, and I get to ask the questions."

"And what questions might that be, Miss Rebecca, that has you all excited?" Eli was walking with us to the elevators being very inquisitive, Mama looking on with a kind of royal detached interest. The doorman usually didn't accompany the residents to the elevator. But I figured he was genuinely interested in my stardom; besides, Mr. Eli always took time to talk to me, unlike some of the other doormen.

"You know. The question that begins our Seder, isn't that right, Mama?"

"That's right, Becky, now tell Mr. Eli what the first question is. I'm sure you have it memorized."

"Oh, I do." Looking up into Mr. Eli's chocolate brown face, his bushy eyebrows arching slightly to show he was listening intently, I recited my line very professionally (so I thought): "Why is tonight different from all other nights?" The elevator doors opened with its usual ping, Mama and I stepped in very quickly, and Eli waved to me.

"Everything will be just fine, Miss Rebecca, just fine." And he gave his usual laugh as the doors closed, and we were riding up.

"Why didn't Mr. Eli know the question?" I said out loud, somewhat mystified as I had been practicing the questions for weeks.

"Eli isn't Jewish, Becky; he won't be having Pesach."

"Oh, that's too bad." I was lost in my thoughts, as much as a six-year-old can be lost, I guess. I thought everybody had Pesach. I felt sorry for Mr. Eli, at least as long as the elevator was moving up to our floor where I think everybody had Pesach. I couldn't wait till sundown tonight. All the big holy days seem to begin at sundown; I wonder why? Sundown must be a favorite time for God. Rabbi Lieberman once told us in Hebrew class that the ancient Jews marked the time of sunset when the evening star appeared; it was called the *vespera*.

Tonight, when the *vespera* star would appear, Mama would light the Passover candles. I was so excited, not because I would be wearing a new cyclamen pink dress with a Chantilly lace collar and not because I got to sit next to Papa tonight, but because it was my first time to ask the questions. It always goes to the youngest child in the family, and it was my time now. I was not the youngest; my little sister Ruthie was only three years old and although she was capable of stringing words together in a pleasantly audible way, the nonchalant formality of the setting called for a more grown-up questioner. Rebecca Abigail Feinstein could do it just right. Mama even said so when I practiced it for her. Next year I'll sing the question in Hebrew, if I practice enough. That's what Mama says: "Such a blessing our Rebecca who can sing the questions in Hebrew."

My older brother, Joshua Hiram Feinstein, had done it for as long as I could remember, and now it was my time. I knew in my child's mind that it was a question first asked in ancient times, like over a hundred years ago. It was *Pesach*... Passover. Poor Mr. Eli, I thought, as Mama lifted me up to touch our mezuzah, and walked into our apartment. It smelled so clean and everything looked so tidy.

Last night Joshua, Sally, and I searched the apartment for any food that had leaven in it. I wasn't sure what "leaven" was, but we couldn't have any of it in the apartment when Pesach began. Mama called it "*chametz*". She always sounded like she was clearing her throat when she pronounced it: "Haaah-mets." And we always found chametz in the oddest places. I found a whole bagel under the throw pillow on Papa's chair. Sally, my older sister, found half a loaf of the challah from last Shabbat under the pillow of Mama and Papa's bed. I wondered if they ate bread in bed every night, and why couldn't I? Papa said we shouldn't be surprised to find chametz because he prayed that we would before we went searching for it. And I knew that God always answered Papa's prayers.

Papa always found crumbs on the kitchen counter, and would brush them into a wooden spoon with a feather, which he kept just for this night before Pesach. He said the feather used to belong to his grandfather—imagine!

This morning Mama had us put all our chametz with Papa's crumbs in a brown paper bag, and we went with her to the trash cans in the basement where we threw it all away. She said next year if we're in Jerusalem, we'll burn all the chametz. Actually she would say that every year. And every year we'd still be on West 79th Street in New York, in the cellar. Some of our neighbors burned their chametz in the backyard. I don't know why they didn't wait to go to Jerusalem. We didn't have a backyard, of course, but there were lots of trash cans in the basement, which was closer than Jerusalem. I think there was even one can marked "for chametz." Maybe the super took it to Jerusalem.

Tonight was also different from all other nights of the year because tonight Mama would use our special china which only came out once a year, at Pesach. I learned when I was older and could understand these things, that it was porcelain china from Austria. All the plates and serving bowls were creamy white with a staggered trim in blue. Some had

Hebrew words on them too. They once belonged to Mama's grandmother, my great-grandmother, whom I never met. She must've been very old when she gave her Pesach china to Mama, but I don't remember. It was before my time.

I was also a little nervous. I wanted Papa to be proud of me. Papa would be sitting at the head of the table with his tallis on and his special yarmulke only worn for the eight days of Pesach. He was like our own rabbi. He could even sing the *Kiddush,* the blessings, in Hebrew, like Mama would do every Friday night when she lit the candles for Shabbat. After all these years, I can close my eyes and remember the sound of Mama's voice praying with her eyes closed, and then she'd open them on the Sabbath, and greet us: "Good Shabbos."

When I was six years old only David, the eldest, could help Mama set the table with her special porcelain china. There were even coffee cups and saucers and a gravy boat, and a special enameled pottery Seder plate with indented places for all the special foods. Even the matzah was in its own *matzah tosh*, or decorated bag. I love matzah—it's like a huge cracker!

Then, in a flash, I was twelve years old helping Mama and Sally set the table. I was nearly a teenager. I was wearing a cyclamen pink dress with a Chantilly lace collar, and saying, "I hope Ruthie doesn't make a production out of singing the questions tonight." Ruthie had been asking the questions at Pesach for four or five years. She could be very dramatic about it, which made Josh and me giggle till we saw Papa's solemn frown telling us to be quiet and listen. The rabbi hath spoken.

Sally and I were setting the table. I had the large Seder plate, which was heavy even when empty. Our Seder plate was different from that of all our neighbors, and Mama was so proud of it. She said it would go to Sally when she got married. Sally was always afraid to carry it, but I wasn't. I was just carrying it in from the kitchen, and I saw Eli sitting at our dining room table, big as life, smiling at me, his gold tooth flashing like a light. "Good evening, Miss Rebecca. Everything's gonna be just fine, Miss Rebecca, just fine…" I jerked with surprise, and the plate slipped out of my hands and crashed on the dining room floor.

***

I suddenly jumped awake in my choir stall and scared poor Sr. Mary Angela half to death. I must have hollered out loud when I jumped, hearing the smash on the hardwood floor. It was only a dream, only a dream. My pocket rosary was on the floor…again. I was dozing in choir and dropping my rosary a lot recently, or so it seemed. "*Poor Sister Mary Baruch,*" they'd be thinking, *"falling asleep during her rosary again."* The Sisters were used to it, but young Sr. Mary Angela was new. It was her first time to be alone with me in the chapel. She was doing her "hour of guard," that is, adoring our Eucharistic Lord in the beautiful, but plain, weekday monstrance. It was close to 10:45 p.m. I had remained in the chapel after Compline. I liked that quiet time in the semi-darkness to pray a rosary.

It is so quiet at night. There's a calmness that settles over the monastery in the evening, unlike the other times of the day. If I stay after Compline, I like to lean against the Heart of Jesus and just rest there in the silence. I don't use a lot of words anymore to thank Him for everything that happened that day. He knows what's in my heart; I just sit there and lean against Him. Most nights I'll take my pocket rosary out because I know there is a special quiet presence of Our Lady with me at that hour too. And I like to hold my rosary in my hand; it's like a connection to her. Sometimes I imagine her walking the hallways of all the hospitals comforting the sick and dying. She hears our "*Hail Marys*" over and over, and she knows each of us personally and individually. I surmise that it is a special gift given to her at her Assumption into Heaven. I suppose or wonder if it's one way we will participate in the Divine Nature: being able to listen to people's prayers and knowing each person on an individual basis, all at the same time. Our Lady not only listens to the rosary being prayed by children in every language all over the world, but also old folks in nursing homes (especially those who feel abandoned and alone), and even old nuns who fall asleep in the middle of the second decade. She is the Comforter of the Afflicted for every age and state in life. I still stay in choir and silently pray my rosary, and sometimes I fall asleep. But I remember that night years ago, maybe because Sr. Mary Angela still reminds me of it. I also remember that dream—which is unusual, as I don't remember most of my dreams.

I also remember that I asked Our Lady to look after Mama who was still living alone in our old apartment on West 79th Street. She never made it to Jerusalem to burn her chametz, and I doubted she would even try now. I was especially grateful to Our Lady that Mama came to visit me. After a few years she took to hiring a car service to come to

Brooklyn Heights, which was so much easier than the subway. "Such a blessing, Moshe's Car Service, they give an old lady a discount!" Mama was still sharp as a tack, and I think actually enjoyed being a regular at the monastery. The extern Sisters all made a fuss over her, and she would bring them pastries and/or chopped liver from Zabar's, Mama's favorite Jewish deli on Broadway and West 80th Street.

And I'd often pray for my agnostic brother, David, that he would find it in his heart to visit me. And I'd pray for my older sister, Sally, that she'd find her way to the Lord. At least she visited me when she was in New York. She lived on Lake Shore Drive in Chicago overlooking Lake Michigan. Mama, David, and Sally. Sometimes I'd give them each their own decade. And every night I'd remember my little sister Ruthie whose sudden and tragic death brought Mama back to me. Funny how that happens.

It's also funny after all these years of praying the rosary, most times I don't really meditate on the mysteries, but think of the graces of each day, or people, or "things" to pray about. And sometimes, I just lean against the Heart of Mary or the Heart of Jesus. After all these years, I knew our life—*my* life—was all grace. Grace upon grace, every day. And I know the graces come to me through Our Lady from Our Beloved Lord. The older I get, the more I realize how much she was part of my life, even years before I became a Catholic: Our Lady of Grace and Mother of Perpetual Help. And sometimes I'd fall asleep—like that night when I dreamed of Eli and the Seder dish and scared Sr. Mary Angela half to death.

Sr. Mary Angela was a novice in her first year. She darted over to me from her prie-dieu. "Are you all right, Sr. Mary

Baruch?" She spoke louder than our usual chapel whisper. I must've been curled up and nearly falling off my seat, when I hollered and jumped. The crash seemed so real!

"I'm fine, dear, thank you. Blessed be God. I must've dozed off a little and was having a strange dream. I'm sorry if I disturbed you."

"You didn't disturb me." Her whisper was a little softer. "I was kind of dozing off myself, a little, and you hollered, and…"

"Would you pick up my rosary for me, Sister, it's here on the floor." Sr. Angela was a lovely young girl, but like so many of the aspirants and young girls coming to see our life, she loved to talk a lot.

"Were you having a nightmare?" Sr. Mary Angela of the Inquisition had no qualms about carrying on a conversation in the chapel after Great Silence, something we would never have done when I was a novice some thirty years ago. Nor would we ever ask an older Sister anything personal. We probably wouldn't be having the night guard either. "Were you having a nightmare?" she repeated a little louder presuming my hearing was going.

"No, Sister," in my best low-keyed whisper, "I was dreaming about a night different from all other nights, when I was a child."

Having retrieved my brown wooden rosary, and sitting next to me like we were outside on the swing, she whispered: "Was it your senior prom?" And she giggled. She's asking me about my senior prom? Oy.

"No, it was not my senior prom. Goodness. Sister, I don't even remember my senior prom." I knew she was just being nice. The young Sisters like to tease us older Sisters, again, in a way we would never have done when we were young Sisters. I could never imagine saying such a thing to SCAR—Sr. Catherine Agnes Russell. She was my postulant mistress who taught us all about the enclosure, being on time, doing what we were supposed to be doing, when we were supposed to do it, and most of all keeping silence. She was quick to correct and very rarely, if ever, smiled. Sr. Anna Maria and I called her SCAR, because one always felt wounded after Sr. Catherine Agnes taught obedience and humility.

I knew Sr. Mary Angela was just teasing me, and I could have played along, but we were in the chapel after all, and it was getting late. "I'm off to our cell, Sister, now you pray for me, okay, that I won't have any more scary dreams; I wouldn't want to wake up the whole dormitory."

Sr. Mary Angela thought that was hysterical and laughed out loud till she saw the shock on my face, and she became very repentant right there in front of our "week-day Jesus," as Sr. Gertrude would refer to the monstrance, more than the Lord. I smiled back to reassure her I was not upset. "Pray for my old bones," I said, making my way out from behind the form in front of our seats. I was still thinking about the night different from all others. I really did drop the Seder plate. To think the memory of that still comes up in my subconscious…

Walking down the cloister alone at night brings back many memories and a comfortable spirit of peace and contentment. The Great Silence settles over the house like a London fog. I was just twenty-five years old when I entered, and I have grown old here; or maybe, I should say, I'm on my way to growing old. There are still Sisters much older than I; they still live the life as best they can. We haven't had as many entering the last ten years, but we have some wonderful young Sisters too, coming to our way of life from the crazy world they have grown up in. They probably don't realize it, but it's all the work of grace.

Outside in the garth—our monastic garden surrounded on four sides by the silence of the cloisters—there's a light in front of the life-size stone crucifix which stands in the middle. It's a beautiful sight to gaze on, especially in the winter and on very dark evenings when the moon is waning or the sky is filled with clouds. It's stark. It says all that one can possibly say about our life because it's in union with Him and Him crucified. I know that can sound very pious at times, but His night, the night before He died, was a night different from all other nights. I guess the Scripture scholars debate whether it was a Seder the Lord ate with his twelve apostles in that upper room, or just a kind of festive meal. But I believe it was indeed a Seder. Even Mark's Gospel has two disciples ask Jesus where they should go to prepare to eat the Passover with the Lord. There is a set "order" (Seder) to the accounts from the washing of the disciples' feet (in John's Gospel only) to the Kiddush (blessing) over the cups of wine, and breaking of the bread without chametz. It was the Feast of Unleavened Bread.

I was passing the door to our infirmary where the elderly and infirmed Sisters live, and sometimes a young Sister if she is recovering from the flu or an operation. It is one of my favorite places in the whole monastery because of the Sisters who are there, and I still go there often just to be with them and help out however I can. Someday, I know, I'll be a permanent resident, and we can all talk about our senior proms, if any of us remembers them.

But I don't live in the infirmary...yet, although I'm showing signs of getting ready. Picking up dropped rosaries and tying my shoes are not the easiest things for me to do any more. The rosary is dropped because of arthritis in my left hand, but I try to offer it up. The shoes are hard to tie because, well, I'm just a bit plump.

Sr. Anna Maria used to tease me and laugh at my trying to tie my shoes from a seated position. I am on the verge of asking for soft comfortable loafers, but I really like the black gym shoes we're allowed to wear now. No longer black lace-up oxfords with thick heels; now we wear Nike and New Balance! Vatican II footwear for nuns. I'm also grateful we don't have to wear stockings anymore; good ole white socks are much more comfortable. Such a blessing, the renewal!

We have a rocker in the cloister walk outside the doorway leading to the infirmary. It's not as nice as Squeak—my own antique rocker that I had rescued from the curb on Amsterdam Ave and 75th Street about forty-five years ago! I dragged it home, cleaned it up, stained it with a nice maple brown varnish, and sat in it to read. It squeaked. But I came to know the Lord in that squeaky rocker. I was doing *Lectio Divina* and didn't even know it. I'd read my *New Testament* each night, and close it and think about it, and I began to talk to Jesus about what I was reading, and what He was saying to me in those books.

When I left West 79th Street and my family's home, I took Squeak with me to the East Side. Greta Phillips shared her apartment with me during that crucial time in my life. We went to Mass together every morning, and both worked at the New York Public Library. She had entered the Church a week before me; we met in our Instructions Class at St. Vincent Ferrer Church on East 65th and Lexington. She was a retired missionary; she and her Lutheran husband, Pastor Paul, served for many years in Mozambique. She was a wonderful roommate and dear friend although she was almost thirty years older than I. My sister Ruthie said she looked like Grace Kelly. Dear Greta…

When I left for the monastery, I left Squeak with her. And after nearly twenty-five years, when Greta died, she left me Squeak. I offered her (Squeak) to the infirmary, but Mother Agnes Mary said I should keep her in our cell till I went to the infirmary myself.

The rocker outside the infirmary door is a more modern distant cousin of Squeak. It doesn't make a sound when someone is rocking back and forth. It has thick corduroy covered pillows for the seat and back, and wider arms than Squeak. It's comfortable for tired old bones, so I indulged myself and had a seat which had a beautiful side view of the stone crucifix in the garth. It was a kind of memory rocker… it lent itself to taking a sentimental journey, as the song says.

Christmas Eve 1999 was a night unlike any other. For one, it was the first time we had midnight Mass at eight o'clock. It got changed, maybe because two older Sisters complained in the kind way older nuns have learned to do. It goes back to Mother John Dominic's days when we would only have a couple cookies and Christmas eggnog after Mass and then hurry off to bed. Mother John Dominic taught us that joy is a great ingredient in Dominican life, often expressed in what we call a *Gaudeamus* (Latin for "we rejoice"), which is a community "party" after a big liturgical celebration. So if we had Mass earlier, the elderly Sisters argued, we could have more time for our *Gaudeamus*. (I am among the "elderly" Sisters!)

With the end of 1999, not only would a new century begin but a new millennium. The year 2000 would be a big one for us as Mother's second term would be coming to an end, and we would be electing a new prioress. Besides that, a lot of things happened or changed in 2000.

For one thing, we never used to get personal gifts at Christmas. For years, on Christmas morning, everyone would find an orange, bright as California sunshine, at her place in the refectory, along with her Advent mail. Later in the day, a candy cane, and maybe a lovely holy card of the Holy Family. Thirty years later, now we get gifts from the Prioress and her council like Santa and his elves.

The Christmas of 2000, we got new sheets for our beds—colored ones with prints and form-fitting, which made us feel so modern it came up in Chapter whether we should keep them. The argument against them was that they were too worldly, too distracting, too pretty, too expensive, and too unbefitting to a nun practicing austerity.

The "*sed contra*" cleared it up by calling on the transcendental of beauty in which we lie down and sleep comes at once. This time it was the younger Sisters who won the argument. We kept the sheets and were so used to them by Ash Wednesday that it gave some of us something to give up for Lent. They were kept in the common linen closet, so again each one was free to choose what sheets she wanted.

At the beginning the colored sheets were a novelty, but the plain white seemed to be most used. I used to try to take the purple and pale violet sheets during Advent and Lent. Being "liturgical" erased the guilt of being "worldly."

In 2002, after our eight o'clock-midnight Mass and Gaudeamus, we went to our cells and found small poinsettias at each door. These were truly lovely and brought a little Christmas into each of our cells.

Rocking in my time-machine-rocker, I thought about how things had certainly changed in the last thirty-five years, since I knelt at the enclosure door and it opened to welcome me inside. I still remembered it like it was yesterday. The community was all standing there in their black cappas, holding lighted candles. They were all smiling, even "one tough old bird," an expression I learned from the tough old bird herself; SCAR once called herself that when we were chatting about the old days!

At one Chapter, when we were discussing changes in light of the renewal of Vatican II, it came up to do away with this little welcoming ritual and just introduce the new postulant in the *De Profundis* line before meals. But it didn't pass; we've kept the custom, and even added chanting another psalm along with Psalm 122, the pilgrim psalm which welcomed the newcomer: *"and now our feet are standing within your gates, O Jerusalem."* Little does the newcomer know how much *chametz* will be burned up, or burned *out* of her in the year ahead. Spiritual leaven puffs us up with pride, like we're on steroids.

My entrance way back in 1970 was not dramatic except to me—and I'm sure to Papa who was there to "give me away" because he thought of himself as the father of the bride.

Much more dramatic was Sr. Mary Mannes, ten years later, who was just plain Charlotte when she entered. She was kneeling at the enclosure door as prescribed, on her knees, smoking a cigarette (not prescribed). I even knew which brand: it was an Old Gold spin filter, which my sister Sally smoked.

When the enclosure door opened, Charlotte ceremoniously stood and squished out the half smoked tote in a cut-glass ashtray which she ceremoniously handed to Sr. Paula, our extern Sister standing beside her, her mouth agape with disbelief. The prize, however, went to Mother Agnes Mary, who had a lovely smile as she watched this little farewell to cigarettes ritual. Charlotte stood up, and Mother took her by her now empty hand, and said: "*Let our prayer rise before You, O Lord, like incense in your sight.*"

Charlotte never had another cigarette (that I know of) and became a model novice and an excellent cook. When she received the habit, she received the name of Mannes, St. Dominic's blood brother who entered the Order. I guess Old Gold spin filters were ole Charlotte's *chametz*...burned up and lying in an ashtray.

When I was librarian, Sr. Mary Mannes checked out a book of the writings of Edith Stein. She didn't know much about her but was curious about her being Jewish and dying in Auschwitz. I told her she would find her early life interesting. She used to smoke Gauloises, those strong (awful) smelling French cigarettes, when she drank wine and beer in the local pubs and argued over philosophy. Sr. Mannes smiled and said: "I never knew anything about philosophy."

Christmas Eve 2004 was different from all other nights as my gift after our midnight Mass at eight o'clock was two new cushions for Squeak. They were called Evening Champagne with the Blues because they were a light beige corduroy with dispersed powder blue stripes throughout. Squeak never had it so good!

We aren't keen on decorating our cells; we are not a college sorority house. Simple and plain is the preferred décor, but a hint of beauty was allowed, like our colored sheets and maybe a plant. Over the years we acquired blond wooden blinds on the windows, which muted the color in the room at various hours of the day. Squeak was really a prayer-chair and could be turned to the corner where I had hung an icon of Our Lady of Perpetual Help, and to the left of that, Ruthie's comedy theater mask. I inherited it from Ruthie after she died. Well, I didn't really inherit it as much as I took it. Mama insisted, and I didn't want to spoil the mood of reconciliation between my mother and me which Ruthie's death brought about. Mother Agnes Mary thought it was quite extraordinary but since our cells are very private, she said I could keep it. It is older than Squeak actually. When we were kids Ruthie and I shared a bedroom. We were great fans of the theater and the movies, and we had gotten the theater masks, comedy and tragedy, as a joint Chanukah gift. Ruthie pursued a life in the theater. Rather eerily, the tragedy mask fell off our bedroom wall just after Ruthie's death.

Many years ago now, Ruthie offered them to Sr. Gertrude because of Sister's great love for the theatre and Ruthie's career in particular. Sr. Gertrude was very touched by the gesture, as was I. Ruthie had great awe and wonder at Sr. Gertrude because she had given up Broadway for a monastery in Brooklyn Heights. She gave up the lights of Broadway for the obscurity of the "Narrow-way." Sr. Gertrude thanked Ruthie and told her that she had her own theater masks—a picture of the Sacred Heart of Jesus. Mercy, joy, and suffering.

I'm happy to have them in our austere cell with pale violet sheets. They feel at home here, and they help me remember to pray for Ruthie, whose poor life was comedy and tragedy. She was starring in a musical revue at Penguin Pub in New York's Greenwich Village when she died of an overdose of crack cocaine. She was quite the comedian, I'm told. Comedy and tragedy. It's also ironic how much my meditation has flowed from those masks, as our life is certainly happy and sad, or full of joy and sorrow. Our Lady is one whose soul rejoices in God, while her Immaculate Heart was also pierced with a sword. The masks have been "converted" from the theater to the monastic life. Sr. Gertrude certainly fills that analogy out to a tee, but many of the Sisters do in their own way.

Ruthie thought our life in the monastery was "sad." But I've often thought how few are the people who really get to know and love and share life with others as intimately as we do. It can often be an intense life, especially in the early years when one is learning all about oneself, but it's not sad. The interior world is a whole universe we've got to explore with its own landscape. Hills and valleys, mountains and deserts, and lots of flat plains without much of a view. It has moments of comedy and sometimes tragedy, but we "travel along, singing our song, side by side." And we burn up our *chametz* in the flame of love of the Sacred Heart.

Well, enough of this sentimental journey. I got out of the infirmary rocker and made my way around the cloister corner. Passing the refectory, I was tempted to make a quick peanut butter sandwich, but I prayed to St. Michael the Archangel and the temptation passed. I can't imagine why, with the world in such a precarious state. St. Michael must be on overtime, and he saves me from falling into the pantry. I guess I still hang on to some old *chametz.*

Two

Shanah Tovah: "May it be a good year"

The Lord said to Moses and Aaron in the land of Egypt: This month shall mark for you the beginning of the months; it shall be the first of the months of the year for you. (Exodus 12:1-2)

It was a crisp September day nearing the even crisper and more colorful month of October. We have one apple tree in the professed garden which yields a crop of crab apples. Vespers in the autumn is one of my favorite times. The days are getting shorter, and the shadows are longer in October, pulling us into November. I rarely go outdoors after Vespers, as I like to spend the forty-five minutes we have for meditation in the chapel. But one day I went out to smell the air and to sit on the wooden bench we have under the crab apple tree. I was going to meditate on St. Mark's Gospel when Jesus was hungry and went to the fig tree that didn't have any figs, and He cursed it. I was distracted when a crab apple fell and hit me on the head. I didn't curse, but picked myself up and went to the other bench not under the tree. But then I started thinking about apples, and why Mark made it a fig tree. Fig trees were all over Israel, but this allegory (we learned it was an allegory in our class on St. Mark's Gospel) would have been even more significant if it had been an apple tree, taking us back to *the* apple tree in the Garden of Eden. I like apples…a lot. Maybe that's another reason I like this season of the year so much because we get a whole variety of apples in the refectory…Red Delicious, Macintosh, Golden Yellow, and some new ones with names I never heard. I closed my eyes and could see a whole orchard of apples. I can smell them hanging heavy on the limbs waiting to be picked. Row after row for as far as I can see, an orchard-world, and silent except for the rustle of the September wind and a distant row of bee hives swarming with hundreds of worker bees bringing honey nectar to their queen. And the words *Shanah Tovah* came to my mind. The Jewish new year wish.

It was September 29 and I remembered that Rosh Hashanah began at sundown; I was sitting outdoors in the "sundown." And I remembered my excitement as a kid getting ready for the Jewish New Year. Mama had a whole bag of beautiful apples. Some would be sliced and arranged around the plate with a bowl of honey. "May the new year be a sweet one for you," Mama would say, handing us each an apple slice dipped in golden honey that she bought at Zabar's. Sally and I would help her slice, dice, and chop up more apples and dates and pomegranates for some sumptuous dessert Mama was making…red wine honey cake with plums. Or one year, I remember, Papa's favorite: an apple bourbon Bundt cake. David would joke that Jews eat enough apples for Rosh Hashanah to keep the doctors away for a year. Funny, since he became one. Ruthie would be all excited because there would be a gift for each of us after dinner, to top off the apple cakes and braised brisket with plums and port wine which Mama let soak overnight.

It was a joyful holiday, but maybe not as much as the secular New Year on January 1 which we also celebrated, of course. Joshua, the most religious of the Feinstein kids, reminded us that Rosh Hashanah begins ten days of making amends for the sins and mistakes of the past year, and ends with our high holy day, Yom Kippur. He would be the one to go to synagogue after dinner because he wanted to hear the shofar announcing the New Year. I think he always wanted to be the one to blow the shofar, but it never happened. He had heard the sound of another horn after he graduated high school, and the mournful sound of "Taps" replaced the sound of the shofar for him. May he rest in peace.

That evening after Compline, I was still in my Rosh Hashanah mind, praying for Mama and David and Sally. It's a new year beginning in the Jewish world, but I was thinking about the one we were living in right now. The year 2000. It had been an interesting year. It would be four years come Advent of 2000 that Ruthie died. Crack cocaine and probably a mixture of other so-called "recreational drugs" mixed with recreational alcohol was the cause of death.

Ruthie always wanted to be a star. Since we were kids we studied tap and ballet; Ruthie persevered through both and moved on to modern dance. Sally and I had a year or two and left the dance floor bereft of our *un-fancy* footwork. Ballet was not for me, but I loved tap dancing; however, it was Ruthie who pursued a career on the stage. I don't think I ever shared the brunt or brutality of it all. She was a romantic to her bones, and always talked the talk as so many theater people do. Her visits became less frequent over the years, and stopped entirely when she was actually in a show.

Gwendolyn Putterforth, my godmother and faithful friend, would keep me up-to-date on Ruthie's escapades. Gwendolyn owned and ran Tea on Thames on the Upper West Side, near Columbia and Barnard College. After I entered the monastery, Gwendolyn and Ruthie became friends, and Gwen even hired Ruthie to work at the tea shop. The customers loved her because she would "perform."

"I say, Gov'nor, you've just come from Ascot, I see, and thought you'd stop in for a spot of tea. What will it be tonight? The high tea triple tray is on sale if you and your bloke here want to spill a few pounds." The gentleman and his friend would laugh, but they could not be sure if it was for real or put on. Nor did they know the triple tray would be on sale by five cents. But Ruthie was good for business, and did well in tips. They believed her to be right out of Mayfair, till Sidney and Arlene Bergman coming from a little off-Broadway theater on the Upper West Side appeared at the table next to the "Gov'nor."

"Oy, such a night this should be? The Bergmans are uptown on the West Side. Hiding from the spotlight no doubt and craving Lady Gwendolyn's apple strudel with extra honey for the New Year. *Shanah Tovah*, darlings, what will it be?"

Sometimes Ruthie would break into a song. She would have liked to sing and dance, but the tables were too close to each other; she could only do a short soft shoe down the open space to end her rendition of "Tea for Two." Customer population grew, according to Gwendolyn, and if she would be absent for a show, Gwendolyn would put a poster in the window to advertise the show. Gwendolyn would hint to me about Ruthie's "drinking" and, less so, about drugs; but I never stopped praying for her.

It was around 1995 or '96 that Gwendolyn bought a vacant loft on Barrow Street in the West Village, renovated it, and opened the first Tea-Shop-Theater in New York: Penguin Pub. It was in October of 1996 that it opened to great reviews. And the Mistress of Ceremonies was none other than Ruth Steinway (that was Ruthie's stage name). She appeared in a Queen Elizabeth the First costume for the opening monologue. Apparently "stand-up comic" was one of Ruthie's specialties, and the audience loved it.

The infirmary Sisters and I were the prayer-backers behind the entire production. They all knew Gwendolyn and Ruthie, of course. Sr. Gertrude, whose enthusiasm exceeded my own, was Ruthie's biggest fan. Gwendolyn came by for a parlor visit about three weeks before opening night, and I invited Sr. Gertrude, Sr. Gerard, Sr. Amata, and Sr. Benedict to join me in the parlor.

"I am so honored to meet you all in person," began Gwendolyn. She knew all the infirmary nuns by name, but hadn't actually met all of them.

"We're the Ruth Steinway Fan Club; I'm Sister Gertrude of the Sacred Heart, the fan club's president," chimed in Sr. Gertrude.

"You've got a fan club and a president and all?" Gwendolyn was genuinely surprised.

"Oh, yeth," sputtered Sr. Amata who had forgotten to put in her dentures. "Thithter Gertrude ith prethident by default. Thee's an old thow-girl herthelf, you know."

"Thank you, Sister, I think Ms. Putterforth is familiar with my credentials." Sr. Gertrude was nonetheless beaming. "We've been praying for *you,* too, dear, that you'd get everything tip top for the opening of Penguins at the Pub." The Sisters all nodded in agreement.

"Penguin Pub," corrected Gwendolyn. "Just Penguin Pub. The top penguin is Sister Mary Baruch's father…"

"Ruben!" they shouted in unison. (I had them well informed.)

"That's right! Ruben still stands at the entrance on a table surrounded with fresh flowers. He's got a bow tie now and little glass spectacles."

"Ith he loothing hith eye thight?" inquired Sr. Amata, whose own eyes were magnified by thick lenses, like the bottom of Coke bottles. She was most sympathetic to anyone with eye troubles.

Gwendolyn was quite on the rebound. "Oh no, Sister, his eyesight is perfect, the glasses are plain glass, but give him an older, distinguished look. His little glass eyes have not blinked in years." And we all laughed. "Ruben is a real taxidermy penguin, in his natural tuxedo, or as Sister Mary Baruch calls it, his habit and cappa."

Sr. Amata wasn't sure why he was determined to take a taxi, and maybe needed glasses to hail one unoccupied. We let her regress into her little conundrum.

"We are in the middle of rehearsals and some last-minute renovations. The theater is like a dinner theater with little round tables on three levels surrounding the stage on three sides." Gwendolyn went on; the Sisters were all ears. "Ruth Steinway is hidden by a curtain in the rear middle of the stage; the lights go down; and our little combo plays a fanfare and the introduction to *God Save the Queen.* The curtain is pulled aside, and Ruth is sitting on a throne, dressed like Queen Elizabeth the First, with a huge shell-like collar rising from a cartwheel Ruff. Her little scepter is actually a microphone, and she steps down and welcomes all her royal subjects."

"And thingth?" Sr. Amata was back on board.

"Yes, she sings the opening number from the Fantasticks, *Try to Remember.*"

"Oh, now let me think," Sr. Benedict loved a challenge. "Was it *There's No Business Like Show Business*?"

"Sister," interrupted the president of the club with a slightly annoyed voice of frustration, "*Try to Remember* is the name of the song by Tom Jones. *No Business Like Show Business* is from *Annie Get Your Gun* starring..." And she hesitated enough for the three of us to shout: "Ethel Merman."

"Well, yes, although it starred Mary Martin first, but good ole Ethel made it a hit."

And we all had a good laugh, before Sr. Gertrude could break into the chorus with her Ethel Merman imitation. I think it helped to relax poor Gwendolyn, who was looking rather bedraggled by it all. She wasn't a spring chicken anymore, as Mama used to say about, well, about anyone older than herself. Gwendolyn was in her sixties when Penguin Pub opened, but she tried looking younger with her ash blonde hair in a sweep, an array of floppy blouses and plenty of costume jewelry, always with a pin or earrings or charm bracelet of penguins.

"I've brought you a box of almond raisin scones fresh out of the Penguin Pub oven this morning." Gwen put a bakery size box on the turn. The infirmary Ruth Steinway Fan Club hummed with delight and anticipation. They thanked Gwendolyn for coming and promised to pray a novena when they found out the opening date.

"And tell Thithter's thithter we're praying for her and her pet penguin," Sr. Amata added.

"And break a leg," said Sr. Gertrude from her newly acquired wheelchair. "Like I did!" And they all laughed, collected the box from the turn and exited stage right, leaving me and Gwendolyn alone, as they knew we'd want some private time. Sr. Gertrude had not broken anything; she was just getting used to being pushed around in a wheelchair. On her good days, she could still do a little soft shoe across the infirmary common room.

Gwendolyn assured me that Ruthie was doing fine. Having a job to keep her occupied was the best therapy going, along with her "program" of course. Ruthie had been through a month's rehab at Smithers, a drying out place for alcoholics. It was like a celebrity holiday for Ruthie. She was able to be in the last group in the East 93rd Street mansion, before they moved to Roosevelt Hospital. Joan Kennedy, Truman Capote, and Ruth Steinway were among its "graduates."

Gwendolyn's assurance was a good try, but I knew beneath it more was going on than she wanted me to know. But I didn't push it. I was grateful Gwendolyn was keeping her eye on Ruthie. I took it all to prayer, which is what we do. We're the pray-ers behind the scenes asking God to bless them all. To let their talent, their music, their song and dance lift up people's hearts and touch their souls. We pray for all those who don't have the time or the desire to pray or who "fall down" when off stage!

I pray every day for my family and remember them in thought at every Mass—sometimes consciously putting one of them into the chalice by name. Ruthie was put into the chalice many times. I worried about her crazy lifestyle, which I didn't know much about, but my imagination could spin out of control if I didn't learn how to keep it in check. I know they had what they called "recreational drugs," especially in the clubs in Manhattan. Ruthie was a smart kid, but I knew she was also daring, and would try anything at least once. Like the time we saw pickled rattlesnake in a goyim deli across from Port Authority. She got a quarter of a pound and ate the whole thing. I couldn't stomach the thought of it! She said it was delicious, and chewy, but maybe too much pickle.

The year 1996 was a tragic year with an almost miraculous ending. Ruthie died from the drugs and other substances in her body, including bourbon. My dear old mother, who had never once set foot in this monastery in twenty-five years, came in person to tell me of Ruthie's death. Gwendolyn had come with her, but Mama was in the parlor alone when I went in on my side of the grille. Such a reunion we had; I cannot describe it.

Mother Agnes Mary was so compassionate and kind to my mother. I was able to go home with her for Ruthie's funeral and to sit Shiva. My sister Sally came from Chicago, and that was another emotional reunion. The *Kabbala* says that *God counts the tears of women.* Well, He had a flood's worth to count those three days.

The year ended with Ruthie no longer in my life, but Mama back in it. Hannah of a Thousand Silver Hairs. Mama was in her mid-seventies then, and she still looked very attractive for her age. Of course, she had been a disciple of Helena Rubenstein and knew how to put her best face forward. As she would say: "Such a face I should have that a little makeup can't help."

After that Mama became a bi-monthly visitor here. It would be unusual for us to have "family visits" so frequently, but again, Mother Agnes Mary had a heart bigger than all outdoors; she was happy my mother wanted to come every other Sunday to see me. In the beginning Gwen would bring her, as we didn't want Mama travelling on the subway alone, but after a couple months, she began coming on her own by car service or cab.

"I should worry about spending a little money on car-fare to see my daughter, the nun?" (I had become her "daughter, the nun.") "But tell me, where have all the nice Italian cabbies gone? I have to repeat three times to the man in the turban that I'm going to Brooklyn Heights, to Queen of Hope Monastery where my daughter is a nun."

Mama would always bring a "*nosh*" for us. "A little something I picked up at Zabar's." Bagels and fresh chicken liver were a frequent "little nosh" but also something a little sweet so the monastery coffee would have something to wash down.

Mama got used to talking to me through the grille. She would like to sit close and whisper like she was visiting someone in prison. Eventually, I brought up the subject of David, my brother.

"You know, Mama, Ruthie's death, may she rest in peace, Ruthie's death has brought us together again. I am so grateful for that. I'm sure Ruthie and Papa are rejoicing in heaven too. And seeing Sally again was a time of…healing." I didn't know what word to call it. I wanted to say reconciliation, but it wouldn't have the same impact for Mama as it does for us. Probably "atonement" would have done. "But, you know, the only person I haven't seen in all these years is David."

"I know, Becky, dahling, such a schlemiel, that brother of yours. But, you know, Sally has talked to him, and he's coming around. For one, he doesn't like that I comeall the way to Brooklyn Heights to see you. 'She should come to you; she's younger; and she did it when Ruthie died.' For being such a brilliant doctor, he's such a dimwit. I tell him that night was the exception, now they keep you locked up, and they let me visit, so who am I to complain?"

"Is that all he says?" I'd heard that tune of his before. Ruthie would tell me when she had seen David that he never understood "this enclosure thing." Ruthie was getting the vocabulary down. Early on, she used to call the grille, the "cage." The guimpe, the "bib", and the turn, the "lazy Susan." She once quipped, "If they made a soap-opera about your life, they could call it *As the Turn Whirls*." And she'd laugh all by herself. I guess it was a play on words with an actual soap-opera.

Mama continued, "Well, he asks me how you look and are you chubby, and do I think you'll stay?" Mama and I both laugh at that.

"And what do you say?"

"I tell him you look as young as you did when you were in college and of course you're going to stay—it's a life-time sentence…and that, no, you are not chubby, but just right, from what I can tell, under all those robes."

"Do you think he'll ever come see me, Mama? I would love to see him; does he look like Papa now?"

"No, he's taller than Ruben ever was—and heavier, really. He's got that little 'beer-belly look' some men get, you know. He's still got his hair, though, and it's nearly all gray now. He looked very distinguished when it was salt and pepper. And his hairline is receded a few inches. Such a good looking man, our David, he should eat better, I tell him, and lay off the beer."

I laughed. I could just hear Mama telling her son, the doctor, to lay off the beer.

"He's very thoughtful, our David, I'll give him that. He lives, you know, in this fancy-shmancy duplex on Third Avenue and 65th Street."

"I know, that's right up the street from St. Vincent's. Ruthie used to say, 'Thank goodness people have complexes, it's given David a duplex.'"

"I know, I know, that Ruthie could rib him about a lot of things, especially all his girlfriends. But David has made it possible for me to keep my apartment, even helps me when I used to go to Boca till Ester up and died on me. And he comes over for dinner once a week, often for Shabbos, so I can light the candles for him, he says." I could hear Mama's voice crack a little. "He never went to shul, not even on Yom Kippur, but he wants me to light the candles for Shabbos, and he holds his hand on top of his head. Go figure."

"Poor Mama," I said, "he's never married and given you grandchildren, and none of your girls are going to anymore either."

Mama sat silent. Her head down, looking at her feet, I suppose. Then she moved a little closer to the grille and looked up through the grate into my face. "I think it's time to let you in on a little family secret." A slight smile began to break across Mama's face. Helena Rubenstein wasn't able to hide the crows' feet that fanned out from around her eyes, especially when she'd smile.

"David is married?" I kind of whispered back through the grille.

"No, he's not married. He's never been married…but I have a grandson. A teenager." She sat breathless for a moment waiting for my reaction. Mama kind of chewed off her lipstick on the corner of her bottom lip. She was anxious about what I might say.

I sat speechless for the moment, letting this news sink in. Mama daintily took a bite of her raspberry rugelach, and washed it down with monastery coffee. I waited.

"Such a bitter coffee you should have to drink, I'm not complaining, but next time I'll bring you some nice French roast from Zabar's." She took another sip. I hadn't said anything yet; Mama smiled and looked through the grille again.

"David never married, but he fathered a child. She was a doctor doing her residency at New York Presbyterian. I don't know how they met, but David was always dating doctors or nurses from that hospital. I met her once, such a beautiful girl to be a doctor. She's Lebanese. Ruthie met her only once too, when they were all home for dinner. Ruthie said afterwards that of all David's girlfriends, she was the most stunning. She had that beautiful natural olive complexion, you know, and beautiful eyes, and pitch black hair. Such a beautiful woman I couldn't imagine as my doctor!"

"And?"

"And she became pregnant. She didn't want to get married. I don't think either of them wanted that; their careers were their spouses, and she was planning to move to Ohio, of all places. Oy." Mama finished off her rugelach before washing it down with a grimace, and went on. "She wanted to keep the baby, and she said she would always keep in touch with David, and the child would know his or her father. And she kept her word. She moved to Ohio; I think it was Youngstown or Akron, one of those towns out there, but came back and took up residency in Long Island. This was good because David got to see his son. He made me promise never to tell you. I don't know why, if he is still angry with you, or ashamed, or just very private. So I've never told you, and I made Ruthie swear that she would never tell you either. I knew she used to visit you."

"And you've met him?"

"Oh, yes, such a fine looking boy he is. He's got his mother's eyes which will break many girls' hearts down the road. His name is Sharbel. Such a name for a boy, it sounds like a cat's name. I've never heard of anyone named Sharbel. I think it's a Lebanese name. I thought she should have named him Danny Thomas; he was Lebanese. But I was so happy to meet my grandson. He calls me *grandmamma*. Of course he's a Catholic, like his mother, but some special kind of Catholic, like Maryanne White."

"Maryanne White? Oh, you must mean Maronite Rite. That's wonderful; there are lots of Maronites in Brooklyn here. They have their church just down the street. And St. Sharbel is a wonderful Maronite saint. He was just canonized in 1979, I think. He was a monk and hermit in Lebanon, and all kinds of miracles occurred after he died, like a light coming up out of the ground where he was buried; and when they exhumed the body, he was completely incorrupt and exuded a sweet smelling liquid." Mama just sat silently listening to all this.

"You Catholics have all the neat stuff. I wonder if Sharbel knows all that."

"Oh, I bet he does, with a saint's name like that. You should ask him about St. Sharbel. Well, I can't believe it… David has a Catholic son…"

"He's a wonderful grandson even without a Bar Mitzvah. And he loves his father, you know. His mother never married, so David's been the only father he knows. He brought him to Shabbat dinner one Friday night, and the boy brought two yarmulkes with him; one for him and one for his father. David wore it without a fuss, just like the old days, I thought. I wished your father was there to see it."

I couldn't help but chuckle, which is not the reaction Mama was expecting. "That's funny after all we've been through, huh? A Catholic son, who's helping David be more Jewish." Mama had to laugh too.

"And not a David, Sol, Irving, or Ruben, but a Sharbel." Mama stomped her foot. "And the boy loves to eat, oy. The four of us went to a Lebanese restaurant for Sharbel's fourteenth birthday."

"How wonderful for you, Mama, you have at least one grandchild. I'm sorry David doesn't want me to know, and I'll keep your secret, I promise."

"Thank you, Becky. I think David is softening a little in his old age. I think he'll come around, and bring me here to see you. Talking to Sally has made a big difference too, and I think he's curious if anything. Besides, Sharbel is dying to meet you. He was thrilled when his father told him you were not only a Catholic, but also a nun. He said he was thrilled to think he had an aunt who was a nun. I think that maybe prompted David to think about things."

Mama would speak of David whenever she'd come to visit. She missed one Sunday due to the weather, and was surprised to learn that we wouldn't be able to visit during Lent, unless there was really something urgent going on.

"Can you talk on the phone during Lent or do they make you keep silent the whole time? I can't imagine not talking for a month. For a month? Oy, I can't imagine not talking for a day!"

"We can talk on the phone, and I even have a phone in my office which I never use, so I'll call you. And yes, we talk among ourselves except on Tuesdays, and on Fridays we don't have recreation and keep a greater silence. Silence is good; you have more silence in your life now than you've ever had."

"Well, I don't have anyone to talk to all day, but I keep the TV on, and Millie Hutner comes over every morning for coffee. And Imogene Levinson pops in once in a while. Her granddaughter, Leah, is giving Imogene gray hair! Poor girl, she lives with her father, after her mother died of cancer, poor thing, and tries to come over to Imogene's every week. You met them, remember? So, I keep myself busy. David calls me every day, I think to check if I'm still alive! And he asks about you all the time—a good sign, I'm sure he's coming around."

* * *

The spring and summer came and went very quickly that year. Mama became a regular visitor. In September of '99, she came with four homemade apple cakes for the community. And after Sr. Paula prepared our Zabar's French roast coffee, Mama pulled out a plastic container full of sliced apples and a jar of Zabar's kosher honey.

"I have a gift for you for Rosh Hashanah," Mama announced as she was putting my apples and honey on the turn. "David's going to come with me next time. *Shana Tovah*, my daughter, the nun."

Three

T'shuvah: Repentance, metanoia, change of heart

...because the heart of this people has become dull—with their ears they barely hear, and their eyes they have closed, so as not to see with their eyes, hear with their ears, understand with their heart, and do t'shuvah, so that I could heal them. (Mt 13:14 on Is 6:9-10)

Afternoon thunderstorms are usually a welcome surprise. It gets dark out, and one hears the distant rumble of thunder like a subway passing underneath your feet; sprinkles of rain sputter outside, and a flash of lightning is seen, and you hold your breath and count, and BOOM the thunderclap crashes over the chapel roof. I was second in line for confession, sitting in the stalls which are designated for penitents who silently go into the nuns' part of the sacristy and to the confessional, which is really an open space between two doors. There is a kneeler on our side, and the door has a screen on it covered with a white linen cloth. Father, of course, is sitting on the other side of the door, his right ear towards the screen.

The thunder made it all feel quite ominous this time around. BOOM.

I liked hearing the rain pouring down on the roof as Father gave me absolution; it's like the grace of the sacrament pouring on our souls in all their brittleness and dry spots. I was halfway through my penance when I remembered I was supposed to be in the infirmary helping the Sisters get down to confession, at least those that could go—unless they would want Fr. Kelsey to come to the infirmary afterwards.

"Father who?" Sr. Gerard said, trying to adjust her hearing aid.

"Father Kelsey, Sister, he's our new Dominican confessor; he comes down from St. Catherine's every two weeks. You went to him last time, remember?" I tried to shout, but I'm never sure these days whether I'm getting through to her.

"Father who?" Here we go again.

"Father Kelsey, Sister, he's our new Dominican confessor; he…"

"Oh yes, I like him, Fr. Kellys. I went to him last time. But I won't go this week; it's raining out."

"It is, isn't it—really hard. But you don't have to go outside, Sister, Father is just in the sacristy confessional. I can push you there…"

"No, I don't have any new sins, although I want to gain a plenary indulgence for my second cousin who died last week, but she can wait; I promised Sister Amata we'd work on a new puzzle." (She and Sr. Amata were avid jigsaw puzzlers.)

"That's fine, Sister, I'm going to check on Sister Gertrude, and then I'll make some nice decaf tea for us all."

Sister fussed with her hearing aid, and waved me goodbye, mumbling to herself something about Tillie, her cousin, who never came to visit her. "She can wait."

Sr. Gertrude was up and in her wheelchair, ready for the trip to the sacristy. She never missed going to the Sacrament of Reconciliation, which used to be called the Sacrament of Penance, or just plain old "going to confession." Sr. Rosaria was already there too, ready to push her. Sr. Rosaria and I nodded at each other and smiled, and Sr. Gertrude was humming a new tune she heard on an album from Taize.

"I'll have the teapot on when you get back," I said.

Sr. Rosaria smiled even more broadly.

"Did you hear that, Sister Gertrude? Sister Baruch will have the tea kettle on for us when we get back."

Sr. Gertrude tilted her head like she does when she's getting ready to sing. "That will be lovely, dear. A reward for getting shriven." And to my utter amazement she sang the opening line of the *Kol Nidre* in perfect Dominican Hebrew chant.

After getting the kettle on, I fixed the cups and sat down at the round table in the infirmary kitchenette, my thoughts wandering, Sister's chant still lingering in my ears…

Yom Kippur was the one holy day that Mama would go to temple. She said it was to hear the sounding of the shofar and the singing of *Kol Nidre* which begins the high holy day at sunset the night before. But I think it was to be shriven, as Sr. Gertrude says. The *Kol Nidre,* always sung in ancient Hebrew chant, very haunting and pleading for God's mercy, marks the Jewish "Day of Atonement." All vows (*kol nidre*) and promises and oaths and resolutions one has made to God are wiped away. It's the closest a devout Jew comes to confession, albeit a "general absolution." It comes at the end of a week—ten days really—of thinking about one's weaknesses, failures, broken promises and "vows". (Kind of like getting a plenary indulgence for the year!) It's a heavy burden we human beings can schlep around—guilt.

For Rabbi Lieberman, I remember, the *kol nidre* was always a form of not keeping a mitzvah, or commandment of the Law. A devout Jew is conscious of being a son or daughter of the commandments, of the Law, the Law of Moses to whom God gave the Commandments, the covenant.

The whistling of the tea kettle brought me back to the table in the kitchenette, with its plastic oilcloth table cover displaying an array of autumn leaves. The "penitents" could be a while, depending on how many Sisters were ahead of them, and Fr. Kelsey tended to talk a little more than former confessors. So I fixed myself a cup of tea from the box of Twining's Earl Grey which was a gift from Gwendolyn, and that I kept stashed in a back corner of the tea shelf.

Thinking back as I sipped my tea…Sr. Rosaria was already a novice when I entered. We weren't especially close in the early years, although we did have a few good laughs, which helped relieve some of the tension. And she was always a wonderful "comic relief" for all the novices because she was so innocent and open about everything. We became much closer after Solemn Profession. I was engrossed in the library for years, and Sr. Rosaria was assistant cook for many years, assistant librarian for a couple years, assistant chant mistress, and an assistant organist.

"I'm a professional assistant," she'd say, "which is just fine because the buck doesn't stop with me. I can always pass it on. I've never been assistant bursar, come to think of it. I think they're afraid I would bankrupt the place." And we'd all laugh.

She was great with the elderly Sisters in the infirmary, and loved baking special treats for them. She specialized in French pastries. One of her words of wisdom is: "One good thing about getting old and infirmed, you'll eat better...and sweeter." We used to joke how nice some of the more disagreeable Sisters were when they'd come to visit the Sisters in the infirmary. We were at the age now when we could reminisce together about the Sisters with whom we lived in our early years, and are now gone. Sr. Rosaria has a great knack for imitating accents and little gestures which marked the uniqueness of each Sister. Sr. Rosaria also has a servant heart; something Mother John Dominic had, our first prioress way back when—and which I believe Mother Agnes Mary has too.

Even before the year 2000, when Mother's term would end in February, there was "buzzing" behind the scenes about who would become our next prioress. I think most of us would not want the job at all, and none of us would campaign for it, unless one did it in an unconscious way. Sr. Thomas Mary, the assistant novice mistress, I think, wanted to be prioress, not because she has or doesn't have (who really knows?) a servant heart, but because her brother was a monsignor in the Brooklyn Diocese. Sr. Thomas Mary was postulant mistress sometime in the nineties. We all thought she'd be novice mistress, but she never was. I don't know if you can say that someone is "too observant." Sr. Thomas Mary was—still is—a model religious. Sr. Anna Maria once said to me, "If the Customary ever got burned up, we'd just have to follow Thomas Mary around to know what we should do." I don't think Sr. Anna Maria meant it in a complimentary way. I know she (Sr. Anna Maria) always made a face at me if Sr. Thomas Mary was assigned to help out in the laundry. She would do it, of course, but always seemed to act as if "assistant-laundry-mistress" (Sr. Anna Maria's words) was beneath her. Sr. Anna Maria had been "laundry-mistress" for over twenty years before she was named sub-prioress.

"I would have loved to have seen Thomas Mary's face when Mother announced that she wanted me to be sub-prioress," Sr. Anna Maria confided to me one day when we were doing dishes in the infirmary kitchenette, chatting about this and that, and slipped into the precarious area of "this one and that one."

Sr. Anna Maria, of course, was an ideal candidate herself, although we'd never use that term. She was a good sub-prioress; she certainly knew the Sisters well, although she was kind of formal with the novices and postulants. They didn't always know how to take her humor. She has a very dry wit and loves puns. She is very clever with words…definitely one to keep an eye on. If we were in the world, I would happily be her campaign manager.

I also liked Sr. Bernadette a lot; she had a wonderful way with the Sisters in the infirmary, and more recently as cook. If it came down to a "servant heart," she would certainly be my choice.

It's possible to elect a Sister from another monastery, but that has never been done here, although we'd surface a couple names each time "election day" was getting close, like six months before! We had an older Sister from one of our southern monasteries come, Sr. Caritas, to rest for a few months with us, and we all loved her. She reminded us (her fan-club, that is, which included me) of Mother John Dominic. Again, we don't campaign for anyone, but Sr. Caritas's name surfaced among more than a few of us. The biggest drawback, I think, was her age, and that she was not a Sister in our community, even though she knew us pretty well. She came here for a rest, and wound up helping out more Sisters than she did in her own monastery. It was like she had to go back to her own monastery to rest from being here! There might have been something of the "workaholic" in her which burned her out, but also kept her going. She died in 2004, the year before her Golden Jubilee.

Even the infirmary Sisters like to buzz about things, at least one in particular, my dear heart, Sr. Gertrude of the Sacred Heart. It was still a month before the election. We were sitting alone together in front of the picture window overlooking our cemetery. There was a fresh blanket of snow on the ground and on each of the gravestones in the cemetery.

"I still pray for Ruthie, you know," Sr. Gertrude said out of the blue. We weren't particularly talking about death, but maybe looking at the cemetery brought it to mind. "I know she didn't always understand our life, and why you were so happy here."

"I know," I interrupted her thought. "She used to think our life was 'sad.'"

Sr. Gertrude chuckled. "I know. But she also saw that the passion she had for the theater was like the passion we have for this life, like you have!"

"Thank you, Sister, but I think you received the Tony Award for that role. Ruthie had a change of heart about us and this place after she met you. That you gave up the lights of Broadway for this…"

"The Narrow-way. Yes, indeed. But I see that passion in you; always have since you were a novice, and I don't mean in your talent, which you are adept at hiding, but in the daily grind. The sacrifices you were willing to make to enter this life and to persevere. And I know it hasn't always been 'coming up roses,' to quote a certain mother of Gypsy Rose Lee!"

I laughed. Sr. Gertrude would quote show people and characters from plays like some of our Dominican Fathers quote the early Church Fathers.

"We older and wiser Sisters like to chat once in a while too, you know. And we think you should be the next prioress." There it was, plop out of her mouth in front of God and all the deceased Sisters snug under the snow.

I nearly choked on my hot cocoa, which really wasn't that hot. Instead I stomped my foot and laughed. "That's a riot! But it takes more than a little passion to be prioress, and I've poured most of mine out in the library!"

Sr. Gertrude didn't respond right away. She sipped her cocoa and took her time with the ginger snaps which were left over from Christmas. Oddly enough, I couldn't abide them. Maybe because they came out of a bag, were bordering on the stale side, and were not very spicy—not enough ginger in the snap.

"I don't know how you can eat those things," I said, hoping to change the subject.

"I know, but we'll eat anything," Sr. Gertrude quipped. "At my age, I'm grateful my taste buds are still working. You've done more than been librarian, you know. And being librarian was a wonderful way of getting to know everybody in the community and what subjects they care about. And you'd buy special interest books to fit the Sister; we all noticed it. You also have a wonderful way with the young Sisters, and before Solemn Profession, they're all saying 'such a blessing' this and 'such a blessing that.' You've got us old-timers saying it too."

"Well, you all are! Such a blessing you bring to the community!" And Sister would laugh.

"Look out there," she said gesturing with her hand to the cemetery. "There's our blessings. For over a hundred years the show has gone on without a single intermission. Oh, the scenery changes and the leading roles come and go..."

"But the corps de ballet keeps on dancing," I added.

"You've got it, kiddo," Sister said with the old twinkle in her eyes.

We talked of other things, and I noticed Sr. Gertrude would tend to repeat herself a lot now, but I didn't mind. I guess we shouldn't have favorites, but it happens. It's human nature, and Sr. Gertrude was one of mine. I would miss her terribly when that time came, and I didn't want to think about it.

Back to reality...Sr. Gertrude and Sr. Rosaria returned from the chapel and the confessional, Sr. Gertrude beaming from ear to ear. "That new priest, after absolution, told me I'm as clean as a brand new whistle."

Laughing, I said, "And what did you say?"

And she whistled our choir response, "Deo Gratias." And laughed.

"Mama used to say after coming home from temple on Yom Kippur, 'Well, thank goodness. *T'shuvah*...we repent and return to a clean slate. Such a blessing, this day.'"

Indeed. I've certainly learned that "the show goes on, thanks be to God," as Sr. Gertrude would say. I've come to realize that repentance is an ongoing disposition of the soul. I look at the young Sisters and remember the initial sense of repentance. It was what we call "leaving the world" or a break with the world, or as Sr. Rosaria would say in French: "*Rupture du monde.*" I suppose we think taking vows is like "graduation" from repentance, without realizing it's only just begun! We come in thinking and feeling much like the world we leave behind. This can be in very subtle little things, like food will make me happy, or excelling in keeping the rules will win me the approval of others; I'll be whispered about as the best novice they've ever had. Letting go of our self-centered way of thinking is a long process of repentance, of *t'shuvah*, or what the Church Fathers always say in Lent, "*metanoia.*"

When I was "in the world" I'd go to confession maybe every month, like before First Friday, one of the first devotions I adopted. I might go during the month if I lost my temper at work and swore under my breath or had all kinds of prejudiced thoughts about some of the people who came into the library. I would trip over "gluttony" once in a while, never seeing the vice or need in myself deeper than having thirds on dessert. Greta was a talented pastry chef which she called her hobby; and I was a talented food-taster, which I said was *my* hobby. We were a great pair! That all gets turned around in the monastery. We don't eat in between meals, period. If I fell in that regards, well, I added it to my usual litany of sins in confession.

It's a wonderful sacrament that accompanies us all along the way, because none of us really lives the life perfectly. We make mistakes. We fall, and we get up. We don't fulfill our vows like we think we should—like we think the saints did, but through it all, we go on. And even though we get on each other's nerves at times, and discover that we can envy others a little, be jealous, get resentful, even discover that we're capable of a little hate, we also discover that we can forgive, and that we need God's mercy and each others', like we said when we lay prostrate on the sanctuary floor and the bishop asked: "What do you seek?" And we said: "God's mercy and yours" *(The community's).* And over the years, dear Lord, we can get very close to some whom we come to love. And even those whom we aren't very close to, in the end, we love. I know I've received a tidal wave of mercy.

We are *T'shuvah*...we_*return* to grace by repentance, not just once a year, but every day really. The Mass—ah, the Mass! Jesus and His Apostles who were gathered with Him at the Last Supper celebrated a Seder, and a new covenant was made in His Body and Blood. And that was truly fulfilled the next day—the true and lasting Yom Kippur, the Day of Atonement. And that act of love is made present to us every day in the Mass. Would that His Passion become our passion, for such a blessing we live in every day. And it does if we simply live the life. Like "repentance," patience is a disposition, a virtue, we grow into. It's not just being patient with the Sister who is slow in the procession, or singing just a little off key (right next to you), or the Sister who sings too loud and isn't told to turn it down; patience with ourselves, bearing up through the colds or flu that may sweep through the house; the heat in the summer when our bandeau is always moist from walking down the humid cloister. The poor Sisters assigned to the kitchen in summer...*patientia*, as we learn in Ecclesiastical Latin 101: bearing with suffering and trials. The word "passion" comes from *patientia.* How close all that is to repentance, to our daily *t'shuva*...returning to grace, the grace of the present moment, which can put everything in perspective.

I go to confession every two weeks now. It seems, at times, to be the same litany of sins, but that's okay. It reminds me that the Holy Spirit isn't done with me yet. I like beginning again, brand new.

Four

Kiddush: "Sanctification." The blessing prayed over the wine of a festival, making it holy or sanctified

Blessed are you, Lord, our God, King of the Universe, who creates the fruit of the vine. (Haggadah)

It seems the older I get the older my memories get, too. I remember Papa in the kitchen with me wiping off the bottles of wine and pouring them into his cut-glass decanter that only comes out for Pesach, and Rosh Hashanah…and Chanukah…and Purim. He would shout *Kadesh,* meaning the first cup of wine, and then he would pray the blessing, the *Kiddush,* over it. We Jewish kids were used to drinking wine from an early age, unlike many of our gentile friends who never even had a sip till they were teenagers. Really little kids would have candy in their wine glasses instead.

Such mental wanderings make me sleepy, and sure enough I had dozed off at my desk in my office. It was just 9:30 in the morning. I hadn't slept much the night before thinking about the day ahead. Today was the day of Mama and David's visit. It was autumn of 1999. I had easy access to Mother, being her "private secretary". Of course, I did a lot of extra things for both Mother and Sr. Anna Maria, the sub-prioress. We would talk about things almost every day. So they both knew of my impending visit with my brother whom I hadn't seen or spoken to in nearly thirty years.

I went in to see Mother as usual after Terce, and to pick up the mail she wanted me to respond to. She was at her desk, which was always so much neater than mine.

"Good morning, Sister Mary Baruch, you're looking chipper this morning." I don't think Mother ever said that to me, or to anyone else for that matter. It must've been the anxious bounce of my walking which she mistook for "chipperness." She should have seen me an hour before: dozing at my computer, nodding off before that little jump-awake in my chair.

"I don't know about chipper, Mother, but I'm feeling nervous about my visit this afternoon with David…today's the day."

"Oh, that's right," she said, glancing down on her calendar on her desk. "I have it marked right here. Now, try not to be too anxious, Sister; think of it as a little miracle. You've been waiting for a long time for this reunion, and it hasn't happened over anyone's death."

"You're absolutely right, Mother. But I'm still anxious. I don't know how he will react. But I prayed about it all week and put him the chalice this morning. I trust that Our Lord and Our Lady will bring about a real reconciliation. I've been praying about it all week."

"Sister, there is nothing here that needs attending to immediately. Take the time this morning to rest and pray. And I'll be praying for you; let me know how it all goes."

"Thank you, Mother, that's most kind of you. They will arrive around 3:30. Please feel free to stop in and meet him; and I know Mama is always happy when you visit with her, even for a moment."

"I will, thank you. I'm glad it's this afternoon. I've got a meeting this morning with a new workman who's coming to fix a couple doors; we'll start with the parlor door on our side. It needs new molding and he's going to attach a rubber runner on the bottom, which will help both with drafts and sound-proofing."

"Why isn't Sister Thomas Mary taking care of that?" She was the Sister in charge of maintenance. Any jobs involving workmen from outside were handled by her. She loved it, I think. She was in charge.

"Sister has a dentist appointment this morning. She's having another root canal. She was going to cancel it when I told her about the carpenter coming, but I insisted she go. I can handle a doorman." Mother chuckled. "Prioresses are not totally helpless." Chuckle, chuckle. This was contagious as I chuckled along with her, and together we had a good laugh, which was just what the doctor (or the prioress) ordered.

I was grateful for the morning off and went first to the cemetery. I know one can pray to the communion of saints anywhere one is, but I liked going to the graveside of my special "communion of saints." First stop, of course, was at Mother John Dominic's grave.

"Good morning, Mother, it's Sister Mary Baruch, as you know. Thank you, Mother, for your prayers. I'm sure you have had a big part in this reunion…you, and Papa, and maybe even Ruthie, and Joshua, and Father Meriwether. It's a little *strange*, I guess is the word, because I've been thinking a lot recently about the last time I saw David. I hate to confess that I'm not positive when that was. He was at the last Passover Seder I went to with my family, but he didn't speak to me. His last words were probably when they had invited the rabbi for dinner to try to talk me into waiting a few years, to embrace Judaism more. David was really the most upset about it all. You may remember me telling you how authoritative he became about everything Jewish; he almost quoted from the Talmud! My 'defection,' according to David, had international repercussions affecting even the State of Israel. Even Sally laughed at that. She knew more about the state of Israel, I'm sure, than even Papa, she being a journalist, you know. That was all over thirty years ago. I know Sally has talked to him since Ruthie's death more than two years ago, and certainly Mama has more than anyone. Maybe he's doing this just to appease her. I can only imagine the monologue from Mama that he's been given over these years. 'Such a son I should have who won't make up with his sister?'" I laughed a little at my own imitation, and hoped Mother John Dominic was laughing too. I hope we can laugh in Heaven. I can't imagine Heaven without laughing. I distracted myself with my own theological conundrum.

"I know you'll be praying for us…it's at 3:30 this afternoon our time. Goodbye, Mother. I love you," I said very quietly. I saw a small smooth stone just a couple feet away. In good Jewish fashion I picked it up and placed it on her gravestone, and I moved on down the aisle of graves.

I stopped by Sr. Mary of the Pure Heart's grave. She was probably the first Sister in the infirmary that I met when I was an aspirant. She called herself a newcomer too: that is, to the infirmary. She told me she was so happy a Jewish girl was entering the monastery. She grew up in Brooklyn, and her best friend through grade school and high school was Judith Morgenstern. "I loved her family as much as my own," she told me. "I was able to be there many times for Friday night supper and still remember how beautiful it was to see Mrs. Morgenstern light the candles for the Sabbath and sing her prayers."

"I know, Sister. That's one thing I still miss. My mother had a lovely haunting voice which we only heard on Friday night." And I sang the "*Baruch Atah*" for her, and dear Sr. Mary of the Pure Heart broke into pure tears. She took my hands and kissed them, and promised me she would pray for me and for my perseverance.

When I received the habit and my new name, there were many cards and notes from the Sisters at my place in the refectory, but one struck me more than any other…it was plain card stock, with an image of Our Lady on the front, and inside, in a shaky hand was written one word: *Mazeltov. Sr. Mary Pure Heart.* Hers was the first funeral of a Sister for me too. I had only known her a short time, not even a year, and I felt like I had lost my best friend. When we received her body, I thought it was somebody else at first. She looked like she was in the most peaceful sleep anyone could have, with a modest smile. I thought her name really fit her: Mary of the Pure Heart. *Blessed are the pure of heart, for they shall see God.* I wanted to be like her. We novices had our hour praying the Psalms back and forth across her coffin;

the songs of Israel which she heard as a child in Hebrew at the Morgensterns.

It was nice to see that the public could come into the extern chapel for a viewing. Sister's casket was moved up next to the grille. There were four floor candles burning at each corner, and on the extern side of the grille was a lectern with a funeral guest book and a pile of holy cards. They were stock photos, four varieties, printed with her name and dates:

> Sr. Mary of the Pure Heart, O.P. (Janice Chesterfield)
> Born Feb. 9, 1891
> Born to Eternal Life: March 24, 1976.
> Requiescat in Pace

Maybe three days after the funeral, the guest book was on the novitiate common room table, having been in the Professed Common Room for three days. There were not a lot of people who came; I guess when you're that old, family and friends wait for you on the "other side." Her doctor had come and a couple local friends of the monastery I was learning by name more than face. And near the bottom in a shaky hand—there it was: *Judy Morgenstern Levine.* I found another stone and placed it on her gravestone.

I had to smile when I passed Sr. Norbert's gravestone. I didn't know her very well either, but she was the one who shocked us when she, as we say today, "lost it" in the middle of recreation. It must've been a solemnity because the novices were with the professed for recreation. Mother announced that a Sister (I forget her name) was going to Rome for a semester to take courses at the Angelicum, the Dominican university in Rome.

Sr. Norbert blew up. "Sister Goody Two Shoes always gets to go wherever she wants. I had asked to go for further studies a year ago, and you told me we don't do that. But your little pet gets to go—well, I hope she flunks and embarrasses us all." We sat stunned; nobody breathed for ten seconds. Even Mother was speechless and red as a beet. "I've had enough of your favoritism, Mother, you should step down; I'm sorry we ever elected you." And she (Sr. Norbert) threw her knitting needles and three inches of scarf on the floor and stomped out of the room.

The Sister going to Rome was in tears. There was a grand silence in the recreation room; not a knitting needle clicked. It was probably the first time I felt sorry for Mother Jane Mary, whom many of us didn't particularly like because she wasn't Mother John Dominic. Mother quietly said, "Sister must be very hurt. She did ask to go to Rome to study last year…"

Sr. John Dominic spoke out, "And I was Mother at the time and told her no. We didn't do that last year and the years before. It would mean a Sister would live outside of enclosure, and we just didn't see any need for individual further studies, especially in Rome. Sr. Boniface many years ago did go to evening classes at St. Francis College to learn English, or rather to improve her English and writing skills, but she was home every evening."

"Thank you, Sister," Mother Jane Mary continued. "It is highly irregular for us, but we're willing to give it a try, and Sister *Whatshername*, did not ask to go; I asked her. She would be best qualified to follow graduate studies, and be able to share everything with us when she returns. Now, if you'll excuse me, I will go and try to soothe Sister Norbert. Proceed into Compline when the bell rings as usual. And pray for Sister Norbert."

We were all kind of shook up about it, and Sr. Mary of the Trinity, the novice mistress, said that Sr. Norbert just needed a little attention. "She's been hurt like this in the past. She'll get over it. And Mother Jane Mary is just learning too, you know, to apply the right kind of glue to hold us all together. So pray for her too. Perhaps you've all learned a lesson too; that we're a fragile bunch at times."

We never heard anything more about it. Sr. Norbert returned to choir the next day and acted like nothing happened. The Sister who went to Rome, went and came back to the U.S., but not to us. She left the Order and lives on Long Island. Sr. Norbert came down with ovarian cancer twenty years later and went through all the treatments, but died before my Silver Jubilee.

I patted the gravestones of a number of other Sisters whom I remembered fondly, even Sr. Boniface, who didn't particularly like me for a while. It took me a while to accept that and to grow to love Sr. Boniface who in the end was quite fond of me, although I'm not sure she knew who I was. She thought I was her best friend in the community, Sr. Hildegard, who was our book-binder and shoe-maker.

Sr. William Joseph was the last in that row. She died when I was in temporary vows, and lived for years in the infirmary, so I didn't know her well. There were whispers about her; good whispers, that she may have had some mystical experiences, but nobody ever talked about what they were. I think maybe talking about them was not allowed. Sisters would go in and pray the rosary with her in her infirmary cell, which they didn't do for other Sisters. I remember the first time I was assigned to help the infirmarian with supper trays, and I was given Sr. William Joseph's tray to take to her. I don't know why I was a little nervous. I thought maybe she could read souls, like Padre Pio or St. John Vianney, and I wasn't so sure I wanted anybody reading mine. Padre Pio would tell penitents the sins that they forgot, and I didn't want Sr. William Joseph telling me I forgot to confess something, like the time that I hid under Sally's bed and listened to her phone conversation. She was the only one in the family who had an extension phone in her bedroom. Ruthie and I wanted our own phone too, but we never got one. Sally wasn't the tidiest member of the family, and there was an accumulation of dust balls under the bed with me. I would have gotten away with being a private-eye, but I sneezed and blew the whole gig, as Ruthie put it.

So I took Sr. William Joseph's tray into her, simply laid out with tomato soup and half a tuna sandwich on toast. "Good evening, Sister, I have your supper for tonight." Sister smiled, looking deep into my eyes, or so I thought.

"Hand me my glasses, Sister, I can't see who you are." They were right there on the bed table within reach, but I dutifully did as she requested, anxious to take my leave.

"It's Sr. Mary Baruch, Sister." I smiled. "Here are your glasses." I turned to leave.

"Sister, you forgot something!"

Oh no, she's reading my soul and sees me under Sally's bed. I blurted out: "I know, Sister, I'm sorry."

"I always get two packs of saltines with the soup. You forgot them."

I was so relieved. "Oh, I'm sorry, Sister, I'll go get them right now." And off I went, bringing back four packs instead of two. She was very happy.

Several weeks after that, we were having conferences on the theological virtues in St. Thomas, and Sr. William Joseph took a turn and was dying. Fr. Bickford was here and in the parlor with a Sister. The infirmarian knocked and burst into the parlor, holding an oil stock, stole, and the *Rite of Anointing of the Sick*. Fr. Bickford and she literally ran down the cloister to the infirmary. Father anointed Sister, gave her the Apostolic Blessing, and the small gathering of Sisters sang the *Salve*.

That was around 11:00 in the morning. By Vespers it was reported that Sr. William Joseph was sitting up in bed and asking for supper. She lived for another six months. We all marveled at the power of the Sacrament of the Sick.

I patted Sr. William Joseph's gravestone and wondered if she could see me now under Sally's bed. Actually, I brought it to confession the next time I went. Fr. Wilcox told me our venial sins are like dust balls under the bed of our souls, and if we didn't sweep them away they would make us sneeze. I liked his analogy, but wondered afterwards what a "spiritual sneeze" might be. If only Sr. William Joseph were still with us, I would ask her; she no doubt knew.

In the next row was Sr. Imelda Mary. Sr. Imelda was an extern Sister when I first started coming to the monastery.

She was more reserved than Sr. Paula, but Sr. Imelda didn't miss a trick, and remembered names and details about visitors which amazed me. When Greta and I went for our second retreat, Sr. Imelda remembered that Greta liked raisin bread toast for breakfast, and that I liked bagels. But maybe that's stretching the miracle too far; I mean, who doesn't like bagels? But she remembered I raved once about onion bagels—and there they were. She also remembered that I liked Earl Grey tea and had it there for me. Only after I had entered and I think was a novice, did I learn that Sr. Imelda kept an index card file on every visitor. When I made my Solemn Profession, Sr. Imelda enclosed "my file card" in my card wishing me a blessed Profession. It wasn't too long after that that she was diagnosed with cancer. I keep her holy card from her funeral in my breviary. I prayed today that she would help me remember any little details about my brother and his first visit that would make him feel welcomed the next time he came.

Sr. Hanna Marie of Jesus Thorn-Crowned had the last grave in that row. I didn't know her, but I loved her name; it was Mama's name without the "h" at the end. Sr. Benedict and Sr. Amata often spoke of her with great admiration. I think she was something of what we would call today a workaholic. She was an extern Sister living inside. She was sacristan for many years and was very fussy about things, at least the things in the sacristy.

She was a native New Yorker; her parents immigrated to this country from Hungary. She had five sisters; only one is still living, but nobody seems to know where. Sr. Benedict once said that Sr. Hanna Marie loved Christmas so much they should have given her the title of Jesus in Bethlehem or the Infant Jesus, instead of Jesus Thorn-Crowned. She knew and loved the Sisters so much that each year she would make each one a unique Christmas card. She did this in her spare time in the sacristy. Apparently she was also big on Christmas decorations and had free rein in the extern chapel. Sometime in the sixties, she was decorating a huge tree she had gotten for the extern chapel. This was like two days before Christmas. She had boxes of ornaments I think that her family donated; some of them came from Hungary with the family. Shewas standing on a tall step ladder, trying to put the star on the top. She wasn't wearing an apron, and she stepped on her scapular, lost her balance, and fell off the ladder, hitting her head on a prie-dieu she had moved out of the way for the tree. She was knocked unconscious.

The Sister keeping guard, of course, heard all this, and ran for help. The ambulance came, and Sr. Hanna Marie spent Christmas in the hospital, without a single ornament. The tragic thing, however, was when she regained consciousness on Christmas Day, she suffered from what the doctor called temporary amnesia. Sr. Benedict was with her and Sr. Hanna didn't know who Sr. Benedict was, nor did she know who she herself was. Christmas, however, she recognized, and she talked about decorating the tree.

"That's right, Sister, you were decorating the tree and putting the star on the top."

"Yes, Daddy was there to do that with me. It was a big silvery shiny star he had had when he was my age, he told me."

"But do you remember a couple days ago in the monastery chapel and the tree?"

"Monastery chapel? What's that? And why are you calling me your sister? I'm not your sister; my sister died of polio."

Sr. Benedict would retell the tale. "She could remember details from her childhood, but nothing of the present. She didn't even remember she was a nun. I would call her Sister Hanna, and she'd look around, 'Who you-a talkin' to? My name is Sophia Gibberish' or something like that." Sr. Benedict would say, "I could never pronounce or understand her last name."

Sr. Benedict could be rather dramatic about it all, but brought everything together saying, "We called it a Christmas miracle. On the Feast of the Holy Innocents, Sr. Hannah's memory was restored. She remembered who she was, who I was, and that she was decorating the tree in the extern chapel. We all rejoiced when we learned she would be coming home the next day. We had a special recreation that night and sang Christmas carols and gave the little homemade cards and gifts we all made to Sr. Hanna Marie who sat by our tree in the community room in tears."

That was part of the "oral tradition," Sr. Hanna and her Christmas Miracle. She resumed her charge in the sacristy, and let other Sisters help her with things, like decorating for the holidays. She never forgot to wear an apron after that.

There was a single Christmas ornament attached to the ground in front of her gravestone. So I prayed a little prayer to her, too, that she would help Mama and David come to know the mystery of Christmas. It couldn't hurt.

Next row. All of the Sisters in this row I only knew by name, and over the years you catch the names that are familiar, the Sisters who are still a part of the oral tradition.

We have a single metal chair off to the side in the cemetery under our beautiful oak tree which was in glorious golden yellows and red that day. I remember sitting down there for the length of a rosary, asking all the deceased Sisters to pray for me and my encounter with David. "Our Papa is with you all if you want to learn about David." I thought that said it all. Although I thought Ruthie was probably filling them all in on how mean and belligerent David was when I became a Catholic.

I remembered Sr. Mary of the Trinity's words: "We're a fragile bunch at times." And I thought about my family…a fragile bunch at times indeed.

Next I went to visit the Sisters in the infirmary to ask for their prayers, especially Sr. Mary of the Trinity who was then our oldest in the infirmary, almost a hundred years old…former novice mistress, former sub-prioress, former prioress for two terms. Strong for all of us, and now, among the fragile bunch. Like my dear Sr. Gertrude whose prayers I've always depended on.

Sr. Mary of the Trinity was sleeping comfortably in her room; Sr. Gertrude and Sr. Amata were playing Whist at the card table, the latest craze to hit the infirmary.

"Where's Sr. Benedict?" I inquired of the Whist players.

"She's stepped out for a moment." Sr. Amata was concentrating on her hand. Sr. Gertrude looked up at me with a smile.

"I offered my Holy Communion for your meeting with David today. *Another opening, another show*—don't be nervous, kiddo, you've got the Lord on your side."

"Thank you, Sister, I knew you'd have just the right words for me. I could go for a cold glass of apple cider, ANY-ONE WANT SOME?" All hands went up, including Sr. Mary Bruna and Sr. Sarah who were sitting on the sidelines engrossed in the newspapers.

I went into the kitchenette and fixed six glasses of apple cider. Oddly enough, I thought about Papa and David fixing the wine, and praying the blessings. The first cup of wine always began with a blessing: "firsts" always began by blessing God first. Maybe David will have a kind of amnesia that forgets the hurts inflicted years and years ago, the old wine skins the Lord talks about. And coming here will be new wine skins. David likes his wine, and I know Mama does too. Maybe it is really prayer and mercy and kindness, and a dash of humor, and sweet apple cider that is the wine of our life. All these things, we sometimes just call God's "grace." I was ready and waiting to welcome my brother into my home for the first time: dust balls and all.

Five

L'Chaim: "To Life!"

I have set before you life and death, the blessing and the curse. So choose life in order that you may live, you and your descendants, by loving the LORD your God, by obeying His voice, and by holding fast to Him; for this is your life and the length of your days that you may live in the land which the LORD swore to your fathers, to Abraham, Isaac, and Jacob, to give them. (Deuteronomy 30:19-20)

"WAKE UP, SISTER Mary Baruch, your mother and brother are here." It was Sr. Paula gently squeezing my arm. I had dozed off in my stall in the chapel. I had stayed there to pray right after None, at 3:00. They were expected around 3:30.

"What time is it, Sister?" I whispered.

"Just 3:40, Sister. They're waiting for you in the small parlor."

"Thank you, Sister, I must've dozed off. Oh, could you get my rosary for me, dear, I must've dropped it." I took a deep breath, looked at the Lord in His ever-silent place in the monstrance, blessed myself, and made my way to the parlor, holding onto my side-rosary as I did.

I opened the parlor door and went in, closing the door silently behind me, noticing that it was more snug now with the new rubber runner. I just stood there looking at Mama and David who also just stood looking at me. It was almost like being asleep, but I knew this time I wasn't. I was wide awake. And I heard David's voice crack: "Becky."

If there's one thing we don't see at all in the monastery it's grown men crying! But there he was. My brother was a sixty-two-year-old New York psychiatrist who practiced on the Upper East Side of Manhattan. For thirty-five years he was immersed in people's mental and emotional turmoil and learned to be stoic and stalwart, rational, and emotionally put-together. And he put his head down, and let out a sob that filled the room like an emotional implosion. Maybe that was his spiritual sneeze. I began to shake, and let the floodgates open, and Mama and I, both crying, made our way to the now familiar grille.

It was Mama who broke through the sobbing. "Don't be afraid, David, come and touch your sister; she's still our Becky." Mama was holding on to my fingers through the grille. I was searching for a handkerchief with my right hand. David came within a foot of the grille and looked at me with tears rolling down his cheeks.

"I wasn't expecting this," he managed to get out. "You look so…"

"So beautiful," Mama blurted. "Such a blessing, I told you, look at her, your sister, the nun." Mama was on a roll. "All of us have gotten old and gray; my oldest daughter lives with a girlfriend and gives haircuts to dogs; my youngest daughter, may she rest in peace, kills herself in the middle of

New York stardom; my son, the doctor, such a blessing, can't talk to his little sister for thirty-five years, and she looks like she's the same age as when she left us." It was all disjointed emotion, but it was Mama!

"That's true, Mama, that's true." He took a deep breath and put his left hand on the grille and encircled my right hand fingers, a little too tightly, but I didn't let him know that.

"David." I managed to get his name out. I thought my emotions would mature with age, but it's been just the opposite. I tried again. "David, thank you for coming here," and I took two steps backwards, spread out my arms with a slight bow and said, "The nunnery." And he laughed and cried at the same time, if that's possible. The "nunnery" was his word for the monastery, with the scornful tone of Hamlet to Ophelia.

I don't know where it came from except from the deep recesses of the soul, or maybe the spirit of Ruthie hidden by the invisible curtain of eternal life and playing the prompter, or the prayers of Sr. Gertrude sitting in the rocker outside the infirmary door, but I took another two steps backwards, spun completely around, and assumed the character of Ophelia.

> OPHELIA: "O, help him, you sweet heavens!"
>
> (David remembered the lines by heart.)
>
> HAMLET: "If thou dost marry, I'll give thee this plague for thy dowry: be thou as chaste as ice, as pure as snow, thou shalt not escape calumny. Get thee to a nunnery, go: farewell. Or, if thou wilt needs marry,

> marry a fool; for wise men know well enough what monsters you make of them. To a nunnery, go, and quickly too. Farewell."
>
> OPEHLIA: "O heavenly powers, restore him …"

And all three of us burst out laughing. "Such a blessing, my children should know Shakespeare by heart."

Mama was amazed, and as always pulled up a chair closer to the grille, and David followed suit. Of course, I sat down too. Mama went on: "And look at the two of you, both well past middle age."

"Ruthie would be so proud," I said. "When she played Ophelia, you used to help her memorize her lines. But I must say our chastity is not ice, but warm and joyful, especially after fifty." (I winked at Mama.)

"Hamlet was not a happy man when he said that. Anyway, I always thought that I made a dashing Hamlet, although I was never sure how to psychologically interpret him. I've had a few Hamlets over the years on my couch."

"And probably a few Ophelias! But I must say, you've aged well, David, *past* middle age." I glanced at Mama. "You've kept your hair, which is very distinguished looking."

"Yes, I think I have Mama's genes to thank for that, including a few hundred of her thousand silver hairs."

Mama actually blushed. "Such a blessing, Helena Rubenstein." We laughed.

"Do you have hair under your…your…" "Veil," Mama said.

"Yes, of course, I do. We don't shave our heads, David. My hair's like yours actually, maybe just a bit shorter, and nearly all gray." I smiled. There was an awkward silence. David was staring at me through the grille work.

"I understand you made quite a splash at Ruthie's funeral, and even came home to sit Shiva with Mama and Sally." His tone was not cynical, but kind.

"Yes, I was hoping Rabbi Lieberman would come in." And David laughed, remembering the staged scene with the esteemed rabbi who came to dinner.

"I know. We did kind of put him up to it. But I was sure if anyone could change your mind it would be him. I presume he wasn't at Shiva; I don't know if he's still living, but I'm sorry I wasn't able to get home on time. A seminar in Amsterdam..."

"Brussels." Mama interjected. "It was Brussels. And Rabbi Lieberman retired and moved to Miami Beach and had a stroke and died. May he rest in peace! Your father liked the man; I couldn't stand him, or his prissy wife."

Ignoring the last remark, David went on. "You're right. About my seminar, it was Brussels. We have these seminars every year. It was the Brussels one, now I remember, that I was giving one of the talks, and couldn't leave everything and come home. I wouldn't have made it anyway." (This wasn't the kind of amnesia I was hoping for, but I was enjoying it.)

"Such an excuse. Your little sister dies of an overdose, and a paper is more important?"

Jumping in to save David I asked, "Where are you going next year?" I asked with genuine interest. I was even just a little envious of his world travels.

"Seminar 2000 will be in London, which will be fine. We'll be meeting at Cambridge, which I'm looking forward to. But Seminar 2001, of which I am on the planning committee, are you ready? It's…in…"

And before he could say it, Mama blurted out, "Rome. Maybe he'll get to meet that handsome Pope John Paul."

"Oh, David, that's wonderful. I thought you were going to say 'next year Jerusalem.'" And we all laughed.

"Maybe in 2002? And you'll take me?" Mama sounded like a little girl, her eyes blinking at David like she was flirting with him.

"I will, Mama, if we can persuade the committee." Turning to me he said, "But do you know where Mama and I are going this winter?"

I honestly didn't know. Mama hadn't been to Boca in a couple years since her condo-friend died. She didn't let me think about it very long.

"It's supposed to be a Chanukah gift, but we're going on a two-week cruise all over the Caribbean. David told me last night so I can start to get a new wardrobe. Just the two of us. Sally and Mitzie are coming to New York for two weeks and can have the apartment to themselves, I told them, if they don't bring any dogs with them. I don't want dog hair all over my parlor."

"That could all change, Mama, you know. There might be four of us."

"Four?" Mama exclaimed. "Now you tell me there may be four? You're not bringing a floozy along with us, are you? Oops, I'm sorry, Becky, such words should not come out of my mouth in this holy place." Mama kind of bowed her head like she was afraid the ceiling was going to fall in on us.

David put his head back and laughed, a little louder than most people laugh in the parlor...in this holy place! "No floozy, Mama, unless I'm lucky..."

"Such words, David!" Mama was being herself again, not realizing she had said it first!

"No, Mama. I'm sorry, Becky, but I'm sure you've heard worse." I just nodded in the affirmative, trying to recall if I ever heard that in this parlor. "I'm trying to talk Sharbel's mother into letting him come with us; it'll be his seventeenth birthday, and I think he should get to spend some time with his other grandmother."

"Before she kicks the bucket," Mama added, but quite pleased with the news. "Oy, that would be such a blessing. They play shuffleboard on these boats, don't they?" Mama was already planning her on-deck activities with her grandson.

"But you said 'four.' You aren't going to bring his mother, are you?"

"No, of course not, Mama." And he turned his gaze towards the nun in the cage. "I don't suppose you'd be allowed to be released for two weeks?"

Now it was my turn to put my head back in a grand guffaw. I laughed louder than I ever remember laughing in this parlor, and that's with years of Gwendolyn and Ruthie's visits.

"I am very moved by your offer," I said, getting control of myself. "But I don't think even Vatican II would include that in the renewal of the contemplative monasteries." I laughed again. "Not that I wouldn't love it. Can you imagine us, Mama, sailing around ...the islands." I wanted to name one of the big cities down there, but I didn't know any off the top of my head. Even after twenty years as head librarian, our "collection" didn't cover Caribbean ports of call. I knew many of them had saints' names—that was kind of neat.

"Not Sally and the dog-catcher?" Mama anxiously asked. "I could use a drink of water. Becky, can you ring for that lovely little nun who brings us things?"

"Sister Paula, Mama. She's our extern Sister, and I can ask her to bring some water or cider, or would you like coffee? I can't 'ring her.' She's not a servant, although she does have a servant heart. But she's not a servant, if you know what I mean."

"Such a world you live in? Aren't you parched?" Mama had spoken.

"I'll be right back." Sr. Paula of the Servant Heart was not available. I think she was driving back to the dentist to pick up Sr. Thomas Mary of the Root Canal. So I fixed a pitcher of ice water and returned to the parlor and put it on the turn.

"It's called a *turn,*" Mama was explaining to David. It twirls around so you can put things on it from the other side, like cookies and Danishes." Seeing the pitcher of water, she added, "...and glasses."

"There are glasses in the cabinet in the corner." And so Mama fetched them and poured us all a glass of cold water, which did really hit the spot.

"Well, I must say, I am surprised at how peaceful and happy you look." Dr. Feinstein was passing his prognosis of me through the grille. "I can see that this life has suited you well, remarkably well."

"Is this the David who blasted me for becoming a Catholic, let alone a nun?" I said without any sarcasm, I hope. I didn't want to spoil the mood.

"I know, I know. I never could get it through my thick skull what you were doing. And it took a long time. I've had a lot of Catholic patients in my practice, and oddly, it was their faith that was their best medicine...once they got over their guilt. But you know, I think it was Mama more than anything that changed my mind. I could see how much she had come to accept you; even Sally whom I never expected to speak positively of you, couldn't stop raving about you. I guess I had to see for myself." David was being honest and maybe even a little humble, or free from guilt, although he probably wouldn't say that.

"And then there's been Sharbel. I know you know all about him. Mama couldn't hold it in any longer." Mama just smiled and sipped her water. "He and his mother are Catholics, and oddly enough, they seem very happy."

"Well, I've been very happy all these years too, and can't even begin to explain why. Well, I could, but I'm not sure you'd understand." And I smiled my best sisterly smile. "I'd like to try, if you're willing. Sally lives in Chicago, and you're my only sibling close by; we should be friends."

"*Baruch Atah Adonai elohenu,*" (Blessed be the Lord Our God) sang out Mama. And from her oversized handbag, she pulled out a bottle of Mogen David Elderberry wine. "I think this calls for a little toast."

I laughed with delight. "I'll have to get permission, but I think Mother is going to come in pretty soon."

"Well, David and I don't need permission. We'll anticipate her arrival. David, you open the bottle, I'll get the glasses." We didn't have wine glasses in the cabinet, but some rather nice juice glasses with grapes on them. "These 'cheese-glasses' will do nicely."

David and Mama each had their "cheese-glass" filled with elderberry wine, and raised them to me alone behind the grille. "*L'Chaim.*"

And as if on cue, there was a slight knock on the door, which opened, and Mother Agnes Mary came in backwards pulling Sr. Gertrude in her wheelchair.

"Ah, Mother Agnes, thank you for coming in—and our dear Sister Gertrude." Mama was on her feet. David sat just a little stupefied by it all. He quickly put down his glass and stood too, the perfect gentleman.

"I'm Mother Agnes Mary and this is Sr. Gertrude," Mother said directly to David. "And you must be Dr. David Feinstein. We welcome you to our home."

"Thank you, Ma'am, I…we are so happy to be here. It's been a long time since I've seen my sister. We were just toasting our reunion and hoped you'd come in. Will you join us?"

"Oh, I see it's Mogen David, is it? Well, I'm told Mogen David is good for the soul," said Mother Agnes Mary, very coyly. It was Mother at her best.

"And just what the doctor ordered," added Sr. Gertrude who was putting her fingers through the bottom squares of the grille. "May we, Mother?" Sr. Gertrude was being very observant.

"Of course we may. It's not every day we celebrate a reunion like this." And with that Mama had our three glasses on the turn, and David's and her glass were refilled. It was Sr. Gertrude who raised her glass, and softly shouted, "*Mazeltov!*"

We all shouted back and drank our wine. David was quite taken aback by it all. I was afraid he would start crying again, which would have been all right, given the company he was in.

David lifted his glass to Mother and Sr. Gertrude. "*L'Chaim*."

And Sr. Gertrude, caught up in the drama of it all, raised her glass again and began to sing: "To life, to life, L'Chaim; L'Chaim, L'Chaim to life." And we all joined in, except for Mother who didn't know the words, but was delighted to listen to our rendition.

"I think we need a little something to nosh," I said after the song ended.

"Such a daughter I should have; she's a true Feinstein, Mother." Mama then pulled out of her bag a roll of Jacob's Water Crackers and a container of chicken livers. "I only live three blocks from Zabar's; best chicken liver in New York."

So we had our little treat. We told Mother the story of taking Mama and Papa to Broadway to see *Fiddler on the Roof* for their twenty-fifth anniversary; and that *L'Chaim* was a song from it. And Sr. Gertrude became instant friends with David by talking about Ruthie and what a splendid actress and comedian she was. David was overjoyed by it all, and at a subsequent visit, told me he couldn't believe how real we were, how down to earth and genuinely joyful we all seemed. (I was thinking, it's better than any seminar in all of Europe!)

Mother and Sr. Gertrude excused themselves for Vespers and Mother told me to stay here with my family. "Epikeia and L'Chaim go together."[1]

I could tell that Mama was pleased with everything. Her children were all talking to each other again. David was very good to her, for which I was most grateful and told him so in later visits. He made it possible for Mama to stay in our apartment where we both grew up. He took care of her medical insurance and even vacationed with her.

As they were getting ready to leave, Mama still hadn't forgotten to ask, "So who is this number fouron our Caribbean cruise? I shouldn't know the mystery person?"

"Well, since Becky, Sister Baruch, can't go, I thought you could ask one of your lady friends who would enjoy the trip and be a good companion for you. Sharbel and I will share a cabin, and you can have whomever you'd like."

Mama was very happy with that arrangement. "I know just who I'll ask. Millie Hutner from next door; she'll love it. We'll have a blast."

David promised he would come back and visit soon, and he told me that he would be more than happy to introduce me to his son who, he said, was dying to meet me. I hadn't thought about that. I was an aunt. And I had David back in my life, and he was more accepting of everything than I ever expected. I must visit the cemetery after Vespers and thank everyone.

---

1 Epikeia: A liberal interpretation of law in instances not provided by the letter of the law. Etym. Greek: epieikes, reasonable. In short, when "charity" replaces another already standing virtue. Cf: Summa Theologiae, Secunda Secundae, Question 130.

I sank into my stall that afternoon a half hour before Vespers. I looked at the Lord in His weekday monstrance. "I love You, Lord. Thank you for getting me to this nunnery. I thought I would go to my spot in our cemetery without ever seeing David again, and now he wants to be friends, and come visit me. Sometimes, Lord, Your ways just overwhelm me. Maybe You'll use me, Lord, to soften David's heart even more, and maybe he'll come to know You. Maybe someday You'll be Number Four on Mama's and David's vacation trips. You know, Lord, You've always been my Number One. *L'Chaim!*"

Six

Charoset: A sweet, dark-colored paste made of fruits and nuts eaten at the Passover Seder. Its color and texture are meant to recall mortar (or mud used to make adobe bricks) which the Israelites used when they were enslaved in Ancient Egypt. Clay.

THE PASSOVER WAS still six months away, but because of our grand reunion, Mama brought us a couple quart containers of *charoset.* It brought back a flood of memories in my meditation time after Vespers. Mama would be in full swing preparing for the Seder meal, but put me in charge of the *charoset.* She called it the sweetness of the Seder. It was a mixture of chopped apples, dates, and walnuts, and we'd add blanched slivered almonds…and sweet wine! Mama's secret ingredient was honey and some fresh ground cinnamon, just a pinch or two, or three. One year she added raisins, but not in this batch. I knew it was supposed to represent the mortar which the Hebrew slaves were forced to use to make bricks.

It's not really mentioned at the first Seder, nor is there a blessing for it in the *Haggadah*, the "prayer book" of the Seder. Really good *charoset* was sticky and sweet. It held life together...the bitter and the sweet; the really sad times and the times of rejoicing. Tragedy and comedy.

"Becky, don't eat the *charoset* yet."

"Yes, Mama." I almost caught myself saying out loud in my choir stall.

Funny how my short little daydreams can be so real and so reminiscent of my childhood. I did make the *charoset* a couple times. Josh always wanted to do it, but Mama wouldn't let him in the kitchen. Charoset...the mortar holding us together, was woman's work.

Oddly enough, I thought again of Eli. He was kind of like charoset. Being the doorman, he was there whenever we moved from the outside to the inside. Summer and winter. He was like the building's charoset, holding us together in this brick building on West 79th Street. And what is the charoset of this stone building in Brooklyn Heights? I think "the faith" is the charoset of our life. It has certainly been the one thing, both bitter and sweet, that holds us together. It is the only thing that makes sense in the impossible world in which we build our bricks...our lives.

That evening after Vespers, I grabbed a jacket by the side door and made my way out to the cemetery. I thought about Our Lady making her charoset for Passover and delighting in Jesus's delighting in it. Maybe Mary herself is our charoset, after all we do call her "our life, our *sweetness,* and our hope." It was in her immaculate womb that heaven and earth were joined together in the Incarnation of the Word. I found my way to the bench where I sat this morning. It was truly dusk; the long shadows of the afternoon faded into that in between light before nightfall. Despite the slight drone of traffic wafting over our enclosure wall, it is very silent and peaceful here.

My meditation, however, got interrupted by thinking about my next parlor with Gwendolyn. She was coming to see me tomorrow! Of all people on the outside, she would be the one that I'd want to share everything about my reunion with David. She kept in telephone touch with Mama, but not as regularly as a couple years ago. It's fitting that she's a part of this all.

Thinking about Gwendolyn stirred up a new worry for her. She was in her mid-seventies now and still working. She went from running her British tea shop, Tea on Thames, to Penguin Pub and the new millennium; I didn't know how she did it. But this was her "charoset", the sweetness and joy in her life. Gwendolyn was a widow at age thirty-two. She and her young son came to America and lived in a small walk-up apartment on West 75th Street. Her son, Christopher, was killed riding his bike when they were vacationing at Seaside Heights on the Jersey shore. I said a prayer for both of them before going in. I was looking forward to supper and then to going to the infirmary to thank everyone there for their prayers. It had been quite a day.

* * *

Gwendolyn arrived on time. She always travelled by cab now. She settled into the wooden chair with arm rests, close to the grille, as always. She waved to me as I came through the doorway on my side of the parlor.

"Your fairy-godmother is here bearing gifts." Already on the turn was a large bakery style box filled with something from the Penguin Pub Ovens. “I’ve created new autumn biscuits called ‘Falling Leaves’—you’ll love them; they have three different flavors in one biscuit.” By “biscuit” Gwendolyn meant “cookie.”

“Do you get all three flavors if you stick the whole biscuit in your mouth at once?” She thought I was being facetious, but I was actually quite sincere.

“You won’t do that with these, M.B., they’re too big.” Gwendolyn always called me by my initials. I think it was a British thing, like the “biscuits.”

“And what are the three flavors, pray tell?”

“There are two varieties, in flavor and color. Mint chocolate with mandarin orange and lemon twist. Or Cocoa cream, pumpkin spice, and yellow corn.”

“They sound disgusting. I can’t wait to try them!”

We laughed. It was good to see her and hear her laugh—her costume jewelry collection clinking and tinkling as she brushed back her hair with her hand. Three of her five fingers had rings on them, and her dangling penguin earrings swung back and forth.

“So tell me, how did it go? Did David rant and rave and call you names?” Gwendolyn knew what I had gone through with David and my family.

“It was very emotional, as you can imagine. But old age has certainly mellowed his anti-Catholic fire. We didn’t talk about religion at all. He and Mama are going on a cruise, and he’s taking his son, Sharbel, and a friend of Mama’s, Mrs. Hutner, her neighbor. She didn’t live in our building when I was growing up, but I met her when I went home for Ruthie; you met her too; she was the nice lady who kept the coffee up to date and sorted out the food as it came in. Millie Hutner, which I think is short for Mildred. She's also a widow and around Mama's age, so they will have a lovely time aboard the cruise ship. David didn't go into any song and dance about Sharbel; he knew that I knew. Mama had filled him in on a lot of stuff, I think. But he wants Sharbel to meet me. Mother Agnes Mary and Sr. Gertrude came in too, and David was the perfect gentleman. They even had a glass of Mogen David with us."

"David brought Mogen David with him?"

"Mama."

"Of course she would! Such a blessing, my son Doctor David, *and* Mogen David."

"David said he will come and visit me, if that's okay…that we've got a lot of catching up to do. He looks quite distinguished, I think."

"I could look quite distinguished if I lived on 65th and Third Avenue." We laughed. "Well, I've got some news for you, M.B., and need your prayers."

"Uh oh. Don't tell me you're getting married or something." That set all the jewelry and penguins in full swing again.

"Not me, dahling, that's not a cocktail I plan on drinking! No, I'm getting out of the business. We had a big slump, you know, after Ruthie died, and it took a while to get back on our feet, but old Ruben the Penguin was back in business. Jimmy Oliver took over as MC and was a big hit; and we had some big names beginning to 'appear nightly' at Penguin Pub. I've made a bundle of money, and now it's time to retire. My sister Jacqueline wants to retire too, and wants me to move back to England and get a bungalow together, or something. She's my only relative left, you know…maybe like you and David, we've got a lot of catching up to do. I'm leaving after the new year."

There was a dead silence. I couldn't say anything; I couldn't speak. It all came back to me in a silent flash. I didn't have the opportunity, or good fortune, or luxury, whatever, of having lots of friends. When we walk through the enclosure door, we leave family and friends on the other side. We may become acquainted with some very nice people over the years, but we lose most of our friends. Some maybe, we get Christmas cards from, and once in a while a parlor visit. But I really had only two dear friends: Greta and Gwendolyn.

When I was losing my other "G-friend", Gracie Price, I wandered into St. Vincent's and found Christ…I wandered into Tea on Thames uptown, near Barnard College, and found Gwendolyn. She was there when Ezra, my only really close male-friend, came into my life when he came into Tea on Thames. Gwendolyn was my godmother when I came into the Church, and my anchor and support when I was a young Sister, worried about her little sister and her mother. Gwendolyn's were my arms that hugged Ruthie and my eyes that watched out for her; it was Gwendolyn who brought Mama here when Ruthie died. It was Gwendolyn who kept the honor of my father alive for me—Ruben the Penguin King.

I know there were tears rolling down my cheeks and onto my guimpe when I finally looked up at her. "I will miss you." That's all I could say. And Gwendolyn, who was never at a loss for words, was as mute as I was.

Minutes went by. There were no words to be found on either side of the grille. It's when silence says it all. Broken by both of us sniffing and blowing our noses…Gwendolyn louder than me. "It sounds like a foghorn when you blow your nose, Lady Gwendolyn. Honk Honk, the Queen Mary is about to set sail." And that did it. It started as a simpering giggle and burst into a roar of laughter.

"Well, you're no nose-blowing prima donna, little Sister Barrrruuuucch. Once I thought you had brought in a shofar from Temple Emmanuel."

We got hysterical laughing. I thought Gwendolyn's penguins would come undone and go flying across the room. The bell calling me to Vespers brought our hilarity to a sudden sober halt.

"I'm not leaving till the new year…and it may not be permanent; I'm subletting my apartment here," she said as she got up and straightened out her autumn shawl, which was falling off. "You are a blessing, M.B.," and she turned and swept towards the door. "Don't forget your Falling Leaves. I'll probably choke on them…" And she fled out the door. Vespers came right in time to save me...from putting a whole Falling Leaf in my mouth. (St. Michael to the rescue again!)

I dropped off the Falling Leaves in the kitchen, resolved to take a batch to the infirmary, and made my way into Vespers. I carried Gwendolyn in with me, of course. We do that automatically. She was probably sitting back in a cab right now, crossing the Brooklyn Bridge heading into Manhattan, and we gathered all the world up in our Evening Prayer. *May our prayer rise before You, O Lord, like incense in Your sight; the raising of our hands like an evening oblation.*

As I settled into the sentiments of the evening's Psalms, I realized it was the Divine Office, now called The Liturgy of the Hours, which was the charoset of our daily lives. Day after day, season after season, year after year—it holds us together. And every night the Church puts on our lips the Canticle of Mary: "*My soul magnifies the Lord. My spirit rejoices in God, my Savior, for He has looked with favor upon the lowliness of His handmaid. From this day, all generations will call me blessed.*" The light at the beginning of Vespers changes in choir when we end with our *Deo Gratias*. Our mood changes too. We can come into choir full of the day's work and anxious about this or that, and leave at the end a little calmer. A little sweeter, perhaps.

We are so blessed. We are not conscious of that much of the time. We get caught up in the routine of the life, living out, not just an evening oblation, but a daily, every-minute-of-the-day oblation. And it all only makes any sense when the Lord Jesus is at the very center of it all. I'm so happy we keep the adoration of the Blessed Sacrament all day and night. He is the Host, the *Victima*, the one and only perfect oblation of love.

I think our awareness or consciousness of our oblation matures as we do, with every new substance added to our offering, like homemade charoset. The nervous young aspirant offers herself when she walks through the enclosure door and it all begins.

Each step of the way marks a new oblation, a new "ingredient": novitiate, temporary profession, Solemn Profession, and all that follows. We work, we play, we pray, certainly; and we do other things. Some may get terribly sick, or depressed, or misunderstood—it's the stuff of what we offer today to the Lord. The young ones offer their youth and the years when they would probably be etching out a career, getting married, having children…that's the most natural "path of oblation" and sacrifice.

Others live in the world as single men and women, or widowed, and live out their faith with great devotion and selfless service to others; and there's us, who offer ourselves with faith and hope, and love, whether we're young and just beginning or elderly and getting near the end.

Our voices sing out the praises of Israel and of Christ and His Bride, the Church. Christ has transformed the Jewish Psalms into His prayer; the prayer of the "new man."

We constantly listen to His Word, that it may dwell abundantly here, and we offer our prayers of petition…every morning and every evening. *Like incense in Your sight; the raising of our hands like an evening oblation.* Such a blessing.

Seven

Maggid: The second cup of wine and the telling of the story of Exodus.

I WAS JUST TAKING a little snooze in Squeak before Sext. I had finished my morning correspondence for Mother and was doing my morning spiritual reading in our cell, and kind of nodded off. My *Three Ages of the Interior Life*, by Garrigou-Lagrange, was lying on the floor in front of me. Next to Squeak was my little bookcase and a Rosh Hashanah card from Mama. Being reunited with David was wonderful, but Gwendolyn's leaving in a couple months had me a little down. I was missing Fr. Matthew too; that's Ezra, who was back in Africa after a home leave of two years. His health was failing, but he begged his provincial to let him go back to Zimbabwe to finish his pet projects, especially his orphanage. I prayed for him every day. I knew he struggled with lots of things for lots of years. He will be sad to learn that Gwendolyn is leaving New York. And he will be thrilled and excited to hear about David, whenever I get around to writing him. I miss our talks we had during the two years he was back here. He's like a brother to me.

And now I didn't have anyone to talk to on the outside, except Mama, of course, and now David—but I mean someone to talk to *about* Mama and David! I missed Greta too, and thought how she would have known just what to say to David if he got off on religion.

Sr. Anna Maria was a very efficient and busy sub-prioress. We were able to chat a little in between things, but certainly not like her "laundry days" or my library days. Not to mention, that over the years the "observance" takes over, or has its effect on you without you knowing it. Silence becomes more ingrained and a natural part of one's life. There are moments when I'm either sitting in the chapel or sitting in our cell when I think about all the noise in the "world." We've also read a couple articles in the refectory on the prevalence of "multi-tasking" and how much technology is becoming the modern addiction. We thought it was a huge improvement when we got a computer in the library (that affected me the most) but also in the bursar's office, and then in all the offices. Then we got pagers, which were a big luxury and change from the old bell system. If a Sister got a phone call, for example, or was being called to the parlor, the house bell would ring her number…twice. Sometimes it reminded me of shopping in Macy's, but even Macy's didn't have long number codes. It meant one would literally have to stop and count.

Sometimes we can hear cell phones ringing or playing music or whatever they do—in the extern chapel. We've succumbed to house cell phones, if one is outside of the house, like at the doctor's. But I think the biggest invasion of the enclosure has been the Internet and email. It's like we've opened up a huge hole in the grille and let in the world. Maybe this is the twenty-first century challenge to enclosure.

The way that silence becomes a part of one's life, so does the enclosure, and the mindfulness with which one does things. I have to think about it a little more, but I'm beginning to see that it's invading our lives. These are the new challenges facing all of us. Is all this the wave of the future and I'm just resisting because I'm older and don't like change?

Settled in Squeak, I put Garrigou-Lagrange aside and picked up a journal of mine that covered our first election in the new millennium. New Year's 2000 did not come in with a bang for us; it was as any New Year's was, more celebration of the Solemnity of the Mother of God really than the party atmosphere of a New Year. We had a lovely baked ham dinner—which, I thought to myself, Our Lady would never have had! And breaking with all tradition, Mother Agnes Mary suggested a rich cabernet wine, golden yellow, and sweet enough for the approval of most of the community. Was this the wave of the future? I think I could live with this more easily than everyone having her own computer. We rarely had wine in the refectory, but the movement into a new millennium was something none of us would ever experience again. We weren't "scared" like some religious articles we read about a computer blitz affecting everything; we didn't store extra food, or build bomb shelters. We had a glass of cabernet in the refectory! It reminded me of the second cup of wine which marked the beginning of the Passover Story, the Maggid. Passing over to a new year and even more a new century, and a new millennium—wow—this was a real Maggid time.

After we were seated in our places, the prayers and grace being said, and before the music for the meal, which replaced the usual table-reading, Mother stood holding up her glass of cabernet, like she was a toast-mistress at a wedding, and said: "Sisters, we have moved with Our Holy Father John Paul II into the new millennium. As he has crossed the threshold of hope may we join him with our prayers and hopes for this new year of grace. May Our Holy Father Dominic and Our Lady, Queen of Hope, intercede in a special way for us this year. God bless us all with His peace, unity, good health, faith, hope, and love. Happy New Year."

We all lifted our glasses and said "Happy New Year" in a "refectory-tone" which was perhaps more joyous and amplified than usual. We smiled at each other, and enjoyed the meal, the music, the cabernet, and the company. It wasn't contrived or overdone. It was us. As I glanced around the refectory, I thought of how each one must perceive this in her own way; certainly the eldest among us have a peacefulness and deep joy which the youngest will grow into, while they also have their joy and contentment too. I watched Sr. Catherine Agnes sip her wine. Smelling it for a second or two, her eyes closed for a moment, maybe relishing the moment or remembering something or someone from years past. And old Sr. Benedict, carefully bringing the wine glass to her lips with both hands, took a good gulp, and smiled with approval as she carefully put the glass down. The younger Sisters all seemed to eat quickly, and drink quickly, while the well-seasoned Sisters took their time, and savored the moment. I think, maybe, that's how they lived the life too…savoring the moment. Mindfulness.

I thought about Ruthie, as I often do, but especially at times of celebration when we seemed happy to be with each other. Ruthie used to think our life was sad, and I hoped maybe now she could see these moments we had. There was Sr. Alice Marie across the refectory from me who suffered from depression and never seemed to smile. I used to think I was invisible to her and couldn't figure out why she didn't like me, but that wasn't it at all. Depression can be very isolating, I'm told. I'll have to ask David about it, maybe he can help me understand why some people seem to retreat from life. I know she got help a few years ago, and she's been doing much better. She saw me looking at her, and smiled. She tipped her water glass towards me in a silent toast. Sister didn't drink; I don't know if it's because of the medicine she's on or if alcohol was a problem, or if she just didn't like it. I don't know. I tipped my wine glass back to her with a big Feinstein smile, and hoped she's happy now. She smiled back.

Even Sr. Jane Mary down the row from Sr. Alice Marie looked happy. She was never depressed, just very strict with us and with herself. She held things together when she was prioress, but lacked a human warmth, I guess. She wasn't really charoset, like Mother John Dominic and Mother Agnes Mary. She was a good administrator and is still a good teacher. She gives the novices classes on the history of the Order; she's amazing, actually, with names and dates. But maybe she's overly intellectual and lives in her head. I think she's happier being an older Sister-in-community, not in charge. The novices say she has a unique sense of humor. I'm happy to hear that because I never saw it in her. But maybe

I'm just looking at her through my own filter. I guess we all do that, don't we? We all welcomed the New Year, the new millennium through our own filters. In a real sense, that's all we've got. We live with ourselves all the time. We tell our stories through the filter of our own lives. In the end, the "ego" is a very personal filter; there are other larger filters.

It dawned on me that I've probably had more New Years in the monastery now then I had in the world. And how different from the world is the "monastic filter." It's really a liturgical filter, which is wonderful. Beginning each year with January, which is a wonderful month liturgically. The liturgy is our telling the story of the Paschal Mystery in all the seasonal shades and colors that make up this wonderful "filter." After the Solemnity of the Mother of God, there's the Solemnity of the Epiphany of the Lord. All the candle light we have, all year round, but especially at Christmas and Easter, reminds us of Christ the Light who came into the world, and becomes a light of revelation to the gentiles. Then, we have our American saints like Elizabeth Ann Seton and John Neumann; and special Dominican saints this month: Raymond of Penyafort and, of course, St. Thomas of Aquinas. There's the Baptism of the Lord after the Epiphany which sadly ends the Christmas season. January should go slowly and let us savor each feast day, like fine wine, like this lovely cabernet, imported from California.

* * *

February came in with a nice snowstorm, surrounding us with the extra silence to celebrate the Presentation of the Lord. We also began praying in earnest for the election which was actually postponed till March 2 due to the bishop's schedule—but still within the month since Mother Agnes Mary's term was up. The election would be on the Thursday, six days before Ash Wednesday. The regular table reading was suspended the week before and the Rule of St. Augustine and The Constitution of the Nuns were read, especially the chapters on elections. I remember that it was Sr. Beatrice who was the reader that week. I interiorly groaned (I'm sorry, Lord) because she reads so slowly, but it was one "job" shecould still do well since moving over to the infirmary. So she read the qualifications for the nun to be elected prioress:

The nun to be elected prioress should 1) *be charitable, prudent and conscientious regarding regular observance*; (pause) 2) *have sufficient knowledge of the laws and traditions of the Order;* (pause) 3) *be able to participate in the community exercises.*

She also had to be solemnly professed for over seven years, be over thirty-five years old, and not have been prioress for two consecutive three-year terms. It is quite a solemn undertaking; not on the scale of a Papal Election, of course, but marked with similar elements.

We had the Mass of the Holy Spirit in the morning, and at 8:30 a.m. the vocals—all those in Solemn Vowswho were eligible to vote—assembled in the community room. Sr. Anna Maria, the sub-prioress *in capite*, then entered with the bishop. The tellers were elected and took their oaths of secrecy; the Holy Spirit was invoked again; the bishop reminded us that no one was to vote for herself, and the first ballot was taken by writing on a paper: *"I elect N or I postulate N."* The ballot was folded once, and each Sister went to the table where there was a large wicker basket and placed her ballot in it. There was profound silence during this little procession; only the swish of our tunics and rattling of our rosaries could be heard. The two tellers went to the infirmary and collected their ballots. The more able-bodied Sisters were with us—just a few remained in the infirmary. I was watching Sr. Gerard in her wheelchair fussing with some hair that was sticking out from her coiffure, and I had a sudden flashback of Mama the morning that President Kennedy was elected. She couldn't get an appointment to get her hair done before going to vote: "I should go to vote with my hair looking like this?"

The still-folded ballots were counted to see if they matched the number of Sisters voting. If the number did not exceed the number of vocals, the ballots were unfolded. The tellers and the bishop read the ballots privately, recording the names. Blank ballots or an invalid ballot are not counted. The bishop then reads out loud the names of the Sisters nominated. Sr. Anna Maria wrote each name and number of votes on a white board. When a brand new prioress is being elected, there is rarely a majority on the first ballot.

This election was interesting because, one, it was the first in the new millennium, whatever difference that really made; and, two, names emerged which had never been nominated in previous elections. To my surprise, I was one of them. On the second ballot my numbers had increased, but not to a majority.

I felt a certain tightening in the back of my neck; this happens when I'm anxious. I don't know if I was flattered, shocked, amazed, scared, or all of them together. I never dreamed in all my life that I would become "Mother." Well, if I'm honest, I admit it crossed my mind a few times, especially after Sr. Gertrude mentioned it. I think I spent an entire meditation period thinking about it. Mother Mary Baruch. Would I be kind and insightful like Mother John Dominic and Mother Agnes Mary? I would try to be. I knew how important it was to be able to listen to each Sister and to try to understand where she's coming from.

Get real, Baruch, this is not going to happen; Sr. Gertrude is a dreamer and producer, not a prophet. And I snapped myself back to reality and prayed the Jesus Prayer fifty times on my rosary.

So I never thought it could actually be happening, and this election-stuff was serious business and can alter one's whole life. I only remember sitting alone in a chair in the corner and praying. After the second ballot we only had one more. If no one won on the third ballot, only the top two names went to the fourth ballot where it took a relative majority. And I prayed.

"Dear Lord, I never expected this to happen. I cannot imagine being Mother; really, Lord, I don't know if I could do it. I would have to depend entirely on You, Lord, You know that. But really, Lord, don't You think Sr. Anna Maria is much more qualified; she knows how to figure out all those things on the computer; Sr. Rosaria has a bigger heart than I; she would be more understanding of all the problems that would come her way; and Sr. Bernadette, Lord, You know what a great infirmarian she was; she'd be perfect with the elderly Sisters. Even Sr. Thomas Mary, Lord, her numbers were down in the second ballot, but You can bring them up;

she really would like to be prioress. I think she'd be kind of aloof and strict, but You know just what we need, Lord. Your will be done."

Those Sisters were among the names proposed; they were all Sisters around my age who had "come of age" and were now in positions of leadership. Being secretary to the prioress is not such an important charge; the sub-prioress is much more qualified to take over things. Sisters would know that, surely. I was good behind the librarian's desk all those years, but I've never been novice mistress, or even assistant novice mistress; I've never been sub-prioress or in charge of anything big like the refectory and kitchen, or maintenance. If Sr. Anna Maria becomes prioress, oh my, she might name me as sub-prioress and secretary besides.

The full impact of what it would be like to be prioress hadn't really hit me yet. At times, over the years, okay, I may have fantasized about being prioress a few times, even before Sr. Gertrude said it. It was usually when I wasn't happy with what the prioress was doing! But this was for real! I was praying within myself to Mother John Dominic: "Mother, if you have any influence in all this, please help us elect the prioress whom the Lord wants. Amen." There wasn't much time to pray, but time doesn't always matter, does it? In that brief time, I was able to surrender everything to the Will of God. It didn't make it less scary, I suppose, but more spiritual. For a brief instant one can see how the Holy Spirit weaves the tapestry through the most ordinary threads of our lives. It usually takes a little distance and reflection back on it all to see that, and we certainly have that opportunity, if we don't distract ourselves with all the demands on our time.

Mama used to say: "There's a little bit of *maror* and a little bit of *charoset* on our plates, both can be delicious if prepared well." Electing a prioress is a kind of "Passover" from one "regime" to another. Mother Agnes Mary has been one of the kindest, big-hearted, prioresses I have lived under; I will miss her terribly. I'll always remember her kindness to my mother. If I'm elected prioress, I would want to be just like her and Mother John Dominic.

The election went to the allowed four ballots, and at 10:45 a.m. we had a majority. We had a new Prioress. Blessed be God.

Eight

Matzah: The unleavened bread of Passover.

In the first month [i.e. Nissan] from the fourteenth day of the month at evening, you shall eat unleavened bread until the twenty-first day of the month at evening. (Exodus 12:18)

It wasn't a dream, but my meditation that evening almost seemed like a dream. I thought about the matzah which was/is the most important food of the Passover Seder. The house is clean of chametz and replaced by the pure and humble unleavened bread. It is a mitzvah to eat it, and so it is eaten exclusively for the eight days of Pesach. It binds the Jews together with all other Jews all over the world, in Jerusalem and in the diaspora. It is also the bread of freedom. The slaves fled Egypt with matzah in their knapsacks. Mama had inherited a beautiful matzah tosh, a silk bag holding three squares of matzah, each in its own "compartment" within the tosh. The rabbis, we were told, spoke of the "three in one." The matzah unified the three patriarchs: Abraham, Isaac, and Jacob. There's so much more to that, but that night, my meditation concerned only how the prioress is like matzah.

By our vow of obedience we submit ourselves to God, the Blessed Virgin, St. Dominic, the Master of the Order, and the prioress. It is the unifying vow, that makes us one: equals, "Sisters." For the Jews it was the bread of freedom and the bread of affliction. Our vow of obedience unites us in a wonderful freedom, even if it feels like affliction. I'll always remember Fr. Kitchens, our retreat master one time, who told us that we were the freest women in the world.

In Christ, we are one and free because the Lord Himself fulfills all the Laws and the prophets. He is the pure (sinless) and humble Bread of Heaven; He is the unblemished lamb whose blood is sprinkled over the door lintels of our souls, and the Evil One passes over us; His blood saves us; His body, the Eucharistic matzah nourishes us and makes us one with Him in a Holy Communion. The monastic community that we are is the church in miniature, and the first among us is the prioress, the first, the channel of grace poured out in loving service. Like the Mother of God, she "mothers" the body.

It was a rich meditation with many branches to explore. At 10:45 that morning the chapter chose the new Mother. Thus we sang our thanks to God, our *Te Deum*, as we processed from the chapter room into the chapel, and the sub-prioress with the bishop led the prioress to her stall: Mother Rosaria of the Mother of God. And the first thing Mother did was the venia (prostration) before the Lord in the Blessed Sacrament. When she rose and knelt on the kneeler in her stall, she led us in the prayer composed by St. Thomas Aquinas, which we pray before each Divine Office when prayed in the presence of the Eucharist:

> O sacred banquet, in which Christ becomes our food, the memory of His Passion is celebrated, the soul is filled with grace, and a pledge of future glory is given to us.
>
> V. *You gave them bread from heaven.*
>
> R. *Containing every blessing.*
>
> Let us pray. O God, in this wonderful Sacrament You have left us a memorial of Your Passion. Help us, we beg You, so to reverence the sacred mysteries of Your Body and Blood, that we may constantly feel in our lives the effects of Your redemption. Who live and reign forever.

The bishop was unable to stay for dinner, but we had planned a small reception after the installation. Two coffee urns were moved into the community room and a tray of doughnuts brought by the bishop himself. Apparently he anticipated this too. We had Krispy Kreme from the Jackson Street Subway Plaza…thank you, Bishop. I had a minute by myself, sitting in the corner with my coffee and chocolate Krispy Kreme. Anyone watching probably thought I was saying grace when I blessed myself, but I was saying a prayer of thanksgiving to Mother John Dominic. "Thank you, Mother, if you had any input into this election. Help me to accept that I was not elected; and help me to be grateful for that! And Mother, too bad you left us before Krispy Kreme Doughnuts came to Brooklyn; they are to die for. Amen."

Our new prioress looked very happy, if not a little overwhelmed by it all. The Holy Spirit did a wonderful job again.

Mother Rosaria Mary of the Mother of God. She was born in Defiance, Ohio, south of Toledo. She is the youngest of eight children. She went to St. Mary's Church and grade school. She had Adrian Dominicans for teachers. One in particular, a Sr. Mary Humbert, taught sixth grade. She was the prettiest nun Sharon (Mother Rosaria) had ever seen, and so she wanted to be a Dominican Sister since sixth grade, until her freshman year in high school! The lasting memory she has is not from school, but from church. Waiting for Mass to begin one knew when the Sisters came into the church. The swishing sounds of their habits and chain-rosaries brought a mysterious reverence while watching them move to the front pews, always kneeling on Mary's side, or what we called the Gospel side. After Communion, Sr. Mary Humbert would bury her face in her hands and not move till the final blessing. Sr. Mary Humbert wasn't mean and grouchy like some of the other Sisters. Sharon knew it was because she loved the Lord so much after Holy Communion. When Sharon was in eighth grade, Sr. Mary Humbert didn't come back to St. Mary's, and Sharon became disenchanted with it all.

After high school, in which she was a cheerleader for three years, and in the Girls' Glee Club, the Latin Club, and the Projectionists' Club, she wanted to move to New York City and maybe become a flight attendant. She thought this was a very glamorous job and would provide lots of travel to exotic countries around the world. She had also studied French for two years at Defiance High School, and wanted to visit Paris and see Notre Dame Cathedral, which she had written a term paper on. She never became a flight attendant, but she did become an *au pair* for a well-to-do French family on the Upper East Side of Manhattan. They were both in the Fashion Business, working for one of the famous French fashion houses with stores in New York, London, Toronto, and Paris. They had three children, ages eight, six, and two, when she started as *au pair*. It was wonderful because she could practice and use her French; and she went to France with the family at least three or four times a year.

She told me once that she didn't have much of a social life for herself at that time. She couldn't very well date and be at home to mind the kids. The parents were often out in the evening, and she had to go through the night-time routine with the kids and get them all tucked into bed. She had her own bedroom there in their East Side duplex on 69th Street. She knew St. Vincent's, of course, but they all went to St. Jean Baptiste, the French Church on 76th and Lexington. *Il y a trente ans, il y avait une messe en français tous les Dimanches.* She would show off her *français*, especially when we were alone, usually in the library. She was already a novice when I entered, but we often worked together. She was a great role model for me because she was so humble. She was also accident prone and would accept every little accident with great humbleness. I learned a lot from her, as many times I was uptight worrying what SCAR would say or do if I didn't do something right.

She was also quiet and didn't talk about herself very much. I was always curious about other Sisters' vocation stories, and learned from Sr. Rosaria that she believed the seed of her vocation was planted, or re-planted, at Notre Dame in Paris. The French family she worked for also had an apartment in

Paris on the Quai de Grenelle. She had her own room there, which was very small; but it had a little balcony outside where you could stand and, if you leaned forward enough and looked to the right, you could see the Eiffel Tower. She loved Paris, the City of Lights.

She would take the youngest child, who was not yet in school, to churches or museums around Paris, and especially to Notre Dame where she spent many hours visiting all the chapels and the crypt. She was kneeling in the crypt at the chapel of Notre Dame de la Compassion, and everything became uncannily silent. And in that moment, she knew that God was for real and that He loved her. And she said she knew, kneeling there in front of a statue of the Pieta, that she was going to be a Sister; she didn't hear voices or have a vision; it was simply a quiet interior conviction, or "call." Where, when, and how that would all happen she had no idea. In the stillness, she said, someone had left a vase of sunflowers on the floor near where she was kneeling. When she left, she accidently knocked it over. The water ran all over, the vase cracked, but the sunflowers remained intact. She said she was so embarrassed. She didn't know what to do, but picked it up and put it in a safer place, and made hand gestures warning the people of the spilled water. The little boy she was watching was also making a mess of the candles (tapers) sticking in sand; so she grabbed him and hustled out of there as fast as they could. But she always remembered that moment. She found her way to Rue de Bac and prayed often before the incorrupt body of St. Catherine Labouré. She identified with the saint, who was a kind of *au pair* to her own siblings. Like many pilgrims coming to visit the chapel of the Miraculous Medal, Sharon held on to the hands of St. Vincent de Paul's statue in the alley leading into the chapel. She bought a beautiful Miraculous Medal and has worn it ever since, praying often: *O Mary, conceived without sin, pray for us who have recourse to thee.* She loved the habit of the Daughters of Charity, but she just couldn't imagine doing the work they do, especially in France. "Maybe in America," she thought, "Our Lady will show me the way."

Her faith was sorely tested and strengthened as she remained with this family for seven more years. During the time back in New York, she was on the subway having visited the shrine of Blessed Elizabeth Ann Seton at 9 State Street in lower Manhattan. She accidently got on the wrong train, downtown to Brooklyn rather than the correct train uptown, but she was kind of following two Daughters of Charity who had been at the shrine too. So she took her "accident" as a sign from Our Lady. When the Sisters got off in Brooklyn Heights, Sharon simply followed them. She was not being sneaky about it, and she introduced herself to them, and told them she had seen them at the shrine, and that she often visited the Shrine of St. Catherine in Paris. The Sisters were very gracious and told her they were heading for a Dominican monastery to make a weekend retreat. In her own words: "The Daughters of Charity led me to Mary Queen of Hope Monastery where I met Sister Imelda, the extern Sister, and sat in the extern chapel close to the altar steps and heard the nuns chanting Vespers."

Sharon's French family was making a permanent move back to Paris, and they had invited her to move with them; but she had discovered another Rue de Bac in Brooklyn

Heights. "And the rest is history." Here she was thirty years later, the Mother Prioress, our spiritual *au pair*. At Vespers that night, during the Magnificat, I knew I loved our new prioress and was happy because I knew she would be a good prioress, like unto the hearts of Mother John Dominic and Mother Agnes Mary, and thus like unto the Heart of Jesus. I also loved Sr. Jane Mary in a strange new way, and I forgave her for being more an administrator than a "mother." The Holy Spirit also placed her here and as prioress if we are to believe that our prayers are heard. And I didn't always give her the understanding and acceptance when things didn't go my way. Sitting there in my stall, I also realized in myself how much I had really wanted to be elected, not because I was good at anything, but because it meant the Sisters wanted me. It was my pride that was wounded when the count was given on the last ballot, and I lost. But I also knew I loved this community and every one of the Sisters here, and after all my years here, I wanted to be able to serve them. But I felt so empty. It was another surrender as I felt totally alone, abandoned, just for a minute...maybe five. The Holy Spirit was at work, and I was what? I believe, Lord, I believe, help me to not resist Your Mercy.

My desire to serve was all mixed up, I suppose, with the desire to be wanted and needed. But the desire to serve is good and doesn't have to go away, I knew; it just needs to be re-directed. And the Lord of all consolation reminded me that I was very much loved and appreciated...one doesn't have to be elected to anything to prove that. I knew it every day in so many ways from the countless ways the Sisters have had mercy on me: patience with my stubborn attitude at times, and all my mistakes and sins of omission. There will probably be a special room in Purgatory just for those sins; all the lost opportunities to show love and mercy.

I couldn't move out of my stall when the clock chimed after meditation and everyone made their way to the refectory. I was so humiliated by my pride. I have to put on a happy face and go to supper like always; everyone seems so happy with our new prioress. I felt ashamed of myself for feeling so disappointed.

I must've sat there for five minutes. I had my head down, praying for God's mercy on me, without words, with a few seconds of tears, but mostly just dry emptiness. I didn't even hear the swish of a habit moving in next to me, but I felt the gentle arm around my shoulder. And as soft as warm air I heard: "It's okay, Sister. You have not lost the love and esteem of your Sisters."

I opened my eyes, as I knew the voice, and looked on the gentle eyes of SCAR…Sr. Catherine Agnes. "Oh, Sister, I don't know what's wrong with me; I feel so defeated, and ashamed for feeling it."

"I know, child, I know. But feelings are not facts, you know. They're just feelings. Come, now, Sister Bernadette made chocolate chip pancakes for supper and a surprise dessert. I knew you wouldn't want to miss out."

I smiled and shook my head "okay." And together we made our way to the refectory, and knelt together for being late, and Mother knocked and said out loud: "There you are, Sister Mary Baruch, it wouldn't be the same without you. Let's eat." I whispered a quick "thank you" to SCAR, who in all her integrated observance, whispered back: "Blessed be God." The chocolate chip pancakes were the best ever! And the surprise dessert? Two dozen eclairs sent by a Doctor Pierre Lemoine, the youngest son who used to go to Notre Dame in Paris with his *au pair*.

* * *

Bless me, Father, for I have sinned. It has been a weeksince my last confession. I am in solemn vows. And these are my sins. I have been full of pride, wanting to be recognized and chosen in a special way, rather than trusting in the Will of God. I wanted my own will and then was hurt when I didn't get what I wanted. I have been uncharitable in my small talk about other Sisters, and especially interiorly about one Sister who is my good friend, but I didn't want her to be elected prioress. She wasn't, and I was secretly delighted that she wasn't. I missed one of the Little Hours twice and didn't make it up; I'm lazy and full of distraction during the Office. I know that distractions are not sins, but I can go on flights of remembering things from the past. I have passed rash judgement on Sisters; I've complained to the Lord when I should be more accepting; and I've eaten in between meals probably five times. I've interiorly murmured about the food. And if I have lingered on any impure thoughts, I'm sorry, for these and any sins against my holy vows, and all the sins which I do not recall, I ask pardon of you, Father, and a penance.

I had to kiss the floor in the chapel and my stall. I had not had a penance (T'Shuvah) like that since I went to confession to Fr. Meriwether. And it struck me that Fr. Kelsey reminds me of a young Fr. Meriwether, not just in his fervorinos in confession, but in his reverence when he has offered Holy Mass here. Maybe it was a small way the Lord (and Fr. Meriwether) were assuring me that they were still looking after me. Although, Fr. Meriwether never gave me an added penance to forego desserts for three days. Oy.

Nine

Karpas: Parsley, lettuce, watercress or any other green herb and a dish of salt water into which it is to be dipped before being eaten. Also to remember the "dipping" of blood onto the coat of many colors of Joseph, sold into Egyptian slavery.

And you shall eat the meat [of the paschal lamb] on that night, roasted with fire, and unleavened bread; with bitter herbs you shall eat it. (Exodus 12:8)

I WASN'T DOZING OFF or daydreaming at all, but I was rinsing a colander full of parsley helping Sr. Bernadette in the kitchen prepare what we call a "festive meal" to celebrate Mother Rosaria's being our new prioress. It would be on Sunday and actually be a roasted turkey dinner with sweet potatoes, stuffing, and French-style green beans. Rinsing the parsley took me back to my childhood again, helping Mama prepare all the dishes for Pesach. The *karpas,* which was usually sprigs of parsley, was eaten first, very ceremoniously as we all dipped a sprig in a small bowl of salt water. It was combining the hope of spring (the parsley) with the tears of slavery (salt water). It didn't have much significance for us kids except in the context of the "Maggid," the telling of the story of the Exodus. One has to go through some bitter times (*karpas* and *maror*) to fill a bowl with your tears and cling to hope. Someone once said—I don't remember if it was the rabbi, Ezra, or Fr. Meriwether—that the parsley was like the hyssop which the priests would use to sprinkle the altar and the people with the blood. And we know that it was a hyssop sprig with vinegar offered to the Lord on the cross. Such thoughts I should have rinsing off the parsley!

Lent was beginning next week; Mother had scheduled a House Chapter for Monday night to announce the new assignments and charges. I had an appointment in the morning with her...I didn't know what to expect: parsley or salt water! And I had a parlor planned with Mama and David on Tuesday at which I would remind them that I would not see them till after Easter.

Silly, but I broke off a piece of parsley and put it in my apron pocket, and would put it in my habit pocket later and carry it in with me when I had my first meeting with Mother Rosaria. I don't know why. I guess it was like a rabbit's foot for good luck, something which the novices never heard of; or maybe it was just like a relic from my past, for security and luck.

The turkey dinner was a great success. Mother Rosaria was very pleased with it all and didn't even notice that she dripped gravy on her scapular, till she stood up to make a little thank you speech. On seeing the gravy, she said out loud: "Oh look, I've already made a mess of it." We all laughed, given the context of the comment. Recreation that evening was also a little celebration with ice cream and cake, and we presented Mother with a bib from Red Lobster. She thought it was hysterical and said that she would certainly use it, especially when we had spaghetti or gravy. We actually have a box of plastic bibs for the Sisters in the infirmary. It saves on the wear and tear of linen napkins.

The next morning, I stood at Mother's door, thinking that this was my fifth prioress; same door, same place. I took a deep breath and knocked.

"Enter."

"*Laudetur Jesus Christus*," I began with our traditional greeting.

"*In aeternum*, Sister, do come in." And Mother may have been the fifth, but she was the first to come out from behind her desk and embrace me. "Who-da thunk it,huh?" were her first words of wisdom.

I squeezed her. "The Holy Spirit, that's who-da!" And we both laughed. "I can't tell you, Mother, how happy I am that you are 'Mother' and I hope you can lean on me in any way you need to. I'm really so glad it's you behind that desk and not me!"

"Thank you, Sister Baruch. Dear Sister Mary Baruch, we've been through it together almost from the beginning. To think that our dear Mother John Dominic used to sit behind this desk. Could we ever forget her smile and how we needed it when we were novices?'

"No, Mother, we could never forget. I prayed to her to help the Lord choose the one He wanted, so she's smiling upon us."

Mother Rosaria may be behind the same desk, but she had added a couple new things, like two padded straight back chairs against the side wall with a small table between them.

"Let's sit there,' she waved with her hand, and proceeded to the chairs. Once settled she said: "I've been giving a lot of thought to the charges. I think you would make an excellent sub-prioress, BUT, I want to keep Sister Anna Maria there for now. She's much more organized than I am, as you know, and she keeps things under control. She's a born administrator, I think you'd agree." I nodded.

"Now, you have a wonderful way with both the older Sisters and the young ones…I've admired that in you all these years. I would love you to be the novice mistress, But I'm torn by what charge to give Sister Agnes Mary. Next to Mother John Dominic, Sister Agnes Mary was a wonderful prioress, as you know. Like you, she loves the life, and lives it fully. But she's also getting up in age, as we all are…" (I chuckled, and touched the parsley resting in my tunic pocket, not knowing what was coming next.) "I would like to name Sister Agnes Mary Novice Mistress for now, and you as Assistant Novice Mistress. I am telling Sister Agnes Mary that I want her to 'train you' for the job, but actually, Sister, I want you to keep a close watch on her and be able and ready to assist her in any way you can. I suspect the teaching will mostly fall to you, and on your part, the 'sandpapering' of the new Sisters in a way Sister Agnes Mary isn't able to do. Do you understand what I mean?"

"Yes, I think I do, Mother. I am very happy to do this; I am honored, really, to be her assistant, and I'm very happy to be part of the formation of the young ones, if God is pleased to send us some. And I was raised in the sandpapering school here!"

"Weren't we all! My dear, how times have changed, huh? Now, I don't want to lay too much on you, so please tell me if this is all too much, but I'd like you to keep up with the Sisters in the infirmary, not as infirmarian, but as you have been, AND (finally an 'and' and no more 'buts.') if you could still be at least 'part-time' correspondence-secretary to the prioress."

"Of course, Mother, I'd be honored to."

"Thank you, Sister, I'm already leaning on you a lot, but I think we'll make the most of it—a new springtime for the monastery."

She actually said "springtime." I wanted to pull the parsley out of my pocket and eat it right there in front of her, but I restrained. I was good at that now. We can have all sorts of crazy thoughts at times, and even desires, but we learn how to...well, keep them in our pocket.

She stood up, which was my cue to stand too. Again she hugged me, and said: "Such a blessing, this place." We both laughed and agreed that indeed it was. "It's a great life, if you don't weaken." Those were her parting words of wisdom. I left her office elated.

Outside her door, I looked both ways, blessed myself, and ate my parsley on my way to the chapel to thank the Lord for all His blessings. (I'll probably have to kiss the floor again!) Assistant Novice Mistress—imagine that! Please, Lord, send us lots of novices to assist! I was humming *Parsley, sage, rosemary and thyme,* as I genuflected before the Lord waiting for me in our weekday monstrance, hoping He didn't hold it against me for eating between meals again…it was only parsley, Lord.

I had a wonderful hour of guard both that evening after Compline and again in the morning. Being Assistant Novice Mistress would mean I would be moving from our cell to one in the novitiate. It had been a while since I even visited the novitiate floor, so I spent a little time "snooping" around, and seeing what rooms were available. There were too many, actually, as we only had two white-veiled novices—Sr. Mary Kolbe and Sr. Diana—and two black-veils—Sr. Myriam and Sr. Maureen. One stays in the novitiate after taking temporary vows for two years.

Sr. Mary Kolbe was dear to me, as she had a special devotion to both Maximilian Kolbe and Edith Stein. Sr. Kolbe was from White Plains in Westchester County. She graduated from Hunter College which is very close to St. Vincent's which she knew very well. She went to daily Mass there if there was not a conflict with class. It was really there that she first met the Dominicans, and it was Fr. Kelsey, our new confessor, who told her about us, as well as the other Dominican monasteries in New Jersey and the Bronx. She was attracted to the Carmelites because of Edith Stein and St. Teresa of Avila, (more than the Little Flower, my first friend in the faith). She was also deeply devoted to the Immaculata, a title for Our Lady which St. Maximilian Kolbe promoted. She visited a couple Carmels. But in the end it was the rosary that attracted her to us; plus we seemed to study more. This was all in the three years after college. She entered two years ago, and has one more year before profession. We have a two-year novitiate now, which is a change again from my time... the "old days."

Sr. Diana just became a novice after almost a year as a postulant. She's from New Hampshire and was taught by the Sisters of the Presentation of Mary. She worked in various restaurants, working her way up to sous-chef in a French Restaurant in Newport, Rhode Island. She loved Newport and thought she would be there forever and ever. She had a friend from college who worked at Salve Regina University, and for a couple months lived in a carriage house of the Sisters of Jesus Crucified. Clare, her name in the world, was not very religious; she called herself a "Sunday Catholic," and that had been instilled in her from the Presentation Sisters. She found herself joining her friends at the priory of the Sisters of Jesus Crucified, and their living the religious life with such joy in the midst of all kinds of illness and physical handicaps changed her heart about a lot of things. She found herself reading more spiritual kinds of books and after work she began to walk along the Cliff Walk with the ocean splashing below praying the rosary. After the friend moved out of the carriage house, a Dominican Sister moved in for a couple months, and Clare became "Sunday friends" with her. The Dominican Sister was on a long retreat to discern whether to enter a cloistered monastery in Brooklyn, New York, or continue as a Dominican Sister of the Sick Poor. The Sister never joined us, but Clare found her way here and became a regular visitor. She landed a job in another French restaurant in Manhattan, and got a furnished room not far from us.

She reminds me of our Sr. Simon, who is our baker, but has slowed down. It's like God has provided another baker for us, perhaps. Mother was impressed that she put down

"Diana" as her first choice for a religious name. Mother Agnes Mary said, "We have a Sister Amata, but not a Sister Diana. How amazing that she would have a devotion to one of the first nuns at the time of St. Dominic." Only after she became a novice, and Sr. Mary Diana, did we learn she didn't know about Blessed Diana, but was a big fan of Princess Diana, who was killed in 1997, some months before Clare entered here as a postulant.

Sr. Maureen was our *colleen* right from Ireland. Well, she was born in Dublin, but came here with her family when she was just beginning high school. She went to Sacred Heart Academy in Hempstead, Long Island, and then to Franciscan University in Steubenville for two years. Her name in the world was Moira Caitlin Burns. She wanted to keep Moira, but Mother gave her Maureen instead. If she perseveres, she will definitely be one of our chantresses; she's got a lovely voice. She also has a wonderful Irish sense of humor which she learned to temper a bit in the novitiate. For instance, if the priest made a funny remark in his homily, it was okay to discreetly laugh along with a gracious smile directed to him. Sr. Maureen, however, would laugh out loud, too loud, and look around at the other Sisters in sisterly camaraderie. But she learned from Sr. Catherine Agnes: "It isn't our way."

Sr. Maureen loves the life, however, and can be a bit too enthusiastic over little things or get all red-faced when she's controlling her temper. She begins integration the First Sunday of Advent and will help in the kitchen and refectory. Integration is when a temporarily professed Sister moves over to the professed side of the house, and is "integrated" with them; meaning, her cell is now there, and she would attend recreation with them, and be given a more responsible charge. It was also a good way for the professed nuns to get to know her before voting on her for Solemn Profession. She's also great with the Sisters in the infirmary, and can get them all singing together—in harmony, no less—which is no small task.

Sr. Myriam was in second year vows when Mother Rosaria was elected. She was integrated into the senior community before Lent began. She is from Philadelphia. She went to Providence College in Providence, Rhode Island—the pride and joy of the Dominican Friars of the Province of St. Joseph. Her uncle is a Dominican Father, Fr. Aelred Eberhart. Ellen (Sr. Myriam) has her BA in philosophy and a minor in classical languages, namely, Latin and Greek. "Uncle Aelred thought I'd go into a teaching order, but Thomas Merton's *The Seven Story Mountain* changed all that." It was Uncle Aelred who introduced her to Mary, Queen of Hope monastery. We're happy he did. Sr. Myriam is our little scholar, tackling St. Thomas, as she puts it. She'll wind up teaching us!

In 2000, we had one postulant, Sr. Emma, who was from Florida, near Sarasota. She's very humorous and said she always wanted to join the circus when she was young. I think she has a second cousin who is a clown with Ringling Brothers, whom she calls Uncle Bo. I wondered if Uncle Bo would ever appear here in our parlor, if Sr. Emma perseveres. When she was young, she studied gymnastics and modern dance, but her body couldn't take the rigors, so she quit, and abandoned dreams of being a trapeze artist. Her other passion was the clarinet, which she could handle well enough to get in to the Rome School of Music at Catholic

University of America. She graduated from there with a Masters in Instrumental Music, majoring in woodwinds. She was accomplished in both oboe and clarinet. She also played the piano and several other wind instruments, but had never played the organ. We all just smiled. And prayed she'd persevere. She had been with us just a month at the time of Mother's election.

These were the Sisters who would be under our care in the novitiate. They were each unique and different. They had the special charge to pray for more postulants to enter. We were all feeling the decrease in vocations, but tookOur Holy Father's words to heart: "Do not be afraid. Have hope."

Monday evening's chapter went well: no real surprises as everyone knew ahead of time what one would be doing. Sr. Mary George remained Bursar and Sr. Thomas Mary stayed in maintenance, which she (and all of us) were happy about. Sr. Antonia remained in the library, which was also good, as she was converting the entire card indexonto the computer.

I had my hour of guard at 2:00 a.m. Tuesday morning. I loved the early morning adoration time, once I was awake. We were allowed to have a mug of coffee, if we had the time, before our hour began. It was not the kind of coffee Mama would have liked, but it did the trick. I began as usual with reading the Gospel of the day to myself, and then took out my beads. I rarely dozed off when I had the early morning guard. If necessary, one could stand and even walk around a bit, but I preferred kneeling. My meditation, however, was not always on the mysteries of the rosary, but the events of the day, and there were lots of events in early 2000.

Later that day I would see Mama and David. This was still an extraordinary "event," as it had been more than twenty-five years of not seeing either one of them. The reconciliation continued to fill me with such awe and gratitude, tinged always with the realization that it was Ruthie's sudden death that brought about the reunion with Mama.

They had been on their cruise and were planning another. David was so good to Mama, it somehow took the edge off of my judging him as such a worldly hedonist. He *was* that, but Mama managed to keep a corner of his heart open. I hoped that was true with Sally, too. Distance didn't help in Sally's case. I let it all go before the Lord; joining everything to His Sacred Heart. The best I could do in all of it was simply to pray. Just sitting with the Lord without any words was becoming more and more how it went.

Mama and David would be coming around 3:30, so I could visit the infirmary in the morning. After doing correspondence for Mother Rosaria for about an hour; I made my way to the infirmary. Sr. Gertrude always liked knowing if and when I was having company. She and Mama had become friends, and hopefully she could pop into the parlor this afternoon and work her charm on David.

We sat in front of the large picture window looking out on the cemetery.

"The snow has almost melted, don't you miss it?" Sr. Gertrude knew my fondness for snow. Some years ago now, we were able to spend a couple hours "playing" in it, that is, building a couple snow-nuns with carrot noses and sticks for arms.

"Yes, I do. But it's early yet; we may get one more blast of it. It would be nice for Lent."

"Ah, yes. Lent. I'm giving up listening to my Broadway musicals."

"Now that is something! More sacrificial than candy or ice cream."

"Or cottage cheese, which I always gave up for Lent, because I hated it." We both laughed.

"Why such a sacrifice this Lent, if I may be so nosey as to ask?"

"Of course you can." She got silent for maybe twenty seconds. "I don't know how many Lents I have left; this could be my last, so I want to make it a good one."

"Oh, don't talk like that; you've got a slew of Lents left." I kind of slurred it all, making Sr. Gertrude laugh.

"One never knows, dear, one never knows. Changing the subject, are you relieved or disappointed that you weren't elected prioress? Myself, well, I was certainly disappointed, I think you'd be a wonderful prioress, but I'm also happy that you've been named assistant novice mistress; you should be novice mistress, not the assistant, but Mother Rosaria didn't consult with me first!"

"Oh, I'm happy to be the assistant novice mistress, especially with Sister Agnes Mary. And at first I was disappointed about the election. Just between us, I was devastated, and then more upset with myself for being so upset. How could I be so self-centered after all these years? I think my pride was dealt a big blow, but it's just what I needed. You know what I mean?"

Sr. Gertrude always thought before she spoke. "I know what you mean, my dear, just between us girls, I've been there myself, if you recall. I always say I'm happy to be the understudy, but you know, being prioress was the 'lead role.' And it took me a few blows from the Holy Spirit, to accept myself. But you're doing just fine, dear Mary Baruch of the Advent Heart. Like Our Lady in Advent, He looks upon the lowliness of His handmaid. We are reminded of that every evening at Vespers. Our Lady is really the Star of this show, and we should all try to be her understudy!"

"I know. Thank you, Sister, you're always a star to me, you know, and I'd be more than happy to be your understudy. Well, now I'm Sister Agnes Mary's understudy. We've got five lovely dancers in our 'corps de ballet', and we must pray for vocations."

"I know; we're all praying. And I hear there are at least two on the horizon; so you'll have your hands full." A silent moment interrupted our thoughts as we gazed out at the cemetery. Sr. Gertrude picked up the conversation again: "I think Mother Rosaria will make a fine prioress; you two were novices together, if I remember right."

"That's right; she was a white-veil novice when I entered. She was also a part of our little novitiate glee club; you, of all people, would remember that."

"Indeed I do; I even danced to your 'If I were a rich nun' from *Fiddler on the Belfry.*"

I laughed. "That's right; you have an incredible memory, Sister Gertrude. I'd forgotten all about that."

"Thank you. Just don't ask me what I had for breakfast; I don't remember." Thinking again in the silence. I thought she was thinking about the breakfast menu, but came out with: "Tell me, if this is my last Lent, and I'm auditioning for the Hallelujah Chorus on High, do you think Mother Rosaria would allow *'What I Did For Love'* from *A Chorus Line* at my funeral Mass?"

I didn't laugh because I knew she wasn't kidding. "I highly doubt it, Sister, Mother is very open minded, but I'm pretty sure she'd draw the line at a Broadway show song at Mass."

Sr. Gertrude looked down-trodden. "You're right. I really love that song, the words are referring to someone who can't dance anymore, but they speak of our life, and why we do this. If it's not all for love, what good is it? You think about these things when you get older, I know. I've packed my top hat and tap shoes away, but we live the life right till the final curtain!"

I picked up the cue right on pitch: "But I can't regret…" She joined me, "What I did for love; what I did for love." She clapped her hands with delight.

"Sister Gertrude, you know my mother and brother are coming this afternoon around 3:30; it would be wonderful if you popped in to say hello."

"Oh, how delightful. I shall." And she took her wrist watch off her left arm and put it on her right. "So, I'll remember… it's better than tying a string around your finger."

"Let's have a cup of tea," said she. And so we did, in the music room, with a little Mardi Gras coffee cake and the full score of *A Chorus Line.* Dear Sr. Gertrude; always more parsley than salt water. (And how did she know about "two on the horizon"? I hadn't heard a thing about that yet!)

Mama and David arrived shortly before 3:30. Mama was wearing last year's Chanukah gift from David, a car-coat-length mink coat, over a black cashmere sweater with a single strand of pearls and gray slacks. She looked like a million bucks. David put a box of goodies from Zabar's on the turn, and was himself dressed very formally in suit and tie—silk, if I could see it a little closer.

"I saw the sign in the entrance way about ashes tomorrow. It's Ash Wednesday, right?" Dr. David, the observant one.

"Of course, right. Lent begins tomorrow and that means Becky goes into hibernation till Easter. Last Lent she lost forty pounds." Mama was talking about me like I wasn't in the room.

"Not really, Mama. Maybe I lost a few pounds. We fast for the forty days of Lent and don't have meat except a couple times of week, and not quite as many desserts. Not like in the old days! And I don't go into hibernation, but we keep a stricter enclosure which means we normally don't have visitors during Lent; anyway, you two are off on another cruise, so you won't even miss me." I hoped that didn't sound self-deprecating.

David: "Yes, we're going on a 'show cruise'—kind of like the Catskills on water. It's only five days, but lots of fun and lots of entertainment. Ruthie did one a while ago; she was part of the entertainment."

"Oh, I remember that. Our Ruth Steinway, the *comedienne*." We all smiled and didn't say anymore.

I continued with all my news, telling them about the election, and my new charge, and how happy I was about it all—especially getting to visit with them.

"I can see how happy you are. Sally told me a hundred times, I think." David, the psychiatrist making observations. "Sally and Mitzie are coming to apartment-sit while we're away."

"*My* apartment doesn't need sitting?" Mama was "observing." "They want to stay in David's duplex so they play rich old ladies for a week. I'm not complaining, mind you, they'll probably bring one of their mutts with them, so I'm just as glad they're camping out on the Upper East Side."

"Cognac is a pedigree miniature poodle—no mutt, I can assure you. I have to put in a screen on my first floor balcony, lest Cognac falls off to his death."

"Such a fuss you make over that pedigree runt. Cognac, what a name for a dog! But I'm not complaining. I'll be off sailing towards Bermuda in pedigree shorts." Mama laughed. We all laughed.

"Have Sally and Mitzie been here to visit you?" David was asking, although I think he knew the answer. Dr. David, the analyst.

"Not yet. Sally keeps promising to come; but you know, she doesn't come to New York that much anymore. I think she would be fascinated by it all—this life is quite different from what they are used to."

"Why are you two so dressed up? It's just Mardi Gras."

"We're off to the Russian Tea Room for dinner.

One of David's doctor friends is celebrating his seventieth birthday there, and we're invited. The Russian Tea Room, imagine! I've never been there, but Millie Hutner tells me it's one of the most elegant restaurants in New York, like St. Petersburg in 1910. I don't know what St. Petersburg was like, but I don't have to go to Russia to find out. I can eat Russian elegance right on West 57th Street. And then we're going to a concert next door at Carnegie Hall." Mama smiled. And with that, she pulled out a small bottle of Mogen David she had stashed in her elegant handbag.

"This is it till after our cruise, after Lent, and after Passover. So we shouldn't have a little Mardi Gras with you before we go to Russia?" Mama didn't wait for a response; she was getting the un-elegant cheese glasses out of the cabinet.

It was a delightful Mardi Gras party for me, before saying goodbye, and going into hibernation. There was a little salt water going on through the grille which separated us and made such visits bitter-sweet. But my heart was filled with joy, and I looked forward to a wonderful Lent. That evening's meditation after Vespers took me back to East 79th Street as I was remembering that Greta always liked cognac, and it was *not* a pedigree or a mutt.

Ten

Pesach: "Passover" in Hebrew

Then came the first day of Unleavened Bread on which the Passover lamb had to be sacrificed. And Jesus sent Peter and John, saying, "Go and prepare the Passover for us, so that we may eat it." (Luke 22:7-12)

WE HAD A lovely Holy Week. To my great delight, Fr. Matthew was home from Africa and joined our chaplain, Fr. Ambrose, in the liturgies of the Paschal Triduum. Fr. Ambrosc was very grateful for the help as well. Ezra (Fr. Matthew) was the principal celebrant and preacher for Holy Thursday evening.

The novices (this always includes the postulants and temporary professed) and I prepared the Altar of Repose. Sr. Agnes Mary had caught a nasty spring cold, and moved into the infirmary for Holy Week. Mother Rosaria was also extra generous in our "flowers budget," and besides what many friends and benefactors gave, we bought a dozen white lilies, half a dozen pink hyacinths, and a couple potted tulips of various colors.

Mother also let us "experiment" with having the altar of repose in a different place this year. It was always either at the altar where the monstrance is every day, or at the small altar where the tabernacle is—both in the extern chapel. We have in a spare room in the infirmary a small portable altar which we use on rare occasions when we have Mass in the infirmary. One corner of the cloister is without decoration or a statue. We put the portable altar in the corner, and behind it we draped a gold linen curtain that fit perfectly. On the altar we spread an old altar cloth, freshly washed and ironed, which had *Sanctus, Sanctus, Sanctus* in gold Old English letters on the front piece that hung down. We had in the middle a wooden platform held by two adoring angels, both wooden with gold trimming.

We had one plain prie-dieu with a padded kneeler, and on both sides of the cloister fanning out from the altar, twenty padded folding chairs. The ciborium would be placed on the angel-platform, and at midnight, one of the Fathers would come and take the Lord away to a specially prepared cupboard in the extern sacristy. The objections to our doing this was that lay people coming in from the outside would not be able to visit the altar. They could be here for the Mass, but after the procession began Sr. Paula would invite the people to leave. And lock the doors.

I think the majority of Sisters liked the "experiment" because it made it more private for us, and more intimate. We liturgically accompanied the Lord and the Apostles to the Garden of Gethsemane, rather than keeping watch from a distance.

Fr. Matthew did not look well to me; he had lost too much weight, I thought, although he says that's just the "Jewish Mother" in me. But he was in fine voice, and sang the Mass of the Lord's Supper as fine as almost any cantor. In his homily he spoke eloquently about the Seder which the Lord ate with His beloved disciples. He talked a little about the Jewish practice of washing one's hands before the Seder begins, and the importance of the four cups of wine. To everyone's delight he chanted (in his homily) the Kiddush which is sung over the first cup ...the cup of sanctification.

Fr. Matthew paused for a moment. I don't know if he was becoming emotional or forgetful. He said, after eating the bitter herbs, perhaps the most important part of the meal begins. There are three squares of matzah. The Lord, according to the ritual, took the second piece and broke it. One of the halves he would wrap in a linen cloth and hide. The other piece was normally then broken and given to those at the table. And it was here that the Lord changed everything. He broke the matzah, the unleavened bread, and hid the half, and broke the other half, saying: "*Take and eat, for this is my body which will be given up for you.*" The Passover story would be read and discussed, and the second cup of wine drunk. After eating the festive meal, the hidden matzah was "redeemed," and the third cup, the cup of redemption, was drunk and Jesus again changed everything. *Take and drink this for this is the cup of my blood, the blood of the new and everlasting covenant.*

The covenant. This is the bond between God and His People, beginning with Abraham, but seen in earlier covenants with Adam and Noah. And "Jesus changed everything. The covenant—the bond—between God and man is now and forever in Him, in His Body and Precious Blood. What He would do on the morrow, He does now under the sacred signs of matzah and wine. The matzah indeed becomes the Most Blessed Sacrament."

He looked up from his written text, which he wasn't adhering to, and spoke in a personal way which was very moving. He said in words to this effect: "When I became a Catholic, I was joined to the Lord in the Sacrament of Baptism at the Church of the Blessed Sacrament on West 71st Street. When I met a young Jewish Barnard College student who had come to know and love the Lord, we made the round of churches in Manhattan to be present to the Real Presence in all the churches' tabernacles. His Real Presence changed our lives forever—it has changed each one of your lives, for think where you could be this night if you did not know and love Him. He liturgically enters into His passion tonight, and like the first disciples we will accompany Him from the first altar in the upper room to the Garden of Gethsemani, there to keep watch. What He had done ritually in the breaking of the matzah would now be enacted in real time, as we say today. The broken bread, hidden in a linen cloth, like a linen shroud, would be hidden in a tomb, and be found on Sunday following the Sabbath. The eighth day. His glorified and Risen Body is still present for us in this Most Blessed Sacrament, because He gave us Himself in the persons of His apostles—*you do this, to make Me present so you will always remember Me*. What a precious gift we have in the Eucharist and in the priesthood."

* * *

I think the Sisters were pleased with his homily. Not all of them knew that I was the young Jewish Barnard student, but that's okay. It almost seems like another lifetime ago.

On Easter Sunday I had a grand parlor. We were squeezed into the prioress's parlor, as the larger ones were also being used. The extern part could cram four or five chairs only, which was plenty for Ezra, his Aunt Sarah, Mama, and David. We didn't have the table, but I made sure there were plates and glasses and napkins on the turn. It was Ezra's Aunt Sarah's first time here, and she drank it all in. She didn't think monasteries like this still existed and smack in the middle of Brooklyn Heights. She had been to the Cloisters in Yonkers, but there were no real nuns or monks living there. She loved the idea of guest rooms and hoped to come back next fall if she could do the stairs. The big news from her was that Tea on Thames had expanded. "It's owned by two Italian men who bought the store next door and now included exotic coffees in their menu. They knocked down a wall and had an Italian-like bridge joining the two rooms. I think they wanted it to look like Venice. The table space is twice what Gwendolyn had and they added a corner piano on a platform. On weekends there's a piano player and it's very popular. And they changed the name, you know."

"Oh no," came swooshing out of Ezra and me at the same time. "They can't change the name…what is it called now?"

"Tea Time on the Tiber."

"Humph. Sounds to me like they also stole Gwendolyn's idea of having entertainment, like Penguin Pub." Ezra shook his head in agreement with me, and we just looked at each other in amazement.

"Remember Gwen had a framed picture of Queen Elizabeth on the far wall. What do they have, a gondolier?" "Pope John Paul," Aunt Sarah said as a matter of fact. Sounds like she'd been there a couple times.

Ezra laughed, "Well, I'm happy to see you know who the pope is!"

"Such a yutz, this one." (Meaning Ezra, not the pope!) And we all laughed.

This was also the first time in a long time that Ezra and Mama were together, and David, of course, who had met him only once and blamed him for misguiding me.

I had prayed all morning and offered my Easter Communion for the intention that they would all be at peace with each other. I was sharing my anxiety with Mother in her office on Holy Saturday afternoon. As she is wont to do, she listened very closely and chose her words very carefully.

"Life is too short to worry about all that; or to hold on to disagreements and hard feelings. At best we people should be cordial to each other."

"I know, Mother, I'm not worried about Aunt Sarah or Mama, just a little for David and Ezra. I also know I'm powerless to do anything about it. I trust that the Lord will bring extraordinary grace out of it all.

And indeed He did. Ezra (Fr. Matthew) actually kissed Mama hello, and Mama was quite tickled by it. "I've never been kissed by a priest before. Wait till I tell the Hadassah this one!" We all laughed. "You're looking too thin, Father Ezra. Your Aunt Sarah here needs to fatten you up." "I totally agree, Mrs. Feinstein," chimed in Aunt Sarah.

"Please, call me Hannah. And I don't know if you remember my eldest son, David. It's been a long time…"

"I'm happy to see you all again." David stretched out his hand. "I never would have dreamed that it would be here at the nunnery, but who knows the ways of Destiny?"

I wondered if this was David's theological insight or something from his practice…was Destiny with a capital D or a small d? I didn't dare ask. But I was happy that he was so cordial. As Mother kind of said earlier, "Life is too short not to be cordial." Of course, David wasn't very cordial thirty-five years ago; but maybe things like being cordial take time to "mean it."

"Father Matthew has been here since last Tuesday and helped our chaplain with all our 'high holy days' liturgies. It's been wonderful having him here." I wasn't being "cordial," I meant every word of it. "In his Holy Thursday homily, he even talked about our meeting at Tea on Thames a hundred years ago."

Mama joined in the laughter and the sentiment. "Oy, I'll never forget the Thanksgiving when you and Aunt Sarah were with us, and you dropped the Catholic bomb right in the middle of dessert."

David said, "Your career as a 'yenta' flew right out the window."

Aunt Sarah joined in, "And then he runs off to be passionate; I didn't know why he couldn't be passionate right here in New York!"

They were talking about us like we weren't present, which was delightful to see how well they'd all gotten over it, but didn't forget a detail.

David turned to Fr. Matthew and asked, "So are you here visiting or are you here to stay?"

"I'm here to have Aunt Sarah fatten me up. I've had several bouts with malaria, and so I think my missionary days are over. Or at least curtailed. The provincial, that's my superior, wants me to rest and is letting me do it in Manhattan. I may wind up at our retreat house in Massachusetts, but I'll be at a parish in Manhattan for the year. So Aunt Sarah can fatten me up, and Sister Mary Baruch can restore my spirit."

I think I must've blushed, but I was very moved by what he said. "It will be a blessing for us to have you so close. Too bad," I said jokingly, "we can't go to Tea Time on the Tiber…"

"And turn over some tables!" We all laughed.

Eleven

Shulchan Orech: The Third Cup

Now as they were eating, Jesus took bread, said the blessing, broke it, and giving it to his disciples said, "Take and eat; this is my body." Then he took a cup, gave thanks, and gave it to them, saying, "Drink from it, all of you, for this is my blood of the covenant, which will be shed on behalf of many for the forgiveness of sins. (Matthew 26:26-28)

SUMMER CAME AND went without much disturbance. Mother Rosaria was proving to be an exceptional prioress. Sr. Agnes Mary was keeping up as Novice Mistress, but she knew she didn't have the energy for lots of things. I wasn't young myself, of course, but I was renewed in spirit with the new relationship with my brother. I was so grateful to God for everything. Ezra came for a visit in mid-June and was already looking healthier all the time.

We only had less than an hour in the parlor, so I got right to the point. "So tell me, my dear old friend, how are you *really* doing?"

"Physically, I'm doing much better. By the end of July, I was hoping to go back to Zimbabwe, but my provincial informed me that we are pulling out of Zimbabwe. He wants to keep our missions going in Haiti, Honduras, and Jamaica, and, as you know, we've got retreat houses all over. West Springfield is closing, however, as are a few others. We're feeling the vocation crunch, you know."

"I know. We are here, too; although we're holding our own. There's talk among a couple of the monasteries of closing. It's really sad, isn't it?"

"Yes, the renewal after Vatican II was supposed to renew all of us. I don't know what went wrong." Ezra spoke softly and put his head down for the moment as if he were praying.

I waited a moment before responding. "I don't know, but I suspect that some Orders or Congregations of Sisters went beyond what was asked of them, and in adapting themselves to the world, became more and more secular." He didn't respond, sitting there in his khaki pants and a black polo shirt. I thought for the moment that he was looking like a middle-aged junior executive on his vacation yacht, his salt and pepper hair looking very distinguished, and his horn-rimmed glasses making him look very executive; but he didn't look like a priest.

Almost like he was reading my mind, he said, "Tell me about it. Look at me. I look like I'm a college student."

I had to laugh. "A college student? How about a college professor looking to retire and go sailing on his yacht?"

"You're right. Although I'm not so sure about the yacht! Not to change the subject, but I don't suppose you got to watch any of the Pope's visit to Israel last March?"

"No, we don't even have a television, although times are a' changing there, too; so who knows what's coming. But we read all the articles from both the *New York Times* and L'*Osservatore Romano*. It was wonderful, wasn't it?"

"Oh it was, you should have seen him. He began, you know, with a verse from Psalm 31. I carry it around in my college professor's wallet." He pulled it out of his back pocket and read it.

"*I have become like a broken vessel. I hear the whispering of many. Terror on every side, as they scheme together against me, as they plot to take my life. But I trust in you, O Lord; I say, You are my God.* Psalm 31, verse 13." He folded it without comment and put it back in his wallet.

I waited silently for his next words, but then I repeated out loud the opening line: "*I have become like a broken vessel.* Do you feel like a broken vessel?"

He looked up again with a sad face that I had never seen on him before. "I do. I loved my work—my ministry—with my orphan kids, and I loved the missions, period; but over the years it's like my priesthood was squeezed out of me. All the fervor I had in the beginning dissipated somewhere along the way. My prayer life seemed to disappear completely. I was just mouthing the words at Mass, but my heart wasn't in it. I used to be faithful to writing in my journal, you know, ever since I left New York and Greta gave me my first one."

I just sat silently and listened. My left hand quietly went to my side rosary. I didn't want to pray it, just to hold it while Ezra poured out his heart to me.

"That's why you didn't hear from me for months on end. I wasn't really depressed, as I said; I loved my work with the kids, but I was empty…a broken vessel. When I heard the Holy Father pray that, I knew he was speaking of the Lord, but it went straight to my poor heart. It was strange. Like I suddenly had a huge love for the Jewish people. I felt one with them again, although maybe it was just the emotion of John Paul being at Yad Vashem.[2] I didn't lose my faith in Christ, but I felt like I had abandoned Him." He paused for a moment to collect his thoughts. "I was also sick, you know, and my provincial called me home right after that. So, I'm doing much better now. Aunt Sarah has been cooking up a storm for me."

I quietly spoke up, "Yes, it shows even from Holy Week here. What was the last line of the Psalm that Pope John Paul prayed?"

He took it out of his wallet again and read, "*But I trust in you, O Lord; I say, You are my God.*"

"Yes, isn't that powerful too? There've been a few times when I've been scraping bottom, spiritually and emotionally; and in the end, it brings me back to surrendering everything into His hands. *I trust in you, O Lord.* I've had lots of periods when my Jewishness surfaces, and I'm filled with wonder at how blessed I am; it's like I haven't renounced my Jewishness, but really fulfilled it. I say *You are my God*...and I know that is *Yeshuva*..."

Ezra smiled his old smile. And putting his hand on his head like a ready-made yarmulke, he softly said, "*Shema, Israel,* hear O Israel, the Lord our God is One."

We both sat silent for a minute. "It sounds to me like malaria was the least of your problems; I think you suffered from a bad case of Acedia. It's a dangerous illness because

---

2 The Holocaust Memorial in Jerusalem, established in 1953 on the Mount of Remembrance.

one can almost lose one's faith entirely. But it's also curable, you know. Broken vessels can be glued back together." I paused for a moment to collect my thoughts. "I'm blessed, you know, because I have a community right here to catch me when I fall, and a few wonderful Sisters who know how to repair broken vessels. I've thought of it recently as the *charoset* of the life, not chopped apples and honey, but tough love and a dash of humor, and plain old perseverance. I've been thinking a lot about our Seders when I was a kid, and all the foods Mama prepared with such devotion, and how Papa led the prayers. I've even dreamed of Mr. Eli, remember him? He was our doorman, who in my dream told me everything was going to be just fine, when I let Mama's Seder plate smash on the floor. So don't let it all get to you, Ezra Goldman, everything is going to be just fine; you are going to be just fine. Just slow down, maybe, and..."

"And what?"

"And listen to the words when you're saying Mass; it's Our Lord's Seder and it has been fulfilled in you...in us...aren't we the blessed ones!"

I could see the tears flowing down Fr. Matthew's cheeks. "You're right, Becky Feinstein, such wisdom you should have since we met at Tea on Thames."

"I don't know about wisdom, but I know if we let prayer go, we're letting our inner connection with the Lord go, and without that, none of this makes any sense. You showed me that a hundred years ago; you preached about it on Holy Thursday too. There's a real presence of the Lord in the Eucharist, but there's also the real presence within you, and only you can go and adore and commune with the Lord there." He just sat silent, taking it all in. The frown lines and grimace he showed minutes ago faded away. For a second he was my old friend Ezra sitting on a bench overlooking the Hudson River and talking about the Incarnation.

"Thank you for that, dear Sister Mary Baruch." His old smile changed his face completely.

"You're welcome," I whimpered back, adding, "Such a homily I should be giving to a priest?" And we both laughed at ourselves, knowing the Lord was laughing with us.

It was maybe two weeks later that Fr. Matthew came to say Mass for us, and we had a parlor afterwards. He was wearing his clerical shirt with a tab collar. His curly salt and pepper hair was shorn down to a buzz cut, and his eyes had regained a twinkle he had lost before.

"The Passionist Fathers in our province of England and Wales were asking for some help for about a year at their Shrine in Lancashire. Lots of activity going on with pilgrimages. The tombs of Blessed Dominic Barberi and Mother Mary Joseph, the foundress of the Cross and Passion Sisters are there. It's like a retreat mission with lots of time for prayer and in a beautiful location. The Provincial asked me if I would be willing to go."

"And you said?"

"And I said 'Yes, I'd love to go.' I think it's just what I need at this time. You gave me the desire to really let the Lord renew my priesthood, you know. I've always wanted to be a part of a Shrine, and I've never been to see our Fathers in England; they're even fewer in number than we are, so I'm going for just a year, maybe a little longer."

I could only smile and say: "I think it's wonderful. I was hoping you'd be around here for a while longer but I'm really glad for you; it sounds wonderful." I didn't let him know I was interiorly crushed and sad that he would be away, but I knew the Lord was at work in all of it. *I trust in you, O Lord; I say, You are my God.*

"When do you leave?"

"Right after the Assumption."

"And how far is Lancashire from London? Because you know who's there."

"Indeed I do; I've already emailed her and let her know I'm coming. I think she would be a great asset to the hospitality end of the Shrine. Lancashire Penguins can be delicious."

* * *

Late in August, Mama and Millie Hutner were off for a week in the Catskills, again, a gift from David who himself couldn't go, but paid for their transportation and room in the "Jewish Alps." Late summer in New York is always lovely, but the Catskills? "Such a blessing."

David, however, did come to see me on his own for the first time. "I want to discuss a few things with you, if that's okay. Could we meet in both the morning and afternoon?"

"Of course, David, that can be arranged. You can even stay here for lunch, if you'd like."

"No, that's fine. There's a Greek restaurant not far from the monastery that I've been wanting to try; I'll go there for lunch and come back for the afternoon."

We set a date for the last Friday of August. I was a little nervous wondering what it was that he wanted to discuss with me without Mama being present. I prayed that it wasn't anything about his or her health. He always appeared to be in tip-top shape, as Brenda (the second aspirant on the horizon) would say. Usually she was speaking to a Sister in the infirmary who was far from tip-top, but Brenda thought that being complimented was good medication for the soul. She was a nurse and knew these things.

Mother Rosaria was again very kind in giving me the day to visit with him. "It's a good day; the novices are not having class in August; my correspondence is practically nil in the summer; it will be good for you to talk to him without your mother there."

"Blessed be God, Mother, I just hope there isn't anything seriously wrong with him or Mama." Mother Rosaria could read the anxiety on my face.

"He's a good man, your brother. He may be a professional psychiatrist, but he has years of separation from you which he may need to talk about, and didn't want to in front of your mother. *Who knows?*" she said in her best New York Jewish accent.

"You're right, Mother," I responded, laughing at her. "Such a Jewish Mother you could be." And we both laughed.

David arrived on time. He was wearing a sport shirt and seersucker pants that looked very stylish. He sported a Panama hat, which made me think of Papa who loved a straw hat in the summer. Mama had him trained well: he arrived with three dozen fresh bagels for all the Sisters and two cartons of Starbucks coffee, which he claimed was better than Zabar's, but couldn't argue it with Mama.

After the usual small talk about the weather, and the Yankees, which he thought I was still into, he sat down close to the grille. "You know, Becky, I'm terribly sorry for causing you so much pain when we were kids—well, not really kids, but pretty young. We were both at that time in life when we were going to break away from the nest; we all wanted Mama and Papa to be proud of us. Papa was the most open to all four of us—to all five, counting Josh. It about killed them, you know, when he enlisted in the army; it was so contrary to what they believed about family and school and settling down. They laid the groundwork for all of us. Running off to the army was not in their script; and like with you, Papa tried to accept our choices better than Mama did. Her power wasn't in being a boss, or controlling, not even controlling us, but in making a home where one was always welcomed. That's why I made sure Mama kept her apartment after Papa died—it was all of our home, and with all of us gone, it was Mama's security."

I smiled at him. "I'm really grateful you do what you do for Mama; she still feels like she has a purpose and reason to get up. It's for you she can cook supper and go shopping for a new outfit for her cruise. I'm so grateful she comes to visit me now. I think she's come to terms with my life."

"I think so. She talks about you now to all her Hadassah friends, almost in a bragging way, that her 'daughter, the nun,' lives such a life. She probably would never tell you this, but she suffered over Ruthie's life more than she ever did yours. She didn't understand your life, but then, she didn't understand Ruthie's either. The singing and dancing part, yes, but not the drinking and drugs. I think all parents credit or blame themselves for how their children turn out. You? You did something strange but good; 'Ruthie had talent, why did she drink so much?' Mama would lament."

"And Sally's life?"

"As Mama would say: 'Oy, such a life she should live?' But somewhere along the way, Mama didn't understand any of that either, and couldn't figure where the blame went. The good part, I guess, is that Mama came to know she couldn't control our lives. I never married and gave her a wallet full of grandchildren; you ran off to the nunnery, and Sally gave up a prestigious job to become a barber for dogs, as Mama would say. Sally says she runs an upscale Canine Salon." We both had to laugh.

"Well, I'm glad it's not a downscale canine salon." We laughed again. It was true, Mama never really delved into the gist of Sally's life; it was more foreign to her, in a way, than my life.

"We all had a problem with your choice, except maybe Ruthie and Papa. I think Papa actually admired you for becoming a Catholic; it's amazing."

"Between you and me, David, he did. He even told me so. I think he knew that I would become a nun before I knew it. Dear Papa…"

We sat in silence for a moment, each lost in our own remembrances.

David broke the silence. "Mama could never get it in her head that Ezra hadn't brainwashed you; for years she blamed him."

"I know. None of you, I don't think, ever got it, that I had been thinking about Christ before I even met Ezra. It was

Gracie Price's fault, if blame needs to be placed, although, it's really the Lord Himself to blame." I half smiled and waited for his reaction.

"I suppose so, if that's the 'spin' you want to giveto it." He said this without rancor. I hadn't heard the verb "spin" used in that way, but I understood what he meant. It was my way of explaining it all. But I was hoping he didn't want to go into the whole "religious spin".

"I'm not religious at all, as you know. I'm certainly not a very good Jew. Funny, huh? You were probably a better Jew than I was when you became a Catholic. But like I've said, I've had many Catholic patients in my practice, and they really do come around much better than people without any belief in God. It certainly has given me pause over the years."

"Hmmmmmm" was my brilliant response so far. He didn't know it, but I was not chanting Ommmm, but calling on the Holy Spirit to enlighten me and to touch David's soul.

"My whole field, you could say, is dealing with the mind. Like, our lives and personalities, and fears and neuroses all come from the way we think. Somewhere along the way, I think it was from a patient actually, but I don't remember, who dropped the idea that 'God' is the mind behind the design. The design, of course, being the cosmos, the entire universe, but also the very makeup of the human mind, the brain, the electrode forces and synapses involved in simply being alive, as opposed to being 'brain-dead.' I could accept that there is a mind behind every other design in the world—human beings are artists and creators, and we are minds, the brains, behind every design."

"But we didn't create the molecules and the planets with their moons or the solar system, or the human brain itself with all its, what did you call them, synapses?"

"Exactly. Well, I stewed over this one for a while, like for a couple years. I met Olivia, that's Sharbel's mother. She was not only the most beautiful doctor I ever dated, but also the most intelligent. She became a neurosurgeon, you know. She is brilliant."

"Beautiful and brilliant!" I chimed in.

"Indeed." David laughed. "She was also a very devout Catholic. I think that's probably why she didn't marry me, but even before that, you know, we fooled around, you know. She would tell me she went to Confession and didn't want to 'fool around' any more. I tried to respect that, blaming it all on Catholic guilt. Part of the 'Catholic design' was that sex was reserved for marriage. And the mind behind that design was probably an old celibate priest or bishop in Rome, or some pope."

"Uh huh." I didn't comment any further than that.

"Of course," David continued, "the Catholics got their initial design from the Jews. *That* design went back a lot further than any pope, or Jesus himself. This led me to think that all the world religions were just made-up designs by brilliant or charismatic leaders, like Buddha, Confucius, Mohammed, Moses, and Jesus."

"Oh yeah, that's like the German philosopher Feuerbach thought. That God was just a projection of man's mind—like his highest ideal of things." Goodness, I didn't know where that came from. I guess with all those years of classes by our Dominican Fathers, something stuck! "But at least, David, you see that Olivia's reluctance to, I guess you'd say, 'break the rules' didn't come from some old celibate pope, but in the Mind of the one who designed us…or at least designed our human nature."

David sighed, "Ah, but that's the problem, the design is flawed."

"Oh, how right you are, and as Jews and Christians we both know what that's called. Well, at least, we call it the original sin, I guess you say, the original break with the design, and because we didn't make the design to begin with, we can't fix it on our own…our minds are too simple, or too finite, or too—well, how can a broken mind fix its own brokenness? We're all 'broken vessels.'" I thought of the Psalm verse from Pope John Paul II, which Ezra carries in his wallet. David was thinking and after a moment went on.

"I guess, and I'm going out on a limb here," David was speaking slowly and thoughtfully, "that the Mind behind the design would have to fix it…and that's what the Torah is all about."

"Wow! Are you finally becoming Jewish?" I didn't mean that sarcastically; I was truly amazed. David laughed, a good old Feinstein laugh which I hadn't heard in a long time. It brought back memories of Papa.

"I guess I am. I don't really have anyone to talk to about these crazy thoughts of mine, the 'mind behind the design' thing. You know Mama, she gets all tongue-tied with any kind of God-talk."

"Ah, yes, but she certainly knows the blessing behind the mind!"

"True enough." We both sat in silence with our own thoughts.

David said, "I don't suppose you talk about the mind behind the design, inside there, do you?"

"Well, we don't exactly use those words, although I've heard that expression before. We do talk about how human beings are made in the image of—well, the image of the Mind, by having a mind ourselves…the intellect. And we talk about the 'end' of things—like, the purpose or the reason behind the design, you could say. Everything has an end, it would appear…"

"And what you do say that end is?"

"Well, you know, we all want to be happy. It would seem that everything we do, we do because we think it will make us happy. And it's much more, of course, than simple pleasures, because these are all passing pleasures, like fleeting happiness. But you know better than anyone with all your patients who have missed out on happiness along the way and are still broken and wounded from it all. The mind can mess us up. But I'm telling you that? Oy."

David laughed again. He seemed younger when he laughed. "Yes…I see that. You see it so easily and clearly, I must say. I've had years of psychiatric training and study to come to the same conclusion."

"The Mind behind the design…" I said out loud. "I like the analogy of an artist or a sculptor who has the design in his mind, but once he begins to paint or sculpt he has wanted it, the design in his mind, to be formed outside. He creates it, you could say, and does so because he wills it to be so. So the Mind also has a Will."

David picked up on my reasoning here. "So if we are the human design in the Mind then he or it has willed us into being."

"Yes, that's it, isn't it?" I tried to sound like I was thinking these thoughts for the first time. "We don't really call Him the Mind or the Willer, but the Creator." Lord, here I am talking simple Baltimore Catechism with my brother, the doctor, who has travelled and lectured all over the world. Oy vey, what a world we live in!

Saved by the bell, meaning, the bell for Sext rang, and I told David I had to go in for prayers and dinner, which was true. And I think he was ready to take a break too.

"What's the restaurant you're planning to go to?"

"Oh, it's called Athens. Modern Greek cuisine."

"Well, the modern stuff, so I've heard, doesn't come in large portions. I hope you'll find some lunch-time happiness there." He laughed.

"It's a test run. If Mama won't travel the world with me, I'm bringing the world to her, at least the world's cuisine. She kind of got into it on our last cruise. So we've been to a Cuban restaurant, down below 72nd Street on the West Side. Ethiopian where we actually sat on the floor, on a mat, with pillows at the back. Mama did all right for the meal, but we got a fit of laughter, the both of us trying to get up. And she liked a new Vietnamese restaurant on 10th Street in the West Village. So this is a little more western, we'll see. She thinks Greek cuisine is shish kabobs and spinach salad."

"I think it's great you're getting her out of the apartment and eating in places she'd never go on her own. Papa was never one for experimenting or trying new places."

"I know, except for Italian and Chinese. Mama is actually quite adventuresome. And she's not kosher, so I don't have to worry too much."

"Too much?"

"Well, you know, she still shies away from pork and shrimp."

"And bacon! Oh, I've got to run…I'll see you at 3:30." And I rushed out the door, going to Office with thoughts of final ends and shish kabobs running through my head.

After dishes, I went to our cell and sat in Squeak, reviewing my morning parlor with David. And I prayed to Our Lord that He would give me the right words to say. "I know, Lord, that You love David more than Mama and I do. And that Your ways are hidden and mysterious." And I prayed to Our Lady to awaken in David's heart a desire to know the Lord. I prayed to my uncanonized communion of saints: Fr. Meriwether, Mother John Dominic, Papa, and even Ruthie. I still prayed *for* Ruthie, but I knew she could also pray for me. And, I think for the first time in my life, I prayed to David, shepherd and king of Israel. Every single morning we pray: "*He has raised up for us a mighty savior, born of the house of his servant David.*" But I never prayed to David, the head of the household, till now. And the image that came to mind was David and Goliath. Goliath was like the giant world of power, pleasure, money, and all the big ambition my brother pursued all his life, and I was the little David with my slingshot and smooth stone, or maybe, the sling on my side with 150 smooth stones.

With all that in my heart, I began to pray the Rosary for our giant of a world, and for my big brother who is beginning to see that he's a doctor of souls who have lost their design.

David didn't see me at 3:30 that afternoon, but he had come by earlier and left a note with Sr. Paula:

> Becky,
>
> Please pray for a patient of mine who is 20 years old and has attempted suicide for the third time, and thankfully has failed again. She is presently being admitted to Bellevue Hospital. My card was in her suicide note. I am rushing up town to see her.
>
> I enjoyed our conversation and hope we can do it again. Athens was good, but not spectacular.
>
> David

He asked for my prayers. And so I shall pray for his twenty year old and for all those like her who are lost and in despair with life.

I was kind of relieved actually. The morning conversation opened up a few cans of worms, as Papa would say. A little break will give David time to think about it. But still, I was filled with a quiet joy at the *Magnificat* that evening at Vespers. Like Our Lady we have no idea how things are all going to unfold over the years, to where our "yes, Lord" will take us. I didn't have Mama and David, or Sally, in my life for nearly thirty years, and now they fill my later years with great joy; my spirit rejoices in God, my Savior.

It's a waste of meditation time and energy to think about how different things would be if this happened or that happened, thirty years ago, or ten years ago, or if Ruthie was still alive, or David married his Catholic doctor friend. It's better to sit in the chapel, take a deep breath, and accept this is the way it is, here and now. Ezra used to say *"hic et nunc"*. I think he was just showing off, but he kind of got it when we were young. Ah, Ezra, my dear Fr. Matthew Goldman, off last week to Lancashire, England. *Help me, Lord, to accept that if that is what You want, but if You don't mind, Lord, I'd like to ask a little favor. After this chapter in his life, couldn't You arrange a way for him to stay here and be happy? I know I'm being selfish, Lord, but I need him as someone to talk to hic et nunc.*

Twelve

Elijah's Cup: At a Seder, after dinner, an extra cup of wine is poured in honor of Elijah and the door is opened to welcome the messianic age.

It's true to say that over the years, we went through many changes. We have a Constitution, of course, which was revised and approved by the Holy See in 1986. This is followed by all the Dominican nuns worldwide. But each monastery has its own Customary which spells out the "way we do it" in the ordinary life of the monastery. There were bigger changes than colored sheets, like changing the time of the Night Office to allow for a full night's sleep. Other changes came in 2000 under Mother Rosaria's first term as prioress. These would be discussed by her Council and some even voted on by the Chapter, like a major change in the *horarium*. The Advent of 2000 would be our first Advent when we could have visitors and receive mail.

I was looking forward to this my favorite season of the year, as I carry the title: Of the Advent Heart. I realized my "Advent heart" would now have to expand to include the novices and postulants, and any visitors I might have. This all made me very happy, indeed. I made a large Advent calendar for the novitiate with a door that opened each day and gave us a penance to do, or an Advent act of kindness, or a prayer to say, or a Psalm verse to memorize. I had a very special "someone new" to meet in the Advent of 2000; namely, David's son, Sharbel. I had reserved the parlor for the afternoon of the First Sunday of Advent. Mama, David, and Sharbel would come at 3:15 that afternoon. I told them to come before 3:00, however, and listen to our Office of None. It is not as "nice" as Vespers, but it would be a good introduction for Sharbel to hear us sing the Psalms, not to mention Mama and David. I prayed about our meeting at Mass, especially thinking of them with the Advent theme of "*Come, let us climb the Lord's mountain, to the House of Jacob.*" I'm sure they didn't think about visiting me as coming into the House of Jacob.

We were beginning Year C in the Lectionary. *In those days, in that time, I will raise up for David a just shoot; he shall do what is right and just in the land.* That's from the first reading at Mass from the Prophet Jeremiah. David would not hear that reading, of course, but I thought of him immediately. Hopefully David will always do what is right! But if they make it to None, I hope David is listening to the Psalms. The antiphon for None is: *What marvels the Lord worked for us: indeed we were glad.* As Sr. Bertrand would say, "Ain't that the truth." The Lord has indeed worked marvels for us, the Feinstein family. Out of hurt and separation from the past, He brought about great reconciliation and love. Yes, love. Certainly it was always there for me with Mama, but now I can say that there is a real brother-sister love between David and me. And I thank the Lord for that. What marvels the Lord works for us—always in His time!

The second antiphon says: *The Lord will build the house for us; he will watch over our city.* The Psalmist, of course, is talking about Jerusalem, but we all pray it with New York, New York, in our mind and heart. And for us, the house, or home, was always our apartment on W. 79th Street between Columbus and Amsterdam, where Mama still lives, albeit alone, but with her memories.

And if David's listening, and can understand the words, the third Psalm for None is Psalm 127, ending: *May the Lord bless you from Sion all the days of your life! May you see your children's children in a happy Jerusalem.* Ah, it's one of my favorite Psalms. *May you see your children's children...* Mama has that fulfilled in her heart now, and one day, hopefully, Sharbel will be a father, and David will see his child's children.

After Holy Communion I always try to unite myself intimately with the Lord. It is really the holiest moment of the whole day. I'm sure the devil knows that too, and tries to send the most distractions to our souls at that time too. It's usually simple things that are going on, but that day, it was filled with anticipation for meeting my nephew for the first time. Here I am, after Holy Communion, when I should be whispering the Holy Name of Jesus, and I'm wondering what Sharbel will call me. Aunt Baruch? Sr. Mary Baruch? Aunt Becky? Aunt Rebecca perhaps? Oy, such distractions I should have? What difference does it make for Heaven's sake! He can call me Turnip Greens, if he wants; I'm just happy to finally meet him. I hope he likes me. There I was off on another even greater distraction. It didn't cross my mind "I hope I like him." I just assumed I would, but I hardly knew anything about him. Mama adores him, but he is her only grandson. Well, we'll see. What can I do? Nothing. Just expect nothing and be grateful for everything. (Thank you, Greta Phillips.)

Sometimes the post communion prayer and blessing come very quickly. But I settled into my stall after Mass, or I should say, I settled into myself. There were no distractions, no fretting over anything, just a few minutes of silence, absorbed in His Holy presence. No words anymore—most of the time, just silence. Funny, I almost heard old Eli the doorman say to me, "Everything's gonna be just fine, Miss Rebecca." Or maybe that was the Lord assuring me, but I left the chapel ready to meet the world, well…ready to meet my nephew.

Even though it's Advent, our Sunday dinner is always a notch above the weekday meals. We've also suspended the music for the Sundays of Advent meals and have begun a new book in the refectory. I wanted to begin a new book on my own but hadn't taken anything out of the library, so I went there after dishes and surveyed what Sr. Antonia labelled "New Books." Even then, I got distracted and found myself browsing the periodical shelves. Lots of articles on the new millennium. But I picked the latest issue of *National Geographic* and settled into one of the wooden library chairs to glance through it.

The bell for None startled me for a moment, not sure what day it was, but I quickly picked up *National Geographic,* which had fallen onto the floor, and headed out and down the stairs to the chapel. I was coming into the ante-choir at the same time as Sr. Paula. So I discreetly whispered, "Are my mother and brother here?"

She smiled as she nodded 'yes', started to go into the chapel, but turned back to me and whispered, "And a very handsome young man." Sr. Kolbe was making her way into the chapel, and I kissed my scapular in penance for talking. Leave it to me to scandalize a novice on the First Sunday of Advent.

After the Office, I waited for a couple minutes to give them time to make their way to the parlor, and then I looked up at the Lord with my Advent Heart, took a deep breath, and knew it would all be just fine.

Standing by the grille were Mama and Sharbel; David was over by the cabinet where the glasses are. "Such beautiful singing your nephew should hear! Becky, darling, this is your nephew, my grandson, Sharbel."

To my surprise, he blessed himself, and looking right into my eyes said, "I am so honored to finally meet you…Aunt Mary."

"And I to meet you, Sharbel; welcome to my little house." And we all laughed the laugh that breaks the ice and makes everyone suddenly comfortable with each other. "Oh my," I said, "I wasn't ready for this, but Sharbel, you have your grandfather's smile." I turned to Mama and choked up saying, "It's like Papa was standing here."

And with that, David joined us. "He is, Becky, he's smiling down upon us, I'm sure." This coming from my atheist brother who maybe saw Papa still in the design!

"Please, sit down, and tell me all about yourself." They filled in the three chairs across the front of the grille. Mama looked pleased as punch for Sharbel to meet me.

"I'm graduating from Chaminade this year—well, next year, in May—and am applying to three colleges: Notre Dame, Georgetown, and Columbia here in New York."

"Majoring in?" I was all ears.

"Pre-med. But I'm not sure what area yet, or what Med school."

"So, you want to be a doctor; that's wonderful, Sharbel."

Mama chimed in, "What did you expect? His mother and father here are both doctors, their son should be a shoe salesman?" We all laughed, not because there's anything peculiar about being a shoe salesman, but because it was coming from Mama.

"Maybe a vineyard owner, Grandmama, and make New York wine, named for you: Hannah Vineyards Concord Grape."

"It would have to be kosher, my little baklawa." And Sharbel laughed and put his arm around Mama and squeezed her to himself.

"I want to know more about you. I heard you were able to leave and sit Shiva when Aunt Ruth died. And like that was the first time you'd been home in over twenty-five years! And I missed you. I didn't even find out about Aunt Ruth till it was too late."

"Did you know her very well?"

"Dad took me to Grandmother's a few times for dinner, and Aunt Ruth was there a couple times; she was really funny and could make us all laugh. She was always interested in what I was doing in school; did I sing or play an instrument. Oh, and she was in an off-Broadway show probably eight years ago, I was only ten, I think, and Dad took my Mom and me to see it."

"The Fantasticks?"

"That's right, did you see it? Oh, I'm sorry, of course you didn't see it."

"Ruthie and I saw it, when? I think about 1963. It was a smash off-Broadway hit, and is still going strong…almost forty years!"

"It was really great, especially afterwards, and we went backstage to Aunt Ruth's dressing room. She acted like we were royal celebrities coming to see her."

"Well, I'm sure she must've been thrilled that you were in her audience, and that she had a nephew to show off afterwards."

David chimed in, "Oh, she did that all right. She shared the dressing room with four other girls, so she hollers, 'This is my gorgeous nephew Sharbel; so hands off, girls.' The girls all squealed like…like…"

"Chorus girls," Mama added. "That whole crowd acted like teenagers when anybody good looking came into the room. You want to know what it was like? Picture Omar Sharif going to Fanny Brice's dressing room after the show… Sharbel could play his double, don'tcha think?"

Mama was obviously proud of her grandson, and often embarrassed him, I'm sure. Sharbel just sat there and smiled with a slight Lebanese blush.

"Grandmama, I don't look like Omar Sharif; he's much older than I. And I don't sport any facial hair."

"Of course not," Mama quipped, "he's an old man… probably thirty something when he played Nicky Arnstein in *Funny Girl*." Mama continued to laugh on her own thinking this was a riot.

"And you're more 'gorgeous' than Barbra Streisand." Sharbel added, making Mama blush this time.

(I'm thinking, this kid is a smooth operator. I'm happy he makes Mama so happy. He did look like a young Omar Sharif with those dark eyes, square features, and thick black hair. He had Papa's smile, but his mother's eyes and complexion, and a certain serious frown that he probably got from David.)

"You know," I was going out on a limb here, "I only found out about you a couple years ago, so I missed all the growing up years."

"I know, Sister, I mean Aunt Mary; do you mind if I call you Aunt Mary?"

"Not at all, Sharbel, it's unique in all the world; you're the only one that will ever call me that, so that makes it very special. And it sounds better than Aunt Baruch!" We both laughed.

"It also reminds me of Our Lady." This was Sharbel talking! "I think John the Baptist maybe called Our Lady Aunt Mary."

That brought me great delight. "Oh, I never thought of that. I wonder what she called him." And there was a long silence. Mama and David had already faded in the silence of this conversation, and Sharbel looked very intently at me, deep in thought, and then, with a quarter of a smile, he said, "Jackie."

And we both laughed. A good shared-Catholic laugh. "Then I shall call you Jackie."

"That would be swell; my confirmation name is John, for John the Baptist." And he beamed.

"Well, before we have a little bar mitzvah here, let's have a drink." Mama was pulling out her usual Mogen David from her handbag and David was getting the cheese glasses from the cabinet. "You're allowed to have a little elderberry in Advent? Such a meeting should go without a toast?"

We normally wouldn't have wine at all during Advent, for heaven's sake. We wouldn't have visitors or get our mail till Christmas, but this was a special First Sunday of Advent, and our Dominican practice of epikeia fits here very nicely.

When we all had our glasses filled, it was Mama who raised her first: "To this first wonderful meeting of Aunt Mary and Jackie. Mazel tov!"

The afternoon sped along quickly as I told them all about the Sisters in the community, especially in the novitiate and the infirmary. Sr. Gertrude's name came up first and Mama joined in.

"Oh, that Sister Gertrude. Sharbel, you've got to meet her; you'll love her. She was Ruthie's favorite nun—after you, Becky, after you." I smiled.

"I know that Mama, and Sister Gertrude did more than I ever did to raise Ruthie's opinion of our life."

David, looking forlornly at his empty cheese glass, broke his silence. "Ruthie would tell me you were behind bars for a life-time sentence, and loved it."

We all laughed at that. I gestured to the grille. "Well she was right about the bars, and yes, we take what we call

'Solemn Vows' that we will live for the Lord in this manner of life until death."

"It's like you're married to the Lord, right?" Sharbel added.

"That's right, and at Solemn Profession we even get a wedding ring." And I held up my hand.

"Such hands you should have, not a liver spot on them." (Mama's comment, of course.)

I held up my other hand and toasted, "What marvels the Lord works for us; indeed we are glad." And my agnostic brother added, "Hear, hear." Maybe that's his version of 'amen, amen.'

Sharbel promised he would be back soon and bring pictures of his growing up years, as he put it, and asked me in good Catholic fashion to pray for a special intention.

Mama and David were happy, I could tell, the way it all turned out. And Mama left saying, "I'll be back in two weeks with a special Chanukah/Christmas gift for you and something for all the nuns." She wouldn't say anymore. David winked at me and said, "We're eating Mexican tonight. We'll be in touch, okay." And they were off.

Vespers was especially joyful for me. The reading was one of the shortest we have, from Philippians: *Rejoice in the Lord always; again I will say, Rejoice. Let all men know your forbearance. The Lord is at hand.*

Thirteen

Since to live the contemplative life in a monastery is a lofty and difficult undertaking, great prudence is needed in order to recognize true vocations and to ensure the timely exclusion of unsuitable aspirants. (Constitution 122)

During Advent and Lent we have a short Chapter after supper before recreation and Compline. It's a time for Mother to give a little Advent fervorino, or to make any special announcements or request any special prayer intentions.

It was with great joy, as she reread the Scripture from Vespers, *Rejoice in the Lord always, again I will say, Rejoice*, that she announced that we would be welcoming two aspirants who will begin their life with us as postulants. The first would enter next Sunday and the second right after Christmas, before the New Year.

This was wonderful news to me, as they would be my charges. There was no longer a postulant mistress, but the novice mistress now assumed that role. I call them our Advent Gifts of the new millennium.

The first was Brenda Hubbard, who was our first African-American Sister. Brenda is from Manhattan. Her father is a doctor and has been a part of a movement called "Doctors Without Borders" who volunteer their services in third world countries for a month at a time. Brenda herself is an R.N. and worked for several years at Roosevelt Hospital on the West Side. She is one of seven children, and is a convert from the Methodist Church. She told me that a big part of her conversion was that her work got her so depressed that on her lunch break she would go a block away to the Paulist Church on 60th and Columbus Avenue. At first she just sat in the church and absorbed the peace; then she'd read things from the pamphlet rack; then she began reading the bulletin and in there was an invitation to join RCIA...Rite of Christian Initiation of Adults. She was received into the Church at the Easter Vigil in 1995.

A few years later, when she began to look around at religious orders, she discovered the Dominican Sisters of Hawthorne and visited their convent in Hawthorne, New York. She loved it; the hospital section was so different from her regular nursing experience that it literally made her cry, but it was the hospitality and prayer of the Sisters that moved her the most. She spent her summer vacation as an aspirant with the Sisters.

At the time she didn't know there were contemplative nuns in New York and New Jersey till one of the patients she was feeding supper to mentioned Mary Queen of Hope Monastery in Brooklyn Heights. That patient was Helen Parmigano, the mother of our Sr. Antonia. Mrs. Parmigano would talk to Brenda all the time about her daughter, without realizing she was planting seeds of a vocation. When the end drew near, Sr. Antonia visited her mother at Rosary Hill.

She sat by her bedside for hours. Brenda was very impressed by that. She was able to sit with her and pray the rosary together for Sister's mother.

When Brenda's vacation was over, she returned to work, but her prayer now was absorbed by the Sisters and patients at Rosary Hill, especially Helen Parmigano. She called the following weekend and learned that Helen had died the day after Brenda left. Brenda thought of Sr. Antonia, and decided to pay her a visit and offer her condolences. She arranged with one of the Paulist Fathers to have a Mass offered for Helen, and she gave Sister a lovely Mass card. Sr. Antonia shared it with us at recreation.

Sr. Antonia was very grateful for the visit and the kindness of Brenda Hubbard, and told her she would be welcome to come to the monastery for some peace and quiet, and to pray. Brenda had shared briefly that she was thinking of religious life, and thought the Dominicans of Hawthorne were wonderful.

Brenda came to the monastery for several weekend visits, and said she was moved to talk to the "Vocation Sister." Afterwards Brenda went for a walk and sitting, not in the chapel, but on a park bench on the Promenade looking at the skyline of Manhattan she got her inspiration. She said she didn't know if it was the Holy Spirit or just plain exhaustion, but the City was work and nursing and emergency rooms and noise, and she just wanted to be hidden away and pray.

"When I came back to the monastery and was sitting in the extern chapel before Vespers, there was a silence and peace I never knew before."

So Brenda entered on the Second Sunday of Advent, 2000. She was my "first postulant." Like me, she loves to be with the older Sisters in the infirmary, which makes me very happy. She also has a great sense of humor and loves to sing. Of course, I've never heard of the pop singers she admires and tries to imitate. She let go of her pierced earrings; she liked big hoops. I told her there would be "bigger hoops" to jump through down the road! She also had dreadlocks that she kept, although they gave an odd shape to the postulant's veil.

Our second postulant is very interesting, too: Sr. Grace. I first met Grace maybe a month after Ruthie died. Leah was a fan of Ruth Steinway, and Leah's grandmother, Mrs. Levinson, lived in Mama's apartment building. When I went home that first night, Leah and her grandmother dropped off a tuna noodle casserole and creamed string beans with almonds. I'll always remember that detail because Mama was so effusive in her gratitude to Mrs. Levinson for her wonderful tuna casserole, and the minute after they left, she told me to dump it in the garbage, but keep the string beans. Mama liked Mrs. Levinson; she just didn't like her casseroles.

When we were sitting Shiva the next night, Leah and grandmother appeared again. Leah was able to get me aside, and asked if she could come visit me at the monastery with her Catholic best friend from school, Gracie. She didn't know that sent a chill down my spine!

Almost a month to the day, Leah and Gracie came for a visit. We mostly spoke of Ruthie. But I also shared as much as I could about our life. Leah, of course, was all ears and wanted to know how I came to be a Catholic. I gave them the "Abbreviated Cliff Notes" version. Grace was very quiet and seemed shy. She mainly asked about the habit, which she thought was "so beautiful; I've never seen anything like it, in real life."

"I've seen *Sister Act* probably five times, but their robes were all black. Have you seen it?" Grace was sitting on the edge of her chair. "It was with Whoopi Goldberg."

"No, I haven't seen it. We heard about it, though. It came out about five years ago, I think. I did know some Goldbergs but never one named Whoopi. Such a name for a Goldberg." And Leah laughed. Gracie didn't quite get it.

I didn't hear from either one of them for about six months. Then, they came again for a visit in the summer and then again over the Christmas holiday, right before New Year's 1998. They came bearing gifts, neatly wrapped in shiny red Christmas paper. The first was a large coffee canister, and three pounds of Zabar's French roast coffee. ("I know who suggested this gift to you. Thank you both very much; we will all enjoy it tremendously.")

The second was a framed 5x7 photo of Ruth Steinway in her Queen Elizabeth gown which she wore for her show at Penguin Pub. ("I love it, thank you so much. I've never seen Ruthie in this costume that everyone talks about. She must've been a riot with her proper Elizabethan English.") They both laughed and agreed.

The third gift was especially from Grace. I thought at first it was some kind of book, but it was what she called a DVD of *Sister Act* Parts 1 and 2. I didn't have the heart to tell them we didn't have a DVD player or watch movies, but thanked her profusely. "So this is the Goldberg girl? Such a high bandeau."

I didn't have anything for them of course; it was a surprise visit after all, but I invited them to stay for Vespers and Compline. There were retreatants on retreat but they could have supper with them, if they didn't mind eating in silence with a tape playing. They thought that would be "awesome." They stayed for supper, thanked me, and promised they would come back again soon.

They graduated high school that new year. Leah actually went to Israel that summer and lived on a kibbutz. Grace went to New York's Fashion Institute of Technology on Seventh Avenue and 27th Street. I told Sr. Gertrude about them, and she smiled and sang softly: "Two different worlds, they live in…"

Indeed two totally different worlds, I thought, as I continued to have visits from Grace who would share with me letters and what she called "emails" from Leah, who was planting organic vegetables and building houses. Grace was eating organic vegetables and designing casual wear, or whatever the next assignment was. Grace was caught up in the whole world of fashion and design.

I think she made some of her own clothes, and dyed her hair three different colors. I don't think Helena Rubenstein would have approved, but then, who am I to say? I recognized more that there was a big "hole in her soul" and that another Interior Designer was at work fashioning His own design. (David would like that!)

She once said to me on a more serious note: "You must get tired of hearing me talk about clothes; you must think it's very worldly and not a very spiritual career to pursue." I didn't know if she was speaking to me or to herself!

"On the contrary, I've found it all very interesting. We learned in one of our classes in philosophy that Aristotle—you know who that is, right?"

"Yeah, he was married to Jacqueline Kennedy after John Kennedy died."

"No, not that Aristotle. I mean Aristotle the Greek philosopher who lived around 350 BC, who said that a 'thing' that stood by itself, a '*substance*,' had nine *accidents* that belonged to it; these could all change, but the substance never changed...the accidents were things like quantity, weight, position, quality, color, what one was doing or what was being done to you, and one of the accidents was clothes, and it only applied to human beings. Animals don't wear clothes—but we do. And like other things that we even have in common with animals, like eating and drinking, we human beings elevate these things to a fine art...even movement and singing, and cooking. It's because there's a spiritual part of us that stretches upward to the finest form of everything. So creating beautiful clothes can be a very spiritual thing...to do so one must really be an artist, or maybe I should say, the finest clothes designers are really artists."

Grace sat silent taking it all in. She had never heard anything like this in all her life. "That Aristotle guy was really an awesome dude."

I did well in suppressing my laugh. But indeed, he was just that! Grace then asked, "Did he design your outfit?"

I couldn't suppress anymore! Laughing, I said, "No...but he did give it a name, in a way. In Latin the 'accident' that refers to what one wears is called 'habitus'; in English, habit. Our habit is actually part of the fashion women wore in the 13th century, which the first nuns adopted and we haven't changed since."

I could tell that the mystique of our life was beginning to hit Grace, as it does most of our aspirants; some by our chanting, or the enclosure, the grille, the silence, and for many—our 'habitus.' So I showed Grace how most of it was constructed, and promised at her next visit, I would bring a coiffure and veil and show her how it was all put together. I normally wouldn't do that with an aspirant, but Grace was a student of clothes design. She would talk about the textures of the fabrics and colors I had never heard of and how things were constructed.

"It's never changed in eight centuries. That's totally awesome. Everything in my world changes with every season. I suppose there are a few artists in my school; I don't think I'm one of them. And many of the guys and girls are not very nice people…there's a heavy spirit of competition. And some are really weird," said Grace with chartreuse and fawn green hair, and a gold ring in her eyebrow, and only one dangling earring—in one pierced ear, which had two other rings in the upper part.

"Oh, I can just imagine. Our unchangeableness goes back much longer than our habit. It's our faith in Christ that never changes. He is the substance of our lives…and come to think of it, St. Paul once said: *Put on the Lord Jesus Christ* and *you have been clothed in Christ.* He is our unchanging 'habitus' that gives everything else meaning."

There was a substantial pause in the conversation, but I could see that Grace was deep in thought. She started to twirl the fawn green hair around her index finger and thumb. I was watching closely, afraid it would get caught in her eyebrow-ring. I kind of drifted in my thought too…*If I were in the world, I'd like to have green hair too, at least for Ordinary time…and purple for Advent.* Then I snapped back to reality.

"If school is all starting to get to you, you should come here for a weekend retreat, just to get away from the rat-race, and clothe yourself in silence and peace." I hoped I wasn't sounding too pious. But Grace just stared at me, twirling the green locks.

"Could I really do that? I've never been on a retreat."

"Of course you could. We have several very small, but very nice guest rooms. They're not at all color coordinated, but they've got pretty sheets."

"Oh it sounds awesome, but what should I wear?"

"You can come casual…I think you're familiar with that." I was going to say *a large bandana for starts*, but then, I thought it will be fun to see if any of the nuns notice her hair. Probably not, as most keep pretty good custody of the eyes and aren't gawking at the retreatants. Sr. Paula was already used to the technicolor coif.

Her casual wear was something we would never have worn when I was her age. "You're fine just as you are; maybe bring some sweaters because it gets chilly in the chapel, and nothing too tight or too short, oh, and quiet shoes." Grace was into boots up to her knees. You could hear her coming a block away.

And that's how it all started. Grace graduated from the Fashion Institute in the spring of 1999. For all the time and money one puts into a school, she was unable to land a job in the fashion industry; but she did get a job as a sales clerk at a small boutique in the East Village, "Ester's Wear-House." She roomed with four other girls from school, none of whom had jobs as fashion designers.

Grace continued to visit, and made several weekend retreats...they were all "awesome." It was in mid-June 2000 that she popped the question: "Do you think I might fit into this life?" Now at first glance, it would surprise anyone that this young woman with technicolor hair and an earring in her eyebrow, and purple lipstick, would be thinking of monastic life. I was now on the vocation "team" who would interview her and see if there were any "impediments." Whenever I heard that word, I recalled my own anxiety when I was discerning a vocation. I was naïve enough to think that being Jewish was an impediment.

We reserved an aspirant's room for Grace after the Assumption, August 15, if she would be able to get off work for two weeks. She thought she might; she only got a week's vacation, but could probably get two. Ester Easton, the owner of Ester's Wear-House, liked her. In the meantime, I spent at least an hour or two each week with her. Wednesday was her day off, and she'd come for lunch and stay until Vespers.

She was becoming quite devout, and began attending daily Mass and prayed the rosary every day. Sometimes she'd wear a rosary around her neck, which she said was very "Latino"—although Grace Darlene White didn't know a word of Spanish. She spoke of a great feeling of discontent with her life as it was lived; first the attitudes and ambitions of her fellow fashion designers, not to mention Ester Easton and her fellow work-mates. She said she felt "disconnected" from them. She was not dating, although she had had a boyfriend at the Institute. She didn't know if she could live in one place forever and ever, but there was something very attractive about the monastery which she couldn't put her finger on. "I think it may be the Lord, if that doesn't sound too weird."

"No," I assured her, "there's nothing weird about that. I know just what you mean." I think I started praying for her every night at Compline that behind the weirdness of being a cloistered nun, there was a vocation there, and Grace's pierced ears would hear His call.

She listened closely to everything I suggested, and did not argue or resist any of it, at least from what I could tell. She appeared to be a healthy introvert, which most of us are, and could seem to others to be rather shy. But she was also very open and capable of sharing her feelings and fears. By late November, after Thanksgiving, she appeared in the parlor without her usual display of jewelry and the eyebrow ring was gone. Her hair was back to one color, which was not her natural color, but would pass nicely. She called it "dirty blonde".

I asked her about her parents, and she quite honestly said they were very much opposed to such a preposterous idea, especially after all the money they put into the Fashion Institute. Her mother was the Catholic in the family, but she didn't always go to Sunday Mass. "I don't get it," Grace said to her mother. "Would you be opposed if I went to Israel and joined Leah at the kibbutz?" And her mother said she'd prefer that to a cloistered monastery because at least she could live a "normal life."

Grace didn't know how much she sounded like a few of our younger Sisters and even a few of the older ones. She would learn that all of us who enter embrace that cross, heavier for some than others, but God has a way of softening even the hearts of our parents.

"Would you like to join Leah on the kibbutz?"

"Oh no. They have more regimentation to follow then you do here—I think. And they work a lot. I like some things about it, the sense of belonging, but …well, I guess the big difference is that they don't know Christ. He's the big difference; and that's true for the kibbutz and for Americans right here."

There was a lot more going on in her than she outwardly showed. It was after Christmas, two days before the new year 2001, she donned the 'habitus' of a postulant, which reminded her of a 1950s Catholic school girl's uniform, except the skirt was longer, and she had a short veil for chapel and refectory. The change of clothes is just the beginning, but she was ready. Her hair was all a light brown, atop her "ring-free" ears and eyebrows.

Grace kept in touch with Leah, writing that she was joining the "Catholic Kibbutz."

Fourteen

"As Time Goes By"

The fundamental things apply
As time goes by. (From *Casablanca*, 1942)

Meditation time, or what some call "mental prayer," is one of the best times in the monastery. I love the early morning after what we used to call the Night Office, now called Vigils or the Office of Readings. It's the best time to do *Lectio*, reading the Scriptures in a slow, prayerful way. I usually read the readings we'll have at Mass. Sometimes, I confess, I just do the Gospel, especially if we're in the Old Testament in the first reading. I guess that doesn't sound very Jewish of me! I also love the forty-five minutes we have after Vespers before supper. Vespers is really that quiet transitional time moving from the business and noise of the day into a quieter, peaceful time. There's a third period, just after Compline; but that time can also be spent in Squeak in our cell and writing in my journal, usually about the events of the day. Sometimes I think it's more like a diary than a spiritual journal, but it's where I remember so many things from my past, and now can see how God has been a part of it all.

The New Year of 2001 did not have the same excitement and psycho-drama as the year before. We had a festive meal on New Year's night, but no wine, and nothing unusual.

I had a parlor that afternoon with Mama alone. David was spending the day with Sharbel and Olivia. Sally didn't come to New York to see Mama because she and Mitzie were spending the holidays in Honolulu. Mama was fine, though, and not feeling lonely. I think she actually enjoyed the alone time. I had invited her here for New Year's Eve to stay overnight.

"Do you get cable on the television?"

"Cable? We don't even have a television."

"I should have New Year's Eve without Dick Clark? No thank you, darlin, I'll be quite comfortable on West 79th Street."

So when I saw her New Year's afternoon, I asked her if she saw the ball fall with Dick Clark. "I only turned the channel back to NBC and Dick Clark five minutes before the ball fell. I don't like all the rock n' roll music before; it's all so noisy. Not like when Guy Lombardo did New Year's. But earlier I watched a movie on TMC…are you ready?"

"Am I ready? Don't tell me it was some horror flick; no, I know, it was probably *Funny Girl,* or maybe even *The Sound of Music*."

"Wrong, wrong, and wrong. It was *The Bells of St. Mary's*. Your father used to watch it after you came here, but I never did. Ingrid Bergman, probably a nice Jewish girl, made such a beautiful nun, and Bing Crosby, oy, what a handsome priest he made, enough to make you want to become a Catholic!"

"Ingrid Bergman was Swedish; I don't think she was Jewish. She was also in *Casablanca*, of course, and lots of other films. Ruthie and I loved her."

"She also played Golda Meir, so go figure." We laughed.

I could tell Mama was slowing down, but she still seemed very youthful to me. I credit David for that; he keeps her active.

"So, no big trips planned with David and your grandson coming up?"

"Sharbel wants to go to Lebanon. He's never been and he's half Lebanese. And David wants to go to Israel, so they may combine the two; and they want me to go with them."

"That would be wonderful, Mama."

"Don't I know it. 'Next year Jerusalem' could be this year! David said he'd get me a tranquillizer for the plane. 'A tranquillizer?' I said. 'I'm not a horse or a dog.' At my age, I can handle a little flying. Anyway, that's not till summer; Sharbel will be going to college in the fall—wherever he ends up going—and my eightieth birthday is in September, so we'll go sometime before then…too bad Rosh Hashanah isn't in August! So we'll see."

"Oh, speaking of "new" we have a new answering machine for the phone. Mother Rosaria says it was her Christmas gift to us. It will be a great help, we think, and it frees Sr. Paula from being out front all the time and answering the phone when we're in the chapel."

"They're great, aren't they? I've got one myself; it's also a good way of screening your calls. The more expensive ones even show you who's calling."

"Yeah, they're amazing. Ours only has a miniature tape deck which records the messages. I like it because people can call for prayers and just leave the message; I don't have to write them a note back."

"Sally and Mitzie have one too, and can you believe, at the end of their recorded message they have a dog barking. I figure that must be Cognac wishing everyone a happy new year. So I wished them a happy New Year back and barked a couple times for the mutt."

It was nice having Mama all to myself…we chatted for over an hour, and went down memory lane a few times which is a fun thing to do. It's hard to believe that I've lived longer in the monastery than I did at home…that talking about those days is like another lifetime…time goes by and we move on.

* * *

January sped by very quickly. I remember we prayed a lot for our new President, George W. Bush. He was the 43rd president, I think. We aren't particularly political people, but we pray for the people who are.

The winter months gave the novices lots of indoor work to do. We painted a number of the rooms; and updated some of our religious art. This was a project Sr. Grace especially liked, although we were afraid she'd want to put up something abstract or modern. But in the end, she had a classical mind for art. She and Sr. Brenda were both doing well as postulants. And Emma, the clarinetist from Sarasota, became a white veil novice before Lent, around the time of Mother's first anniversary.

Her religious name is Sr. Mary Cecilia of the Immaculate Heart. She looks lovely in our habit and it's as though she glides down the cloister. We had a heavy snow the evening of her clothing which made us all very happy. Well, it made me very happy; I know not everyone loves the snow. Uncle Bo has yet to make a visit. Sr. Gertrude says she hopes he wears his clown outfit.

Our life kind of moves along from one season to another. Lent was upon us again, and I went into hibernation, according to Mama. David had not been back to talk about religion, but seemed to be at peace with coming here, unless it was just a matter of getting used to a routine.

Gwendolyn wrote briefly before Lent began that she and her sister would be spending Easter in Lancashire. They didn't open a Tea on Thames at Ezra's shrine, but did host a hospitality room. She said Ezra was looking very good and was very devout. I brought that to Our Lord every night at Vespers in gratitude.

Mama and David were going on a winter cruise, but I would see them after Easter. Sharbel would graduate in the spring and was accepted at Yale, the one university he hadn't thought about before. I told him about the Dominican parish of St. Mary's right there on the Yale campus, and that we had cloistered nuns nearby New Haven in North Guilford… so he would be surrounded by Dominicans. He promised he would come see me before he left for school. But that didn't happen. Time can get away from us. But he sent me a postcard of the Beinecke Rare Book and Manuscript Library on campus where there is a Gutenberg Bible, dating from 1455:

Dear Aunt Mary,

I thought of you when I saw this Gutenberg for the first time. The campus is beautiful, and I really like St. Mary's. Please pray for me often.

Love, Jackie.

I keep the postcard in the back of my journal.

Our big project—well it was really Mother Rosaria's big project—was converting our plain old ugly rooftop into a garden. We put in artificial turf which looked real, comfortable chairs, wicker tables, and potted plants. There was also a section off to the back where the novices had potted tomato plants. In another far corner she had put in a trestle like we have in our out back garden, and a two person swing with a canopy over it. It was very nice. Mother did a lot of the nitty-gritty work with us, which I think was good therapy for her. It got her out of her office almost every afternoon.

When the summer heat left, like around Labor Day, we were planning a little garden party to dedicate the roof to St. Joseph. I said little but it turned into a grand production!

Fifteen

Betzah: A roasted egg, which symbolizes the Passover sacrifices brought as offerings to the Temple and is a symbol for the wholeness and continuity of life.

It wasn't a recurring dream; it just happened two times, but each was as frightening as the other. Maybe Ezra's visits before he left for England loosened a lot of subconscious memory plaque. I was again around twelve years old in my cyclamen pink dress with a Chantilly lace collar, helping Sally set the table for Passover. I was carrying in Mama's heirloom Seder plate, but each of the empty pockets had a *betzah*, a roasted egg, in its place. They are supposed to represent the sacrifices made in the Temple in ancient times; but these were all colored like Easter eggs. When I got to the dining room, Eli was sitting at the table: "Good afternoon, Miss Rebecca." And the plate crashed on the floor. And I jumped awake, not in the chapel this time, but in the lounge chair in front of the picture window in the infirmary.

Sr. Bertrand was next to me; she had also fallen asleep, but my jump and scream startled her awake as well. "Goodness lands, child, you've frightened me half to death. My poor heart. What are you screaming about?"

"I'm sorry, Sister, I was having a bad dream. I've had it before, I drop the…I drop an expensive plate belonging to my mother, and it crashes on the floor."

"Well, you could've dropped it at another time. I think I need my blood pressure pill." The look on my face must've converted her heart, as she immediately changed her tune. "But don't you worry about it; I have bad dreams all the time. It's the Brooklyn water—it's not good for us." Sr. Bertrand was on one of her pet theories: "Causes cancer, arthritis, lumbago, bunions, and bad dreams—mark my word."

I couldn't do anything but laugh. She was known for going on about everything. "We're not getting enough Vitamin D, cooped up in the house all winter and all that air-conditioning in the summer; it's not healthy, I tell you."

"Have you been on the rooftop garden?" I jumped in. "Mother Rosaria did a fine job fixing the roof this summer; it's been the nicest thing she's done. She's been prioress almost a year now, and I think St. Joseph must be very happy with our rooftop garden." It was named St. Joseph's Garden.

Sr. Bertrand laughed. "Oh, I don't think St. Joseph gives two hoots whether we have a roof-garden or not. Granted, it's a nice change to sit up there in nice weather; it has a marvelous view of the Manhattan sky-line. So, yes, our little rooftop patio is very nice. I've only been up there once, mind you, when it was first finished and everyone was talking about it. It's too chilly up there for me; I like it right here in front of this big window…those trees over there will be turning in another month. Then you can get all the novices out in the fresh air raking the leaves. It'll be good for them; better than being cooped up here." She snorted her little Sr. Bertrand snort.

"I'm looking forward to raking the leaves with the novices. I never got to rake leaves growing up in Manhattan."

"Well, we certainly did growing up in Westchester County; and we'd burn them too. Not allowed today, I hear. That's a darn shame, there was nothing so autumn-y as smelling burning leaves…better than being cooped up here." (snort)

Sr. Bertrand moved into the infirmary in March of this year on the feast of St. Joseph. The move was one of Mother's first decisions. She was a "pip" as Mother told the council when it was decided that Sr. Bertrand was ready. She was getting very forgetful, had fallen a couple times, and could get a little disruptive in the refectory. The more settled Sisters in the infirmary welcomed her warmly and wanted a little tea party in the afternoon to do so. Sr. Amata had a candle and little bouquet of artificial flowers in front of the statue of St. Joseph, and told Sr. Bertrand that she thought St. Joseph must be very happy that she was moving in on his feast day.

"St. Joseph doesn't give two hoots when I move in here; but I hope he's on top of things when I'm ready to move out." And she snorted, followed by a Sr. Bertrand laugh. I don't think Sr. Amata got it. St. Joseph was second in devotion, next to Our Lady, in the infirmary.

It was late August, and Sr. Agnes Mary and our two novices Sr. Kolbe and Sr. Diana, along with Sr. Myriam, Sr. Maureen, and Sr. Mary Cecilia, the Postulants (Brenda and Grace) and I were planning to have a tea party on the rooftop for the Sisters in the infirmary. It was still warm enough that none of them would complain about the chill, except maybe Sr. Bertrand.

It was Sr. Gerard who whispered to me one late afternoon when I was collecting the dishes from our mid-afternoon snack before the infirmary Sisters settled down for a rosary around the statue of Our Lady of Fatima. "Sister, you know that two days after our tea party on the roof it will be Sister Gertrude's eighty-fifth birthday...maybe we could include a cake at the party?" I thought this was a wonderful idea and kicked myself again for not remembering it was her birthday!

That night at the novices' recreation, I brought it up, and suggested we have a theme, something New York, and that we do a couple numbers to honor Sr. Gertrude. Mother Rosaria would prefer that rather than honoring *her* for the rooftop. They all thought it was a great idea, and it was Sr. Maureen who came up with the idea: "Give My Regards to Broadway." It's perfect because we had the New York skyline as our view and everyone already knew the words to the song. Sr. Mary Cecilia became our instant choreographer and said she could easily teach the seven of them chorus line steps, eight counting me. Sr. Diana would bake a cake looking like the Empire State Building—we actually had a mold someone had given as a Christmas gift years ago, and no one ever tried using it. And we set aside tomorrow's afternoon work to quickly make top hats. I borrowed Sr. Anna Maria who brought us wire, foam, felt, silk, and cardboard drums, plus her expertise in putting all this stuff together. I would get Greg to cut six canes from several old brooms he had in the garage, and spray paint them black, and put a white tip on them. I was now grateful he had the penchant to never throw anything away. It made the work garage look like a perpetual yard sale, but he had more than enough discarded brooms and mops to be able to raise canes. (I smile at my own pun.) And white bow ties would be easy to make.

Now I have to confess that I did something I've never done in my whole life, and probably would mention it in confession, but when Sr. Gertrude was down for confession in her wheelchair, I opened her closet door, and scrounged around on the floor which had slippers and shoes, and about five shoe boxes. I opened each box, and bingo—it was the third one, I found her old tap shoes. And on the top shelf, there was her own real wool felt top hat, at the far end of the closet. She wouldn't even notice. I hoped I put everything back as it had been, and I slipped out of her room, tap shoes under my scapular and top hat under my arm. I only passed one Sister on the way who always kept perfect custody of the eyes. She was the one to whom I was always invisible—and I was grateful for it this time.

The big day came on Saturday. The weather couldn't have been nicer. After None, Sisters not involved in "the show" helped to accompany the Sisters from the Infirmary to the roof. The whole community was present except for the Sister keeping guard before the Eucharist. When they were all seated around tables facing the skyline, the first refreshments were brought out. They consisted of pots of tea for each table and trays of finger sandwiches. The sandwiches were just regular sandwiches cut into squares with the crusts removed; but each contained different "fillings" like cucumber and arugula, turkey breast and bacon, cream cheese and sliced pimento olives, and plain old bologna and mustard.

The Sisters found it all very delightful and as Sr. Beatrice said, "It's like being at the Ritz."

"The Ritz?" retorted Sr. Bruna. "This is more like the Plaza."

"Maybe the Plaza to you," chimed in Sr. Gerard, "but it's the Waldorf to me." I thought to myself, even unto old age, we're in competition for who knows the best hotels in New York. And I'm sure none of the above hotels would dare serve finger sandwiches on plastic plates!

With that the Novices Glee Club, each wearing a black or white beret over her veil, opened the program by singing a song in French for Mother Rosaria. It was the popular *Alouette, gentille alouette, alouette, je te plumerai*...and then all the things one would pluck from this poor little bird: the head, the beak, the eyes, the neck, repeating the refrain in between each one. It was a good song to warm up with! Mother loved it—of course, she had sung it countless times with her little French alouettes.

We had arranged the tables and chairs on the rooftop to face the Manhattan skyline, and even had a small rectangular wooden platform laid down that served as a stage. Sr. Kolbe was in charge of the phonograph. We hadn't updated anything from Broadway onto tapes or CDs, but we had the whole collection of Broadway shows on vinyl disks, called "records." I laughed to myself, here we are teaching the new generation how to use a record player!

The music began, and this quieted everyone down. Then the Novices Glee Club came out again carrying plastic tea cups, and singing *Tea for Two* with our own lyrics:

Tea for two and two for tea Oh how happy we will be
When we join the Beati… Above… We will see our family,
Sisters all most loved by me, Oh how happy we will be,
The Lord Himself our groom will be, Tea for two and two for you and me.

The phonograph played *There's No Business Like Show Business,* while everyone helped themselves to more tea and sandwiches. The Glee Club scurried off to make their quick change, praying their top hats all stayed nicely glued together, and no one would trip over her cane.

The Novices Glee Club appeared again, their backs to us, their top hats in their right hands over their hearts, as if they were singing to the City, and began: *"New York, New York"* …all the New Yorkers swallowed their finger sandwiches quickly, took a gulp of tea, and joined in the chorus: "… *it's a helluva of a town… The Bronx is up and the Battery down… New York, New York…* "

Sr. Antonia, who was in charge of Sr. Gertrude, had to keep her from getting up from her wheelchair and joining the chorus line. But they all threw out their arms in the grand finale, and everyone applauded themselves. Sr. Gertrude announced, "That was from *On the Town* in 1944, written by Leonard Bernstein himself." Everyone immediately dove back into their finger sandwiches and into a second cup of tea.

"These cups are too small; you should've used mugs. Where's my mug, Sister?" Sr. Bertrand was nonetheless enjoying herself, with or without her mug. She was wrapped in two sweaters and a blanket over her lap. "These sandwiches are great, but where's the crust? My mother always made us eat the crust; it grows hair on your chest." Sr. Amata choked on that one, and quickly refilled her tea cup, half tea and half milk.

Mother Rosaria came to the little platform we called a stage with a fake microphone in her hand; well, it was a real microphone, but wasn't working: "Ladies and Gentle-nuns, welcome to the penthouse suite at Queen of Hope Home for the Helpless and poor banished children of Eve." The Sisters applauded, and she hadn't really gotten into it yet, but they loved the introduction.

"We have the unique privilege in the whole Dominican world to live in the shadow of Manhattan and have this glorious view of her wondrous skyline. Perhaps our Sisters in the Bronx can also see her on a clear day, but not with this view. Many of you are born New Yorkers and the rest of us have made it our adopted home. And now in honor of and tribute to our special Broadway Baby, Sister Gertrude of the Sacred Heart on her eighty-fifth birthday, because as she says, 'We have given up the lights of Broadway for the Narrow-way'—we thank the Lord for His call to all of us, and still give our regards to Broadway…" She stood aside, gesturing to the stage.

The music began right on cue…("*Give my regards to Broadway*") after the first verse, which everyone joined in singing, the seven Sisters in the novitiate soft-shoed their way onto the stage, with top hats and canes, and white gloves and bow ties. Smiles as broad as Broadway itself; the Sisters refrained from singing and watched and listened, just a little spellbound by it all. You might have thought we had invited the Rockettes themselves to dance, but our Seven-Novicettes were better. They perfectly separated at the break, and onto the stage, I came in top hat and cane, my tunic hiked up by my belt, and wearing Sr. Gertrude's tap shoes. It all came back, like riding a bike, I guess, but I remembered my basic tap steps, to the delight of all present. Sr. Gertrude couldn't contain herself, and stood up with tears running down her cheeks, and shouting "Brava, Brava." At the grand finale we all shuffled along together, arms outstretched, and hats off, to Sr. Gertrude.

The first time in my whole life I have ever received a standing ovation! All of us were thrilled with the "audience's" grand participation.

We turned together, all in a row, our hats now pointing out to the New York skyline, and the music began again for our grand encore: *Give My Regards to Broadway.* Especially meaningful were the words: "*Whisper of how I'm longing, to mingle with the old time throng, Give my regards to Old Broadway, And say that I'll be there, 'ere long.*"

We knew, from a lifetime of doing *Lectio*, that Broadway was like "Jerusalem" in the Psalms; it was Eternal Life…and the *old time throng* were all the Sisters, relatives, friends, and benefactors who have gone before us, and for whom we pray every week.

The "mistress of ceremonies" came back on stage. "Thank you, thank you, Sisters, and a special bravo to Sister Mary

Baruch for filling in for the inimitable Sister Gertrude. Many of the Sisters around our age have grown up here with the joy of Sister Gertrude's dancing at special recreations, and other times, when the Spirit moved her. Thank the Lord that's always been in the community room!" (The Sisters laughed and applauded their agreement.)

"And now, Sister Gertrude, we have two special gifts to give to you to mark this momentous birthday." And Sr. Mary Cecilia in a kitchen apron, but a chef's top hat, rolled out the cake—a beautiful replica of the Empire State Building. It wasn't stone gray, of course, but a light chocolate, and rows of windows made with white frosting and glaze. The spiral antenna at the top was the single candle and protruding out, like King Kong and Ann Darrow (Fay Wray)—the numbers 8 and 5.

The traditional Happy Birthday song was sung (in harmony!) with the second verse added: "May the good Lord, bless you, may the good Lord bless you, God bless you, Sister Gertrude, may the good Lord bless you." The audience held their applause till after Sr. Gertrude bowed her head either in prayer or making a wish—perhaps both—and then dramatically blew out the candle, without losing her teeth.

It was almost a sin to destroy this cake by cutting it… almost. We didn't linger too long on the moral dilemma, and down came the Empire State Building in two-inch slices as if every Sister got her own floor! New pots of hot tea were brought out, the hotel finger sandwiches whisked away, and the background music was a medley of songs all about New York. I think it was one of the happiest times we knew together in that hour on the rooftop garden. We were happy to be together, doing exactly what we did. I don't mean just eating together on the roof, but the whole life: praying, singing, working, studying, and yes, eating together, and holding all things in common, like we do.

Sr. Gertrude was surrounded by the novices, and I made my way to an end row next to Sr. Catherine Agnes and Sr. Jane Mary. "It's a wonderful thing you did for Sister Gertrude, Sister." This was Sr. Jane Mary complimenting me!

Sr. Catherine Agnes added, "We didn't know you had such talent hidden in you all these years!"

I laughed. "Thank you, both, you're too kind, really! You should be grateful Sister Gertrude wasn't a former ballerina!" And I told them about my very short career at ballet school. "I never quite had the figure for a ballerina." They laughed with me. "And besides, I hated wearing a tutu." Sr. Catherine Agnes thought that was hysterical and nearly choked on the 50th floor of the Empire State Building.

Sr. Jane Mary leaned in like this was strictly confidential: "Well, I've never told anyone this in my life, but I hated wearing a tutu too." The way it came out "tutu too" got the three of us laughing.

"Sister, I just can't picture you doing ballet." I was maybe going out on a limb here, but I've never been on this limb before with her.

"Well, you can thank your lucky stars for that—it wasn't a pretty sight." The more we laughed, the more she went on. "They could have changed Swan Lake to Hippopotamus Pond." Sr. Catherine was laughing louder than I ever heard. "After my first *pas de deux*, my partner quit ballet with a hernia."

Sr. Catherine Agnes asked, "And the arabesques?"

"Arabesques? I couldn't lean over on two legs, let alone one, forget about doing it on my toe."

We were laughing so hard, Mother Rosaria made her way over to us. "What's this going on that has you all in hysterics?" She was delighted, of course, to see it. So we filled her in on our dance careers.

"I took ballet too as a girl. I was rather good at it, except I had lots of accidents, like I'd trip over my own feet." We all started laughing all over again. "I could never quite stand straight up *en pointe* without bending my knees and losing my balance." We laughed even more, identifying with every movement. "I loved all the terms in French though, and think maybe that's why I wanted to study French, not to dance, but to speak zee langue de France."

When we calmed down, Mother said, "Come, Sister Baruch, it's time for the second gift." I was the only one who knew what was coming and still couldn't believe it till I saw it.

Back on stage with her fake mic, "Attention, Sisters, er, Ladies and Gentle-nuns, our second gift is most unusual, at least for us. I don't believe we have ever had such a tribute here ever. It is not a common thing in a house of asceticism and humility," (she smiled, and we all giggled) "and so with great humility, we are happy to present to our Sister Gertrude of the Sacred Heart, a lifetime achievement award, direct from the Broadway stage, her own Tony Award."

I don't know how she did it, who she knows, or what strings she had to pull, but she had an actual Tony Award statuette, which was engraved on the base: *Sr. Gertrude of the Sacred Heart, O.P./ Mary, Queen of Hope Monastery/A.D.*

2001. I had never seen one close up, and the engraved image is the comedy/tragedy theater masks. How apropos for Sr. Gertrude of the Sacred Heart. A grand applause again.

We all held our breath, but allowed Sr. Gertrude to get out of her chair and take the stage. Sr. Mary Cecilia quickly handed her a cane to lean on, and Mother handed her the fake mic.

"Ladies and Gentle-nuns." Oh, Sr. Gertrude was a quick understudy! "I want to thank you all for this honor. I never thought in all my days that I would ever hold a Tony in my hand, but here I am. Blessed be God for His gifts." We all smiled and nodded our heads at each other like we were all the recipients. "It's true that once upon a time, I had my heart set on the lights of Broadway. For that I want to thank my parents," and she gestured with her head towards heaven, "they were both in Vaudeville, and so in truth, I grew up on the stage, or rather back stage. The theater, you know, is a whole world unto itself. It has lots of tears and laughter, and lots of hard work, and years of practice, and joy and heartache, and lots of ego getting in the way much of the time—sound familiar? But when you're on that stage, whether you're acting, or singing, or dancing, or a silent part of the scenery, you can see how much you touch people's souls, and lift them up out of their own worlds into something beautiful for just a little while. And your own heart and soul are moved and changed by it all. The applause ends of course, and the house empties, and all the players depart, and left alone on the stage is a single electric bulb burning, so the theater, the stage, is never in total darkness. Many a year, I would put my tap shoes in my bag and head out alone, my feet killing me, but my heart was full except for one big empty spot right in the middle." She stopped to collect her thoughts and to let this all sink in. It worked, because we all sat there without a word or movement. Kind of spellbound, because we knew where she was going with this.

"And one Saturday night after a show where I was just one of many in a chorus line of tap dancers, I stopped at St. Malachy's; you know, the Actors Chapel, on 49th Street. It was always open. It was just past eleven o'clock, I remember hearing a chime clock in the sacristy. And I knelt there at the side chapel of the Sacred Heart of Jesus, looking up at this beautiful image of Jesus pointing to His heart which was all aflame with fire. And I knew it was the fire of love. Don't get me wrong or think I'm some kind of mystic, but I felt a warmth suddenly strike my breast. I caught my breath for a second, afraid I was having a heart attack, but there was no pain, just warmth. I knew I was very tired; we had done a matinee and an evening, and I hardly ate in between. I also realized that I was here, alone. I hadn't gone out with the gang to any of the after-show bars; I didn't have a boyfriend trailing behind me, wanting to carry my tap shoes and talking about how great the show was, and how I was the best dancer of them all. I was content beyond words to be right where I was, and I looked over at the tabernacle, and, burning brightly at its left was the sanctuary lamp. Always burning to mark the Real Presence of Our Blessed Lord. The stage was empty, that is the sanctuary, all the priests and altar boys had gone home, but Jesus remained always there as the light to fill up our darkness, and the food to quench our hunger and thirst. I didn't put that into such eloquent thoughts right then and there, but I knew it all. And I knew my passion for the theater had taken a turn right into the Heart of Jesus.

I left St. Malachy's two hours later and walked over to Seventh Avenue to get a downtown train. Crossing over Broadway I always stood for a few seconds and looked down the street at all the lights like I was a tourist from Kansas, but this night, I knew I wasn't meant for the lights of Broadway, burning alone on an empty theater, but for the light of a narrow-way burning in the sanctuary of a house of God."

We were still spellbound, listening to her every word.

"That was over sixty years ago. I found my way to Mary, Queen of Hope in 1943, and have been here ever since; always a member of the chorus line; always an understudy to someone more…more what? More gifted? More talented? More capable? More lucky? But I've clung to one thing always. My dear Sisters from the infirmary share this with me, and we want to pass it on to you, our young Sisters—and to us, you're all our 'young Sisters.' Keep your eyes fixed on Jesus who is meek and humble of heart, and thank Him every day, every moment, for your vocations; and if you break a leg along the way, well, blessed be God, and let the show go on. Thank you all from the bottom of my heart." She held up the Tony for all to see.

We couldn't applaud instantly. We just sat there in silence and awe at her words. And then in good old New York fashion, the rooftop garden exploded with applause and a standing ovation.

Mother Rosaria let the applause go on at its own length, and gently took the stage again, fake mic and all. "Thank you, Sister Gertrude, for words we will long remember and cherish. Those of us who aren't privileged to remain always in the chorus line, depend more than ever on your prayers. It is all of you (gesturing to the Sisters from the infirmary) who have taught us the steps, and we thank all of you for your prayers and perseverance."

It was Sr. Bertrand, of all people, who shouted out, "And thank you, Mother, for this wonderful rooftop patio." And everyone applauded again. She finally gave two hoots, and we were all in agreement.

"Now, we're not over yet, Sisters, we have one more surprise for you. It is indeed rare that we have a Tony Award recipient among us, and this calls for a special toast, to go along with a special blessing for this rooftop garden." And with that, the novices wheeled out a cart with two bottles of champagne, two bottles of Martinelli's apple cider, a pitcher of plain old lemonade, and hollow stem champagne glasses, albeit plastic ware. When everyone had a glass with something in it, Mother said this time without the fake mic, "Let us pray. Dear Lord, we ask You to bless this rooftop garden in honor of St. Joseph. Bless all who come here to pray, to rest, to be refreshed, to enjoy the weather, or to enjoy the view. Thank you, Lord, for all the blessings in our lives, and may St. Joseph provide for all our needs, bring us an increase of vocations, and bring all our beloved deceased to the rooftop garden of Paradise where we will be with You, and the Father, and Holy Spirit, forever and ever. Amen. To Sister Gertrude, Happy Birthday, *ad multos annos.*"

And we all shouted back, "Amen."

After about fifteen minutes, and a bit of scrambling and rearranging on the stage, Mother calmed everyone down, and took the mic: "And now before we conclude our first *Gaudeamus* on top of our world, the Sisters from the Infirmary, I'm told, have prepared a little somethingfor you, Sister Gertrude, and really, for all of us."

The Sisters moved into place: Sr. Gerard, Sr. Amata, Sr. Benedict, Sr. Beatrice, Sr. Bruna, and even Sr. Bertrand. Sr. Mary Cecilia was on the side with her clarinet, Sr. Bernadette (former infirmarian) and I joined them on the stage; I took the mic: "Sister Gertrude this is a song we have often sung together and acted out when we weren't singing. It's dedicated to you in memory of my dear sister Ruth Steinway."

Sr. Mary Cecilia began with the introduction, the pure baritone sound of the clarinet filling the garden and rolling off into space, and we began quietly singing:

> Try to remember the kind of September when life
> was slow and oh, so mellow. . .
> Try to remember and if you remember then
> follow.
> (Sr. Benedict adding the "follow, follow, follow"
> roll)

There was quiet applause, as everyone was quite moved by the words, but also the beautiful voices of the elderly Sisters. They blended in a lovely harmony. I remembered the joy the song brought to Sr. Gertrude when she learned it was Ruthie's opening number at Penguin Pub. It's a fantastic song from *The Fantasticks*!

The infirmary Sisters took the remaining quarter of the Empire State Building and a bottle of sparkling apple cider with them. The novices and I straightened out the roof; other Sisters took care of the dishes, trash, and all the paraphernalia.

And thus the party was a great success. We were already making plans for next spring: planting even more flowers and maybe even a strawberry patch, which would involve building a flower bed.

The Sisters all seemed to enjoy the view from the roof; for some it was their first time ever on the top of the monastery. We are on Willow Street, two blocks away from the Promenade, and from the roof we can actually see people walking along it. It would have been an ideal spot to watch the fireworks on the Fourth, but we were always sound asleep for that one. If one looked west (left) from our roof we had a great view of the Brooklyn Bridge and the Battery. We could almost see the Statue of Liberty, parked between Ellis Island and Governors Island, though in the process you'd almost fall off the roof. We joked, remembering the jokes that went around before President Kennedy was elected: "If Kennedy is elected, he's going to change the name of the Statue of Liberty to Our Lady of the Harbor." Not far removed from the reality, for us here, located in her shadow, and for many an immigrant she was indeed Our Lady of Hope.

There was a good forty-five minutes free before Vespers. So I just sat in my stall gazing at the Lord who never leaves the monstrance unless we move Him. The melody of *Try to Remember* still played in my head, and I resisted the temptation to go down memory lane, but thought instead of the

Lord who also said: *Do this in memory of Me.* Try to remember Me, as it were, and all the marvels, I have done for you. And we still have Him with us. The soul is filled with grace in His holy presence. The peace of the chapel settled over me; as the sun slowly made its evening dive into the horizon bringing an almost tangible calm to the house beneath the rooftop garden. The Church at eventide…remembering.

Sixteen

Maror: Bitter herbs, horse radish.

Blessed are you, Lord our God, King of the Universe who has sanctified us by commanding us to eat maror. (Haggadah)

Mama's eightieth birthday was coming up and David wanted to do something very special to celebrate. They had already been on three cruises, so David wanted to talk to me privately again to get my opinion on what they should do—perhaps a Broadway show, a nice dinner on the Upper East Side, or a matinee at the Metropolitan Opera. David was into the opera more than Mama, but she would go just to be a part of Lincoln Center.

The early days of September were Indian summer-days and even Sr. Bertrand would venture out to our ground-level garden to sit in the sun, or on the rooftop garden, if another Sister went with her. Either one was better than "being cooped up" inside.

Our Lady's birthday came and went with our usual festivity. We love the feast days of Our Lady and September 8 is one of my favorites. It had been nine months since the previous December 8, the Immaculate Conception. David did call that afternoon, and like before, just wanted to make sure I couldn't get away for the day to join him and Mama. Even Sally was coming in. He or Mama would let me know in a couple days what the definitive birthday plans were so I could be praying behind the scenes. David actually said that without rancor! I don't think he ever talked about prayer when we were growing up. I reminded him about the time we all took Mama and Papa to see *Fiddler on the Roof,* and how much Mama would enjoy a Broadway show. It was so New York.

I told him *42nd Street* had just re-opened and *The Producers* would be two good options. They were both musical smash hits. He probably wouldn't be able to get tickets, but they are two Mama would love, especially *42nd Street*. Of course, David knew that, and was more surprised that I did!

"Are you kidding? I can get tickets for any show. It's a brilliant idea…are you sure you can't get out even for a Wednesday Matinee?" He knew I couldn't, but said these things to make me laugh. "We'll let you know. I want to make a day of it."

The weather was so nice that I "reserved" the rooftop for my meeting with the postulants. Instead of meeting separately, I thought we could just have an informal discussion about things. This would only include them, not the novices or simple professed. The two of them sat on the two-seater swing—which Sr. Brenda politely informed me wasn't actually a "swing" as it didn't swing; it was a glider and glides back and forth on runners. I told her she was being very "Dominican" because we like to fuss over words, and make distinctions. This made her feel proud till Sr. Grace said,

"Well, I'm still calling it a swing." I hadn't realized till I was assistant novice mistress that there can be "sibling rivalry" between Sisters, especially if there are only two of them. I don't remember having that during my novitiate, but we were also not as free to speak our minds—and we certainly wouldn't have been on a glider-swing on the roof for our weekly meeting. We didn't have a weekly meeting!

I wasn't overly concerned about the two of them; they actually got along very well and complemented each other. Sr. Brenda was a little older and was a professional and given to "details" (thus, the swing really being a glider) and Sr. Grace was surprisingly more naïve about many things, being such a product of the pop culture. They were both very prayerful and excited about receiving the habit soon and their new names, and getting their hair cut.

Sr. Brenda talked about her family, especially anold grandfather, and Sr. Grace liked to talk about Leah who was still, as Sr. Grace punned it, "kibitzing on the kibbutz."

* * *

A couple days went by, and I hadn't heard from Mama or David. We rarely had windows open because the noise of traffic and sometimes unsavory conversations could find their way into the silence of the enclosure, but Tuesday morning the eleventh was an exception. It promised to be another beautiful day, clear and sunny; early autumn in New York. A perfect day for Mama's birthday, for whom I offered my Mass and Communion. Our Mass was over and a few of us were having a late breakfast. It was a bagel-breakfast morning. I remember spreading walnut raisin cream cheese on a cinnamon raisin bagel—a treat we didn't get every day. I was standing by an open window looking out on our "Fatima set", a statue of our Lady with the three children and even two little lambs. Our Lady was standing in a bed of pink and white petunias, thanks to the white-veiled novices. And then…

We heard it—we felt it.
God have mercy on us, we smelled it.

There was a boom that shook the ground. We all just froze wherever we were; and then the bell rang—and we all hurried in silence to the chapter room. Mother was white as a sheet and could hardly speak, but she announced that a plane had crashed into one of the towers of the World Trade Center. We could go to the chapel right now and pray, or we could go to the rooftop.

It was Sr. Bertrand who shouted, "Rooftop; we can pray from the rooftop." And we moved like silent roaches when the lights come on…to the rooftop. We could see it; the smoke was a veritable cloud pouring out of the top of the building; and as we stood there speechless, each Sister mumbling her side rosary…we saw the second plane smash into the South Tower, in a fire-ball of explosion.

Mother had brought a transistor radio with her, and we stood motionless listening to the news. I felt my knees suddenly become weak. My New York…our New York. How could this be happening? Some of us had to sit down in the wicker chairs we had bought for the roof-garden. We were stunned.

Mother said Fr. Ambrose had called her immediately. He had a television in his quarters and always watched the morning news. That's when she rang the bell.

I think we probably stayed there on the roof for over an hour; some made their way downstairs and to the chapel. The radio was reporting that thousands were killed instantly. We saw the buildings literally collapsing in a cloud of smoke and debris. We learned that it was a terrorist attack. The Pentagon in Washington had also been hit, and a plane crashed in Shanksville, Pennsylvania. It was almost surreal. The noise and the smell were unlike anything we had ever experienced.

Sr. Paula arrived with several pitchers of ice water and a stack of paper cups. We drank our water, shook our heads, and some of us cried on each other's shoulders. I had to get to a phone and call Mama; she must be terribly upset; she was probably watching it all on her new wide-screen TV… poor Mama, and on her birthday of all days!

I couldn't reach her. She was probably at Millie Hutner's, and I didn't know that number. Or maybe she was out getting her hair done for her big night out. I'd try again in an hour. Many of the lines and communications were all down temporarily. All one heard for hours were sirens; police and fire sirens. We shut the windows and retreated into the chapel and prayed; it was our greatest consolation. Some went to help Sr. Bernadette, a native New Yorker, who couldn't finish dinner in the kitchen; she was so shook-up by it all.

We would have the Office of Sext and dinner (lunch) in about an hour. I made my way to my office, not to work, but to sit at my desk and distract myself. It was then that I saw the little red light flashing…the answering machine. We must have a million calls telling us the news. I would jot them down and be able to let Mother know later on.

The first was from last night…an Evelyn Saccerello wanting a Mass said for her husband's first anniversary…the second from last night…was from Mama.

"This is for Sister Baruch; please tell her that her brother, the doctor, is taking me to see *42nd Street*, the Broadway musical, not the street, and we're having a birthday breakfast at Windows on the World tomorrow morning—he wants to know if she can join us. It would be such a blessing." Beep, disconnect.

I couldn't move. It couldn't be. She couldn't have meant this morning; maybe they were going later; maybe they were stuck in traffic. I didn't have David's number, but I could probably call his office. I grabbed our oversized clunky New York phone book and looked up *Feinstein, David Dr.* Maybe it was too early for office hours; but I called anyway. After five rings, a frenzied woman's voice answered. "Doctor Feinstein's office."

"Hello, is this Dr. Feinstein's secretary? I'm his sister calling from Brooklyn; I'm trying to reach him and don't have his home phone."

The secretary was slow to answer. "I haven't heard from him at all; he isn't due in till this afternoon, but I looked at his appointment book, as I do each morning, and he had written: 'Breakfast with Ma at 8:30 AM'. I don't know this for sure, but he had me call Windows on the World a couple days ago for reservations, I…" And she couldn't speak anymore.

"I understand; I got an answering machine message from our mother. They must've been there." We both gasped at the words.

"I…I…don't know what to say…I can't believe it," came her voice from the other end of the telephone line.

"I know, dear, neither can I. All we can do now is pray. God bless you." And I hung up. If one is able to know the sensation of having a stroke without actually having one, that's what I felt. All I could do, was put my head down on my desk in utter disbelief. I couldn't cry, or scream, or even call for help. Sr. Agnes Mary was going by and saw me. All I could do was point to the phone and say: "Mama…"

The rest of the day is all a blur to me. I know Sr. Agnes Mary got Mother, and together they listened to the answering machine message. Mother wanted me to go to the emergency room, thinking I was in traumatic shock, but I assured her that the only ER I needed was Eucharistic Repose. I remember sitting in the chapel for hours where I was able to come back to my senses, and began to pray for Mama and David, and all the thousands who lost their lives that morning.

There was a "heavy silence" over the house like we were living in slow motion, but the wonderful thing about monastic life is that it drones on, and holds us up, especially the *Psalms* which express the praise and heartache of God's People. The worst part was trying not to think what Mama and David were thinking when it all hit; if they even had time to think…time to surrender themselves to the loving and merciful arms of their Creator.

I couldn't imagine what the poor people on the planes went through, if they even knew where they were heading. It's too much to try to fathom. I would have to pull myself together for my Sisters here; we all felt the impact of the attack on New York; others may have lost friends or loved ones too.

Mother was so wonderful during all this, as only time and reflection on it all would show. Early that afternoon she sent Sr. Paula out to an appliance store, and she came back with a delivery man who installed our new 37-inch colored television. Our most important task was to pray, and this we certainly did, but Mother also knew we needed to know the impact behind all that had happened.

I wasn't able to watch that night. I started to but had to leave. There was a clip of bodies jumping, falling, from the top. Only days later did we come to know that 343 firefighters lost their lives. Many people on lower floors were able to escape, but no one in Windows on the World survived, including seventy-two of the restaurant staff. There were terrible scenes of people covered in white debris running away from the buildings, panic stricken.

Mother also gave us all general permission to use the phones and call whomever we needed. I wanted to call Sally, but had no way to reach her; I did not know her number. I remember David saying she was coming in from Chicago to celebrate Mama's birthday. I tried calling directory assistance or whatever it's called these days, but there was no listing for a Sarah Feinstein in Chicago. I didn't know the name of the dog grooming salon or Mitzie's last name. I was in a quandary over what to do. I decided to just wait, hopefully

Sally would call me, and she did, the next day, Wednesday mid-morning. She had been trying to reach David or Mama all yesterday; all flights into New York had been cancelled; she missed going to *42nd Street* with them. She still couldn't reach Mama; did I know where she could possibly be?

I could just barely get it out. "Sally," (Take a deep breath, Baruch), "Mama and David went out yesterday morning for a birthday breakfast…they were UP…THERE…they didn't…" And I couldn't say anymore, but Sally knew.

"Oh, Becky…I can't believe this…I can't…" and she couldn't say anymore. We both hung onto the phone without a word. "I am coming in as soon as I can. I have a key to Mama's…to our…apartment. I will call you again when I get in, if that's okay, and I will come down to see you…" She couldn't go on.

"That will make me so happy if you do. Please call, and if you get our answering machine, leave a message; I will check it all day long."

The Sisters—well, most of them—watched the news each night for the next five nights in place of recreation, after which Mother put the television away. Our two postulants were visibly shaken by it all; they were both New Yorkers. I also got two long-distance calls that first weekend. The first from Gwendolyn who called from London. She too was a "New Yorker" for many years and loved the city. She was shocked and worried and scared and angry and anxious if I was okay. She was even more shocked when I told her about Mama and David. Her last words to me were: "Hang in there, MB, I'm on the next flight over to see you…if there's a room available, I'll take it, if not, I'm sure Brooklyn Heights has some very nice hotels. On second thought, I'll get a hotel reserved before I come…I'm going to need something a little stronger than Compline."

The other call was from Lancashire. I didn't break down when I heard Gwendolyn's voice, but I did when I heard Ezra's. He was calling only to ask if I was okay. His Aunt Sarah was fine and hoped my mother was too. When I told him, he was too shocked to speak, but promised he would offer Mass for Mama and David that very evening. He couldn't get away, but would be home after Christmas, and would call me again soon.

I felt so utterly desolate. But not alone. I had a deep sense of the presence of the Lord through all this, and that my "family" included all my Sisters here too. We would hold each other up and get through this. We certainly didn't have all the means to grieve as the outside world did, but we had the best. We have the Lord and the Prayer of the Church, His Prayer. *O God, come to my assistance. O Lord, make haste to help me.*

The novices and postulants were very subdued and attentive to me, but I also knew they were carrying their own grief, and I had to be there for them. I told Mother I would not tell the novices about my mother and brother yet; I want them to have their own time to grieve. Along with Sr. Agnes Mary, I suggested we have a rosary novena even though it wasn't October, the month of the rosary; we could devote this one to what we came to call the "tragedy of nine-eleven." We would pray for all the victims and also for their families. They liked this idea, and we did it the forty-five minutes before Vespers each night, which we normally had reserved for class after the afternoon work period.

Our Lady has a very soothing way about her, and our quiet rosary was like a balm of comfort over the novitiate. And over me. Sr. Kolbe seemed the most depressed by it all, and I made a mental note to have a chat with her. She was young; actually they were all young, and the harsh reality of life had never hit them. They are the generation that has had everything handed to them, kind of, although I think they are also stressed out in more ways than we ever were. The rosary helps to concentrate the mind at least for fifteen minutes, although the Lord knows the mind can be doing cartwheels around the globe and on a roller coaster of emotions. We've never discussed him, yet, but I'll have to get her talking about her patron, St. Maximilian Kolbe. He knew the harsh reality of life.

Sr. Diana was older but more fragile. Her faith life was not tested yet by a real crisis, till now. I think she finds certain little things in our life difficult; things she wasn't aware of when she entered, but that's usually true for all of us. She'll be okay, I hope. She was very grateful for the rosary novena.

Sr. Myriam is still with us in the novitiate but will be integrated into the senior community in another month. She's probably been the most emotional about it all. She's also a New Yorker and mentioned after 9/11 that she had been to the World Trade Center several times. She's eaten at Windows on the World with her father who works on Wall Street. He is safe and has talked to her, but still…

Sr. Maureen was hard to read. Her usual light-heartedness was turned into a sullen kind of heavy-heartedness.

Sr. Mary Cecilia seemed emotionally detached from it all, but I think that may just have been a cover-up. Although that's very subjective on my part; I can't imagine someone being detached from it all.

And poor Sr. Brenda seems the most distraught, and spends all her free time in the chapel, which is fine. This is her first major crisis here, and I hope and pray she pulls through it. Being an emergency room nurse probably has lots of disturbing memories. I asked her if she wished she was there now, helping out. And she said, "No, I can do more here."

And Grace, our Fashion Institute graduate, is also very upset; she didn't want to come to the rosary, and I excused her. It took the longest time for her to be able to talk to me about it. She had friends who worked in the World Trade Center.

The rosary novena is not an original idea; this was a common practice among the Sisters in the infirmary. When I went to see them on the Thursday following 9/11 (two days after) they were already praying a rosary-novena. Sr. Gerard, who already suffered from a doomsday-complex, was convinced that the end was coming soon. "The fire will fall from heaven," she said as soon as I saw her. "Get ready, Sister Baruch, the three days of darkness will happen soon." We all certainly hoped not, but Sr. Gerard had everyone in the infirmary half convinced that this might be it. They all had blessed candles in their night tables, just in case, except Sr. Bertrand who didn't give two hoots about all that "end of the world malarkey."

Sr. Bertrand also said she'd never go on the rooftop garden again and that the airplanes could have crashed on our roof. It was better to stay cooped up in the monastery than to risk attack. Getting the attackers' names and motives was going to be Sister's big challenge, but she was up to the task. She had served for four years in the Women's Army Corps. I could tell she wasn't happy when Mother put the television away and told us that we've seen enough. Sr. Bertrand didn't complain outwardly. She accepted things under holy obedience—and whatever *The New York Times* reported. It was almost like *Lectio* for her.

Sr. Amata and Sr. Benedict were the most prayerful and started the novena to calm everyone else down. "It's all in God's hands," Sr. Amata would say. And, of course, she was right. We don't understand why things happen, but we know that nothing is outside the knowledge and love of God.

Sr. Gertrude, my dear Sr. Gertrude, sat silent in her wheelchair. Her eyes were puffy, and her hands trembled a bit. Of all the Sisters who were New Yorkers, and there were many of us, the attack on the World Trade Center affected Sr. Gertrude the most. I didn't have the courage to tell her my mother and brother were among the dead. I would tell her when the time was right; it wasn't time yet.

And at night after Compline, I would stay behind and let the presence of the Lord pour over me, if that's the right word. I didn't feel anything; I was still a bit numb from it all, but I knew He was present, and His presence was healing. And I prayed as consciously as I could for the souls of Mama and David. I sat there for them; it was my Catholic "sitting Shiva," and I would do it for seven nights. I could even slip off my Nike sneakers and let my feet touch the cold floor. I knew I had to pray for them, because, well, because we don't know, do we? Can "baptism of desire" stretch that far to the secret corners of Mama's heart when she wanted to know the truth; when she thought about God in those in-between moments, or when she went to shul and closed her eyes and listened to the *Kol Nidre*; when she kept the Sabbath and drew the light to her face—was it not You, Lord Jesus, who are the hidden Light? All the years that she lovingly prepared the food for Pesach, and ate the Seder every year of her life; listening to Your Word and loving her family. Did she not love You, Lord, in loving us?

How much I would have loved to have seen her come to know You in the fullness of the Faith: the very Word, the One and Only Word made flesh who dwelled among us. Do you not save a piece of broken matzah in your heart for Your Chosen People in all the mitzvahs of life which You kept and fulfilled. I don't know how Mama prayed to You, but I believe she loved You because she saw everything as a blessing. She was always praising You, Lord, in her own unique way. Papa came to know and believe in You; he knew You were indeed the Messiah and Son of God. The grace You sent his way through Mother John Dominic and Fr. Meriwether; and now Mama knows all that; and Lord, You filled her with the grace of reconciliation when she came to me, like the Prodigal Mother, and the love which had been buried for all those years, came alive. Hannah of a Thousand Silver Hairs, and not one of them has gone unnoticed by You; and every salty tear she shed, You have counted, and haven't they counted for something, Lord? Are they not a type of baptism because they sprang from the depths of love? And maybe, Lord, You have put me here to pray for her, in her place, to pray for the salvation of her soul, and to do penance and weep with sorrow for her sins which wounded her at times and which she covered up and hid from us all by her sarcasms and complaints. She made us laugh; she made me cherish the beautiful things of life, and to enjoy the food and drink of earthly families and festivity. She gave me *karpas* but even more she gave me *charoset* and taught me to embrace the bitter herbs and sweetness of life because You are the Lord and Giver of Life. I know You love her so much more than I do, than Papa did, than any human being ever could; You love us more. You love her more, and her heart is bursting with joy to know You now…let her be a catechumen in Purgatory; she'll be one of your loveliest students.

Mother of God, my dear Mother of Perpetual Help, and Comforter of the Afflicted, my dear dear Jewish Mother in Heaven, embrace Hannah Feinstein for me and bring her to your Son. I tried in my own poor way, and I hope it touched enough to stretch her will to desire to know the Truth. Bring her to Papa when the time is right. Mother of God, tell Yeshua that I am willing to undergo any suffering and any cross for the salvation of her soul…and that goes for Ruthie and David and Joshua.

That had been my *Kaddish*, along with a rosary, and the *Salve Regina* each night. Added now to Our Lady's train in our nightly Salve Procession are Mama and David…*Turn then Most Gracious Advocate, your eyes of mercy toward us, and after this our exile, show unto us the Blessed Fruit of Your womb, Jesus.*

And finally, dear Lord, I commend my poor self to You, Lamb of God who takes away the sins of the world, have mercy on me. Fill me with Your Holy Spirit and the fire of

Your Love, for I am an orphan now, Lord, and I feel like I have died. Amen.

Psalm 88

Lord my God, I call for help by day; I cry at night before you.
Let my prayer come into your presence. O turn your ear to my cry.
For my soul is filled with evils;
my life is on the brink of the grave. I am reckoned as one in the tomb:
I have reached the end of my strength, like one among the dead;
like the slain lying in their graves; like those you remember no more, cut off, as they are, from your hand.
You have laid me in the depths of the tomb, in places that are dark, in the depths.
Your anger weighs down upon me: I am drowned beneath your waves.

Part Two

Called by God, like Mary, to sit at the feet of Jesus and listen to his words, they are converted to the Lord, withdrawing from the empty preoccupations and illusions of the world, forgetting what lies behind and reaching out for what lies ahead. (Fundamental Constitution of the Nuns, III)

Seventeen

Because God did not make death, nor does He rejoice in the destruction of the living. (Wisdom 1:12)

THERE WAS MUCH ado made over the first anniversary of 9/11. We didn't see any of the coverage or special tributes, which is fine. I'm sure it will be forever embossed in our memories, at least till our generation passes on. I remember we had silent meals for a week afterwards as we couldn't concentrate on the reading; sacred music was played instead, and it was healing. But thc deeper healing from it all takes time too, and some wounds will probably never heal, or at least always leave a scar. On the anniversary we again had music, but this time it was the *Adagio for Strings* by Samuel Barber, which was played by the BBC Orchestra just four days after the attacks in honor of the victims. *The Adagio for Strings* is so moving, we couldn't eat, but sat in silence and prayer till it was ended.

Tragic events certainly shape the way we think and feel about life, probably more than the joyous and happy times. I know that's so for me when I look back over my life. The death of a loved one becomes the pivotal point, or deepening point that influences the rest of one's life. I wonder why that is? Fr. Ambrose once said to us in class that he preferred preaching funerals more than weddings. We all kind of giggled, but he meant it. And he said it's because people listen differently at a funeral…we are plunged into mystery, and we want a word of consolation or understanding. (We are plunged into mystery at a Sacramental Marriage too, or a Solemn Profession, but they are different. Although, like death, they point to eternal life beyond which they are a sign.) But I know what Fr. Ambrose means.

I thought a lot about this place of "death" in our lives during the year following 9/11, and sometimes it seems that we need to talk about it with others, to make sense of things.

By September 2002, it was a year since my sister Sally came to the monastery for the first time. We had had our *reconciliation*, for lack of a better word, at our sister Ruthie's funeral, several years before that—especially by my being able to spend two nights with her and Mama and sit Shiva with them for Ruthie. There was a "death" that brought about life—a new life, a new relationship between Mama and me, certainly, and also between Sally and me, and through them, eventually with my brother, David. Isn't it strange how "death" which separates one from life, as we know it and live it, brings about union?

At first Sally seemed frightened to be sitting in the parlor, speaking in soft tones like we were in a police interrogation room, being observed through a one-sided mirror. I was able to fill in Sr. Paula before Sally's visit. Sister was a natural for making people feel welcomed. She knew then that Sally lived in Chicago, was Jewish, of course, but didn't really practice her faith, and she (Sally) was nervous about actually coming here to see me. She had been a journalist once and saw a lot of life, but she had never been to a monastery of nuns.

Ten minutes after Sally arrived, Sr. Paula quietly knocked and brought in the usual Pyrex pot of coffee and a plate of (not usual) croissants and orange marmalade. I don't know how Sr. Paula could have ever known that orange marmalade was Sally's favorite, but there it was. She smiled and left as quietly as she came in.

"Isn't she the cutest thing you've ever seen? Oh, I'm sorry, I don't mean that she's cute, cute, but how quietly she came in and left, and look at this!" Meaning the orange marmalade. "She's certainly very young to be a nun, isn't she?"

"Sister Paula? She's almost forty now, maybe older, I can't keep track."

"Forty? She doesn't look a day over twenty. Speaking of age," (*we were?*) "you still look like you're in your thirties!"

This was Sally breaking the ice, of course. She fixed us each a cup of monastery coffee, and a croissant for herself. I had to catch my breath for a moment as she looked so much like Mama at the moment, when Mama would fuss over our coffee. I was half expecting her to pull a bottle of Mogen David out of her purse. She took a swallow of her coffee, and she grimaced the same way Mama would.

"It's the Brooklyn water," I said.

"The Brooklyn water?"

"Our Sister Bertrand blames the bitter after-taste on the water, not the fact that it's institutional over-ground coffee, with chicory mixed in. But it's such a blessing we get brewed now, and not the instant kind." That made Sally relax and smile.

"Oh, Becky, I still can't believe Mama and David are gone and in such an awful way; I can't even think about it; it's giving me nightmares. How are you bearing up?"

"I've had a few bad days and nights, but the Sisters are good—we're all feeling the impact of it, and we hold each other up. Mother Rosaria has proven to be one of the grandest…one of the grandest ladies I've ever met. She's able to express sympathy to each Sister in a way that that Sister needs it, and she does it all without thinking about herself and her own grief." Sally sat and sipped. "I live in the novitiate with the young Sisters, and I am trying to be there for them, each in her own grief. One of the postulants, Sister Brenda, lost her grandfather who was a retired volunteer fireman, who came out of retirement, just to help…and of course, he didn't make it. Like you, I can't think of the details of any of it. I have to keep turning it over to the Lord."

Poor Sally looked quite bedraggled by it all. She probably hasn't gotten any sleep.

"Are you staying in David's apartment or at home?" I asked, trying to change the subject.

"I'm in our old apartment. I'll go over to David's this afternoon. I have to meet with his lawyers; I have a key to his place, however, as Mitz and I have stayed there before. I don't know what's going to happen to any of their stuff. We never talked about that. I know David has a will, and he made sure Mama did too; he was good that way. We're the only ones he's got left, and I don't know…" She hesitated, like stopping to measure her words. "I don't know if he redid his will since you and he were… talking to each other again. You know what I mean."

"Oh, I don't expect anything. I can't inherit anything anyway because of my vows. I haven't even thought about that. And all their things…all Mama's things, what will happen to them all? Isn't it awful—we can't even have a proper funeral and Kaddish, and sit Shiva. Poor Mama. I think she had a girl at the Helena Rubenstein Salon pre-hired to do her hair when she passed."

"Oy." That's all it took: Sally's little forever-Yiddish "*oy*" and we got the giggles which turned into good old-fashioned sisterly laughter, which ended in sobbing for our loss.

We managed to get it all out, and settled for another cup of coffee and croissant with orange marmalade. It calmed us down, and we talked about lots of trivial things, like the traffic in New York, and that Mama and David and she were planning to go see *42nd Street.* She said Mama wanted to go see Elizabeth Taylor and Michael Jackson at Madison Square Garden the night before, on the 10th. It was a 30th anniversary show of Michael's. She wasn't sure that David could get tickets.

"May I ask you something? You don't have to answer it, and I'm not asking to start an argument or anything…it's just that you seem so 'together.' You were the closest to Ruthie and to Mama these last couple years…"

I didn't know what Sally was going to ask. The last of my croissant went down, and I just sat there staring at this poor woman who was my sister, but could easily have been a stranger come in off the street. "Yes?"

"Why would God, whom you say is All Love, allow such a thing to happen? Maybe to really evil people, but Mama? Mama never hurt a fly; she was always kind to people. Granted, she had her opinions and loved to gossip, but she wasn't cruel. Why would God let this happen; she should die in such a horrific way? And David: he was a good man—you saw how he took care of Mama."

I sat for a moment, collecting my thoughts. "I'll take more coffee, if you'd be so kind." I put my mug on the turn and spun it over to her side. I could see Sally's hand shaking as she poured the coffee.

"I've asked myself that question, of course. It's an ancient one, actually. It's the old old question of why is there evil in the world if God is a good and loving God. I can't put it into a clear answer like our Dominican Fathers do, but I know that God doesn't cause evil things to happen; there is not an ounce of evil in Him; the letting bad things happen began with us, and from our human ability to freely choose it...Remember on Yom Kippur, the sound of the shofar? That aching, hollow, blare of the horn that was like the soul crying out to God for mercy. God made us with these free wills, and if we choose to do evil over good, He allows it, because we have to be free. We're not computers or robots, even though we're creatures of habit, thank Goodness, or we'd never know how to dress ourselves in the morning." Sally smiled and sipped and grimaced and stared back at me, listening.

"Sometimes when we choose to do something not so good, it affects, not just us, but other people too. I've wrestled with that one for years, you know. When I became a Catholic, the whole family, except for Papa, thought I was doing something awful, and it affected you all. If you listened to David, my *abandoning Judaism*, as he put it, affected all our relatives for generations of Austrian Feinsteins whom I was betraying, not to mention the State of Israel."

Sally laughed. "I remember that. David, the self-made Talmudic scholar and historian whose shadow never crossed the doorway of a synagogue."

"The evil of the attack on the World Trade Center, the Pentagon, and that plane full of innocent people in Pennsylvania affected thousands of people; it's affected us, in our grief and nightmares. Mama and David did not die that cruel death as a punishment from God, but because there's evil in the world, and we are affected by it." I sat silent for a moment. I'm always afraid I'm going to get preachy.

I went on, "You know, as terrible as it was, I have to think, I want to think, that Mama and David, didn't know what was coming. The impact of the plane was so powerful, their dying was instant. That's too awful to imagine, but can you imagine if Mama had some illness that lingered for years; how she would have hated it all; what she would have deemed 'useless suffering'—for what? Everything sagging and hurting; being bedridden..."

"Her hair all tangled up and greasy," Sally added to my image. "No nail polish on cracked nails and her memory fading."

We both sat lost in our imaginations, not wanting to say it was good Mama went so quickly and so suddenly, because it wasn't good, but she was happy at that moment. She was celebrating her birthday with her son, the doctor, in a gorgeous restaurant high above the New York she loved. She had all her cards in order, as they say, with her three living children…she was a grandma.

"More coffee?" Sally was up and heading for the remains of the Pyrex pot.

"No thank you," I said politely, "another cup of that and my back teeth will be floating." That was an old expression of Mama's. We both laughed to break the seriousness of the air in the room.

Sally added, "Such a blessing, orange marmalade." And we laughed. Funny how we human beings ease the tension of sadness with laughter. I picked up from it to say, "You see, even the good things we do and say affect others. The novices here and half the community see the little things of life as 'such a blessing,' and say so. Mama's had an effect here all these years, and she never knew it.

Seated again with a newly smeared croissant, Sally said, "Do you think Mama's life was…I don't know what word I want… shallow? You know, it was all appearances and what people thought."

"Oh, I guess on one level, yes, Mama certainly lived on the surface of life; most people do. We get caught up in the externals, that's for sure, and what the world thinks is important, or notorious, or meaningful. Some people, I dare say, never get beneath the surface. I'm reading a wonderful book by an old Dominican Father who says that everyone has an interior life—it's our talking to ourselves; we all do this, hopefully silently; but we're always talking to ourselves, making plans, worrying about the future, or brewing over something in the past…that's all an interior life, he says. But when the interior conversation turns to God who is within our heart of hearts, then this interior life becomes a spiritual life. And some poor people spend their whole lives only talking to themselves."

Sally was listening intently. After all, she was always considered the smartest of the Feinstein girls; she could delve into deeper thoughts. She was probably thinking about her own life too, I hoped, but we had Mama to use as our example.

I went on. "I think Mama discovered the spiritual life within herself. She kept it very private, but you know, you have to be able to see deeper than the surface of things to see everything as a 'blessing'…a favor from God. I used to love to watch and listen when Mama lit the candles for Shabbat, and closed her eyes, and prayed. And remember, she was married to Ruben Feinstein, no slouch when it came to the spiritual life, and living life a little deeper than what meets the eye." It was a spontaneous gesture, but I lifted my coffee cup to Sally: "*L'Chaim.*"

"*L'Chaim.*" She responded in good Jewish fashion. "I guess you don't think you live your life on the surface, do you? I think I always judged you and 'it' looking only at the externals, but there must be more going on after all these years to keep you here."

"In the nunnery?" I reminded her. "I think maybe David came to see that too. Some days I'm not so sure, but yes, we try to live life at the deep end. We even have a verse from Scripture where Jesus tells Peter to go out into the deep water and drop your net. And they caught more fish than the boat could haul." Sip, munch. "I'd say that the really deep part escapes us much of the time. We are living in a mystery, not like a murder mystery or a puzzle, but a spiritual reality—we are living in Christ, or He lives in us in a very real way. His life is in us…we spend a lot of time studying and praying and meditating on this, so I can't explain it all in five minutes."

Sally just nodded.

"It's a very Jewish life, you know, although I'd never say that here. But to live in Christ and He in us, is very mystical. He is not just the Messiah, but the fulfillment of all the sacrifices, all the prophets, and of the whole Torah. He is our sukkah in whom we live, and we are His sukkots in which He lives, filling us with the lights of Chanukah all year round... we pilgrim people on our way to the homeland. Next year, Jerusalem…the Heavenly Jerusalem that is. Purgatory…" it just dawned on me after all these years. "Purgatory is where we burn up all the *chametz* before we sit down at the heavenly banquet. And our prayers are His prayers—the Jewish Psalms, we chant over and over. And most of all…" I slowed down and paused so Sally could hear it all. "…most of all He is the true lamb of Pesach; His blood is spread on the lintels of our souls, and evil passes over us when we live in the blood of the Lamb. We pass through the Red Sea of Baptism, and our sins, like the Egyptians, are drowned in its waves and we are saved. The salt water for dipping karpas, remember? Sometimes that's thought of as the Red Sea. And most especially, or as one of our postulants would say, the 'most awesome,' Jesus is the matzah of the new Seder, the new order of the new covenant. His body is broken in death on Good Friday before the shofars are sounded announcing the Sabbath, and He is hidden in the tomb, and found alive again by Mary Magdalen and His apostles on the day after Shabbat…the new Shabbat, the eighth day."

No response yet. Sally drank her coffee and the croissant lay uneaten, so far, on Sr. Paula's guest plasticware. ("Such a blessing, you can drop it, and it won't break or crack or chip." Those are Sr. Paula's sentiments. And I suppose it's all very convenient, but I kind of hate plastic dishes. There's something more real when dishes can get chipped and break, like us. I had a quick flashback of Mama's Seder plate crashing on the hardwood floor. If that had been plastic it would still be with us; but if it were plastic, it would not have been so beautiful.)

"Now that's just part of the depth we strive to live in, but sad to say, we can spend a lot of time living on the surface too. We come in with all our 'chametz.' It takes more than one night to find it all…it takes a lifetime."

Sally laughed, but she was deep in thought. Remembering, she said, "I haven't thought about that in years. I remember when it was just David and I who searched for the chametz, and I knew we'd find some because Papa always 'planted' some. And we'd always have flashlights to search for the chametz."

"Oh, that's right. I forgot that. I think in ancient days it was probably a candle. The light of a candle lights up our way. On Holy Saturday night we begin in total darkness and light a large candle called the Paschal candle, the Passover Candle, and we follow it in the dark, and light our individual candles from it. Oh, dear, I hope in a hundred years they aren't using plastic Paschal candles with electric flames."

Sally was still thinking about the chametz, however, and asked, "Do you still find a lot of chametz in your life? I'd think it was a pretty kosher kitchen by now."

"Well, if I think about it, our whole life here is really like a life-long Pesach. We have times each year, like Advent and Lent, but really a time each day, to search for the chametz, the leaven, St. Paul calls it. It's part of what keeps us from real purity of heart. Ha! The kitchen may be kosher, but the heart isn't there yet. It just dawned me that Cassian, I think, says the ultimate aim or ultimate end of our life is Eternal life, but the immediate end, like the daily aim—is attaining purity of heart."

"A kosher heart!" That was my intelligent sister catching on!

"Yes, a kosher heart," I said. "That's very good."

"But even then, it seems like such a waste. Like you aren't *doing* anything to help people—you know, like Mother Teresa."

"A lot of people think that, probably even within the Church. But, again, it's the affecting-others-thing, like evil, but the opposite. And actually, I've realized over the years, that Catholics have a specific and maybe a unique understanding of the Church, very different from Protestants. It's more than an organization or institution, it's also an organic body—we call it the Mystical Body…the Mystical Body of Christ. And we become a living member, or cell, of that Body at baptism—it's that Christ living in us again. What we do or don't do, affects the entire Body. And we here, like other monks, nuns, and even hermits, devote our lives to prayer and penance and sacrifice for others—for their eternal salvation. So it's not a 'selfish' or self-centered life, but a hidden life lived for others. We don't see the fruit of our prayer and sacrifice as a teaching Sister or hospital Sister might see it. Even Mother Teresa, you know, also has a contemplative branch of her Order. They are not strictly enclosed like we are, but they live a life of prayer and sacrifice."

"No, I didn't know that. But, back to you, your life is so regulated, doesn't it get boring? Don't you wish you could get away from it all, you know, go out for dinner, have a few drinks, go to a movie, go dancing, go on vacation?"

I laughed. "All of those have passed through my mind; I miss the theater, certainly, and the beauty of the ballet, and the symphony at Alice Tully Hall or Carnegie Hall—not that I went so much, but it was always nice to know it was all going on. I miss walking down Fifth Avenue, especially at Christmas. Yes, I miss a lot of ordinary things, and our life is very 'regulated' as you put it, but that holds us up when we're going through the slouchy periods. And actually the life is never boring; it may be tedious at times, and repetitious, but it's never boring."

Sally sat silent for a moment, taking it all in, along with her croissant and orange marmalade.

"We also have classes, and retreats, and special lectures to fit different seasons of the year, but the rhythm of the life comes from singing the Psalms and reading the Scriptures… we're like an All Girls Catholic Yeshiva." Sally laughed at that, as I thought she would.

"Well, I can see you're not bored; your face gets all animated and lights up when you talk like this. I'm glad David got to see this before…before it was too late."

Our thoughts were interrupted by the bell for Sext. "That's the bell calling me to prayer, and then we have dinner or lunch, although it's really our main meal. You're welcome to stay and have some lunch here in the retreat dining room, and I could meet with you afterwards."

"Maybe the next time; I've got to get back to Manhattan and uptown and see what's what with the apartments, and I'm meeting with the lawyer, I hope, this afternoon. Can I come back in the next couple days? I'll have more information then."

"Of course you can, just call ahead of time and let Sister Paula know when you'll be here."

"She's the cute one, right?"

We laughed. "That's right...she's also the portress, the extern Sister, and the phone-Sister when the machine isn't on. Good luck with the lawyers...I'll keep praying at this end."

Sally didn't quite know how to respond to that, but smiled, squeezed my index fingers through the grille, grabbed the last croissant on the tray, and exited saying, "Later, Sis."

I just stood there speechless. I don't think she's ever called me "Sis" even when we were sisters.

Eighteen

Now when Job's three friends heard of all this evil that had come upon him, they came each from his own place... They made an appointment together to come to condole with him and comfort him. (Job 2:11)

I KEPT OCTOBER 1, 2002, as the first anniversary of Gwendolyn's visit. I'll always remember it as it's also the feast day of St. Thérèse, the Little Flower. St. Thérèse was the first Catholic saint that I met and with whom I became friends. I guess I'd have to say St. Vincent Ferrer was the first Catholic saint that I met, but I didn't know him as "a friend" like I came to know Thérèse of Lisieux. I first "met" her riding the crosstown bus after visiting my Catholic friend, Gracie Price, at Mt. Sinai Hospital. I had stopped that day to light a candle for her at St. Vincent's, and helped myself to a handful of the pamphlets and booklets on the rack in the vestibule. The first one I read had on the cover, the picture of a young nun in a brown habit holding a bouquet of roses. It talked about her "little way" of doing everything for the Lord with love.

I don't know the full extent of everything that happened to me that day, but I always remembered little Thérèse as being a part of it. St. Thérèse loved little things. I still pray to her to help me find the Lord in the little things of each day.

Maybe she helped me find Tea on Thames, owned and run by a lovely woman from Yorkshire, England, named Gwendolyn Putterforth. Little did I ever suspect then that Gwendolyn would wind up being my godmother!

Gwendolyn was about fifteen years older than I was. She seemed so worldly wise and full of fun, and she genuinely enjoyed owning and running a tea shop. She was not an artist, but dressed like one; there was always a bohemian flare about her, something rather like an English gypsy—if there is such a thing. I don't mean that in any insulting way; she was like a cross between a hippie and a country lass from Yorkshire. She loved costume jewelry and penguins. The penguins were actually the "obsession" of her son, who collected penguins of all sorts: not real ones, of course, but toys and penguin bric-a-brac, including a large flock of them waddling their way to the crib in their Christmas nativity set. Christopher was killed by a drunken driver about ten years before I met Gwendolyn. The penguins became a lasting memorial and tribute to him.

Only after Gracie's death did I come to know that Gwendolyn was also a devout Catholic, and that certainly made our friendship even closer. Funny, but Gwendolyn became the link between me and other members of my family. She befriended my father and named her best penguin, a real taxidermy penguin who stood at the entrance of Tea on Thames, after him—Ruben. She always loved my little sister, and after I entered the monastery, it was Gwendolyn who went to all her recitals and plays. She played a big part in

Ruthie's later career, as she became the Mistress of Ceremonies in the new tea-shop-pub in Greenwich Village, called Penguin Pub. Maybe Ruthie filled in the emptiness of Christopher; they were about the same age.

Even when you live in a cloister, the loss of loved ones and friends is felt, perhaps even more intensely, as we carry them in our thoughts and prayers in a way we never could were we living with them in the world. Gwendolyn's returning to England left a big empty space in my life, which seemed to be just one more cross the Lord was asking me to bear. One more sand dune in the desert I found myself in, with only a few oases scattered about. I try to remember that, as I think the young women entering think it's all one big oasis, when it turns out to be one big desert.

Gwendolyn was a transplanted New Yorker; she loved the city and all its crazy neighborhoods and diversity. I knew it was a real sacrifice for her to leave it and return to London. It may just be a temporary thing, I'd tell myself. She was in her mid-sixties when Ruthie died, but I always thought of her as being in her forties or fifties. I guess people we love always stay young in our eyes.

I knew she was coming, but I didn't know when. She had called me shortly after 9/11, and when she learned that Mama and David were in Windows on the World, she said she'd get the next plane over the pond; but it ended up being a few weeks, which was good. It gave time to let things settle down.

On October 1, we had had a very nice Mass for the feast of St. Thérèse, and Fr. Ambrose gave an inspiring homily on her. We needed a little up-lifting: even three weeks after the

Towers fell, we were all a little depressed. It's like the aroma of 9/11 lingered in the air and in our minds. Our two postulants, Sr. Brenda and Sr. Grace were still very sad over it all and finding the life a real struggle. In our life we have to find our own way of dissipating emotions, or they'll push us out the door.

So I was thrilled that morning when Sr. Paula called the extension in my office and announced "Lady Putterforth is puttering around the parlor." Sr. Paula's precocious punning pleasantly pleased me profusely. I went in and there she was—donned in a black blouse and slacks for mourning, and wrapped in yellow and orange scarves and floppy hat for October. She wore dangling earrings and at least seven bracelets on one arm; and just one on the other, a medley of penguins.

"MB…MB…you are a sight for sore eyes!" There was the usual tearful squeezing of fingers through the grille. "Now, I'm not going to cry; I'm here to keep you company and mess up your schedule for a couple of days—I've got a lovely room at the Promenade Hotel with a northern view, so I can't see the Manhattan skyline. I can't bear to look there, my darling, how are you holding up?" It all just flowed out of her like a torrent.

Without being able to respond, she went on. "They're not homemade, as you'll instantly know, but they are all fresh and kosher—from your deli down the street." She was referring to the boxes of whatever were piled on the turn. "I want to hear everything once Sr. Paula arrives and leaves."

Almost on cue, Sr. Paula appeared and did her serving thing with the Pyrex and a tray of good old apricot rugelach from Solomon's Deli. "I told her I'm staying for lunch if there's room, so we can meet this afternoon too…how is your sister Sally doing?"

Finally getting a chance to speak, I filled her in on all the recent details. "It would appear that David had taken care of things, thank the Lord; we weren't sure what to do if he hadn't. His own duplex he has willed to Dr. Ghattas and her son, Sharbel, with the title to be transferred entirely to Sharbel when he reaches twenty-one years old. Mama's apartment was also co-signed a couple years ago (she completely forgot this) under Sally's name, Sarah Feinstein. So Sally has inherited our apartment, which I'm really happy about. She and Mitzie are planning to move to New York after the first of the year. She calls her 'Mitz'. I haven't met Mitz yet, but Sally says she's excited to meet me. Sally says she's the spiritual one between them. I think she was or is involved in some kind of New Age cult, so that should be very interesting, don't cha think! Oh, and Mama left me something, which I'll show you later…you will love it."

"Oh, that is all good news. That Sharbel boy is certainly a lucky young man! That sounds terrible; I don't mean he's lucky except that he's inherited a New York duplex; he'd much rather have a father, I'm sure, but you know what I mean." Smile, nod.

"He's a serious kid, and I think he wants to be a doctor; he's at Yale University. He called me but got all choked up and couldn't talk. I told him I wasn't going anywhere and would be here next time he got home. David, Mama, Sharbel, and Mrs. Hutner, Mama's neighbor, all went on a cruise together a couple years ago. Mama was in her glory, having a grandson finally, and able to show off his pictures. She said that Sharbel told her she's much more fun than his other grandmother. That, of course, made Mama's day."

We laughed. It was good to hear Gwendolyn's laugh and to hear her jewelry making a commotion. "How is *your* sister?" I inquired.

"Oh, she's a blooming mess, as I expected, but she's good company. She's nearly sixty now, and acts likes she's in her twenties, well, maybe her thirties. She's still running her theater club in Soho, which has kept both of us busy. I thought I was retired from the business, but I enjoy it. The young people are very talented; different from American kids, you know, but still kids, really. They have a worried carefree-ness about them—I haven't figured it out yet. It's like they live hard in the present and yet, are oblivious to the future, and not conscious maybe like we were of air raids and atom bombs. But it's much more a reality than we ever imagined. There are days when I wish I were twenty-five again, but then, other days when I'm glad I'm in my seventies. And of course, you know, we've gotten over to Lancashire a couple times to see Father Matthew, whom I still call Ezra! He sends his very best and said he will be home here just after the new year. He looks very austere, you know, with his hair cut and his cheeks kind of sunken in. He said he misses you and all the Sisters." That all cheered my heart to hear, except the sunken cheeks.

"Speaking of Sisters, our two youngest are delightful; you would enjoy both of them. One is named Grace and graduated from the New York Fashion Institute; you would have loved her outfits, before she entered! She's quite content,

I think, with her postulant's plain jumper and blouse; but she would fit in with your Soho crowd. I don't know about their being oblivious to the future—I'll have to think about that one, but I do notice a hesitation to make a permanent commitment. The permanence of this life frightens her, and others who have come and gone. It's hard to imagine living in one place for ever."

"Yeah," said Gwen, sounding more American than British.

"Brenda is a little older and more solid. She is an African-American with dreadlocks that she knows will be snipped off come vestition, but she's looking forward to it. She's an RN and a convert from the Methodist Church. She lost her grandfather on 9/11 whom I just learned was also a deacon in his church besides a retired volunteer fireman. She hasn't been able to talk much about it yet."

"And how are Sister Gertrude and all the nuns in the infirmary?"

"Devastated as you can imagine. They have the right perspective on everything though; they still pray about it all. Most of them were children during World War II, you know. They've been through the Korean War, Vietnam, and now this…this *war on terror*. It's never struck quite so close to home, however. Sister Gerard is predicting the End Times are any minute now. Sister Amata doesn't say too much; Sister Benedict is still sharp and keeps up on the news in the paper; and Sister Gertrude is quiet, for Sister Gertrude, and weeps easily. I'm amazed how they each take it in their stride in their own way. Sister Bertrand and Sister Gerard are the gloomiest, but very funny in their pessimism. Sister Bertrand says that *we* could be the next target: 'What's to keep a crazy

Islamic terrorist from coming into the extern chapel, coming up to the grille, and mowing us all down with a machine gun?'

"Sr. Gerard immediately picked up on it: 'Glory be to God. I know it's the chastisement. It's gonna happen; we should keep the chapel door locked.' And Sister Amata, very thoughtfully and with a slight smile, said: 'We'd be the Dominican Martyrs of Brooklyn Heights.'

"And Sister Gertrude rallied to the cause: 'It would be a Feast Day for all of New York; our relics could be displayed in a side chapel of St. Patrick's.'

"Then Sister Benedict: 'St. Patrick's? We'd be in the Cathedral of St. James—our own Basilica. Brooklyn and Queens—Manhattan will have their own martyrs.'

"Sister Gertrude: 'But I want a little side chapel in St. Patrick's, and maybe one at St. Malachy's in the theater district.'

" 'And St. Vincent Ferrer.' I added my own two cents.

"Sister Benedict: 'I hope our feast day will be in October or November…'

"Sister Amata: 'It will be the month whenever we're all mowed down.'

"Sister Benedict, pensively: 'Oh yeah, well I hope it's October or November.'

"And we all laughed, turning our doomsday into a feast in a New York minute! I remember that night praying very earnestly that I hoped the Lord wasn't listening to us and taking us too seriously. It would be wonderful to be martyrs, but not just yet. I know I have a lot more work to do! I know that's very Pelagian; I'm sorry."

"I don't know what Pelagian means, but I hope it doesn't happen at all—period." Gwendolyn's penguined hand brushed back her hair, and she looked me square in the eye. "Now, listen, M.B., I have some *not* very good news."

The bell for Sext rang. Gwendolyn stood up. "It can wait till this afternoon."

"Oh no, don't tell me you're sick and dying…"

"You'll be late for your prayers. I'll see you at 3:30…ta-ta." And off she went clinking all the way, waving her usual wave at the parlor door.

Nineteen

Sext: The "sixth hour" of the Divine Office, around 12:00 noon. Second "little hour."

"Come to me, all who labor and are heavy laden, and I will give you rest. Take my yoke upon you, and learn from me; for I am meek and humble of heart, and you will find rest for your souls." (Matthew 11:28-29)

I ATE MY DINNER with enough anxiety that I couldn't enjoy it—nor could I concentrate on the reading. Then I got impatient helping with the dishes afterwards, which I know is not a good example for the novices; I wanted people to hurry things up, which was stupid because Gwendolyn wasn't coming back till after 3:30 anyway. Whatever could Gwendolyn have to tell me? She certainly looked healthy for seventy or seventy-one. I never knew her exact age.

Maybe she was going to tell me that Tea on Thames was now Tea on the Tiber, which I already knew. There was a nostalgic ache every time I thought of it; that tea shop was like a personal historical preservation society home of my early years: my conversion, my meeting Ezra, my meeting Gwendolyn! Maybe Gwen will tell me that it's stopped being a tea shop entirely and was bought out by a coffee chain, like Starbucks, and renamed Coffee on the Hudson.

Well, whatever it is, I can't do anything about it, I told myself. I will simply accept whatever it is, if it's not sinful, of course, or contrary to the Faith. She certainly hasn't become Church of England.

We have grand silence from 1:00 to 2:00 p.m. I usually go to our cell and either lie across the bed or sit in Squeak and doze, pretending to read. For the first couple weeks after 9/11 I couldn't doze at all. One can do work as long as it doesn't make noise or disturb others. The first week I went to the infirmary. The Sisters would all be taking their after-dinner naps, but there were bound to be dishes to be washed in the kitchenette or things to be straightened up in the common room. One day that week Sr. Gertrude was sitting alone in front of the picture window. I fixed us each a cup of tea and sat beside her; we didn't speak, just sitting together was comforting enough. When the silence was over at 2:00 we said a few words to each other. That's when I told her about Mama and David. And she couldn't say anything, but took my hand in hers and gently patted it. "I can't imagine what you've been going through; thank you for telling me. With your permission, of course, I'll tell the others when we come to pray our rosary."

"Of course you may; thank you, Sister. I wanted to share it with you because I knew you would pray, and because you knew Mama, and Mama thought you were the most extraordinary woman she ever met." Sister smiled and squinted over the top of her old-fashioned frameless glasses.

"Your Mama was an extraordinary woman, Sister, but you know that. And our dear Lord knows that...He has a special place in His Heart, you know, for mothers. I know it was a heartache for you all those years not seeing her, not being able to share our wonderful life here with her; but she came around, and that has filled your heart with great joy these last few years. Many of us don't have that extraordinary opportunity."

We didn't say anything more for a couple minutes. Sister continued to pat my hand. "And now she is gone, and your brother whom you have come to know again, but you have the memory of their love for you. I can hear your mother: 'Such a blessing, my daughter, the nun.' What a memory to carry with you for the rest of your life."

Sr. Gertrude was very serious in a way she only reveals in the most poignant moments. There was a depth in her which she kept hidden with her show-biz antics and talk, but I knew she lived in the 'deep end.'

"Sometimes life comes crashing down on top of us, and we can't pick up the pieces. And life is never the same when we pass over to the way life will be after that. And so we go on. We begin anew...that's what we do."

Sr. Gertrude didn't realize her words were more meaningful to me than she could imagine. September 11 was like the Seder plate crashing down, and I couldn't do anything to change it; I couldn't pick up the pieces and put them back together. I suddenly remembered the dread of that moment, in not just what I did, but in what I feared Mama would do. This was her prize possession. This was the plate that held all the suffering and joy of her life, her faith, her love for her family, and her years of preparing the foods for Pesach. And what did Mama do?

She forgave me; she wasn't angry, but felt sorry for me and what I was going through, and she poured out her mercy on me. It was my first experience of real mercy. I cried more than she did, picking up the shattered pieces.

"Don't worry, Becky, our Seder will still go on tonight… that's the whole point, isn't it? We break, and we begin again. I have another Seder plate which you've never seen, but we shall polish it and use it tonight…such a blessing, it's made of silver. And Papa will be very pleased because it belonged to his Mama."

She made it all better. Like sitting quietly with Sr. Gertrude in front of the picture window looking out on our cemetery.

"Doesn't it depress you, Sister, sitting here every day and looking out at the cemetery?" I was rather pensive when I asked her that.

"Oh, no, dear. This is where I meditate best. It's not depressing or morbid. I know many of those Sisters whom we have laid to rest; I used to watch their every move and listen to their every word, like a good understudy. Isn't it something when you think about what God did for His people at the time of the first Passover. And to think it was all in preparation, like a dress rehearsal. God's Chosen People knew the oppression of slavery early on in their story, and they stood in for all mankind since the first crash—when Adam and Eve fell from grace. Mankind had chosen to know evil and thus suffering and sickness and loss, and separation from God came about—the worst part, death would come to every human being, fallen from grace, cast into darkness, our minds and our hearts covered with a…a what? A veil." And she pulled on hers and smiled. "Not like our veil really, but a veil of ignorance and falsity. How awful to not know why we are here, why we were created, and what it all means? Can we never know what life is really about, or are we to be slaves of ignorance, obeying the taskmasters of power, money, fame, manipulation, meaninglessness?"

She paused to collect her thoughts and take a sip of her now-lukewarm tea. "God Himself prepared mankind for a new way, a new life, a new union with Himself unrealized before. He gave His People His Word…His Torah." I smiled. "The most precious thing mankind could have, God's Word to reveal to us the truth about life and God Himself, and to begin a new relationship with Him. And wonder of wonders," Sister's face lit up and her eyes sparkled, "this Word became a man…His humanity, His flesh and blood and human soul, would belong to the Divine Person, the Word, the Son, the Beloved. And from the first instant of His human life, He became a sacrifice; He was set apart to fulfill in Himself all that God the Father had prepared for mankind."

I added quietly, "He became our Seder Plate."

"Not just the plate, my dear, He became the whole meal. He was the Lamb whose blood would save mankind, and the Evil One—death itself—would pass over the souls marked with the blood of the Lamb. He became the matzah, and the wine, and all the prayers, and bitter herbs and tears, and mortar—He was it. He took upon Himself all the sin of all the world before and to come…and it came crashing down on the Friday before the Sabbath Passover would be celebrated."

I just sat stunned by her words, more eloquent than any rabbi could preach. Her hidden depths all these years was imbued with Judaism and all it meant for the world waiting for the Anointed One to come. It was/is the greatest love story ever told, ever lived.

"I'm amazed at how much you've integrated Judaism into your...your what? Your theology."

Sr. Gertrude smiled at me and giggled a little. "Remember, I grew up in New York and the theater crowd. We were a very Catholic family, given today's standards, but we had lots of Jewish friends. I'd been to more than one Seder in my life. And I suppose the Mass, or, as we say today the *Liturgy,* always drew me deeper into my own faith. It was like a beautiful drama unfolding before our eyes, and when I read a little about the history of the Mass, well, I saw how much Our Divine Lord fulfilled the greatest of Jewish feasts." She stopped and looked out at the cemetery again, thinking about something, and humming to herself. "I think we should all be a little more Jewish and a little less Protestant! *How do you like them eggrolls, Mr. Goldstein?*" quoting from the Broadway musical *Gypsy.*

"Sr. Gertrude, you are too much! I wish Mama and David could hear you; and the novices, yes, the novices. You'll have to come to one of our classes and share all that with them. I think they are having a tough time coming to terms with death."

"I'd be thrilled to come to talk to the novices, and maybe teach them a song or two. Death..." After another couple minutes of silence, Sr. Gertrude gestured toward the cemetery. "We don't think on these things often enough; oh, we hear it said in sermons; we read about it on our own and in the refectory; we have retreats every year to ponder it all more deeply, but it's in moments of death, isn't it, that the Truth of Life and the glory of the Faith—that we live in Him and He in us—all comes to mean something. The veil is lifted, as St. Paul says, and we behold the glory of the face of Christ—risen in glory, who lives now with us, within us, in the glory of Heaven and in the Eucharist and in the sanctifying grace present in souls. Death remains a mystery, but it's really our Passover to eternal life, and it's been done already in Christ."

The bell for None was sounding, and I didn't want to go, but to stay and absorb more of Sr. Gertrude's wisdom, but she patted my hand with the gesture of "it's time to leave." Even something as little as a "Little Hour" of the Office calls us to obedience and joins us in every little way to the love of Christ.

"Thank you, Sister, you don't know how much that means to me. I feel like I can begin again, and even the tragedies of 9/11 can't rob us of faith and hope…and love." And I kissed her on the top of her head, and dashed off.

*Christ is our Seder Plate and the whole meal…*I kept repeating silently in my head. My dreams were not nightmares but realizations of how my whole life was fulfilled in Christ, and in every "crash", in every death, there is a fulfillment and a "blessing." What may appear as a disaster, and may actually be one in reality—the plate really smashed to pieces—is a pass-over to something new.

I genuflected and moved into my choir stall; set my choir book for None; and turned and faced the altar, repeating to myself: Christ is our Seder Plate and the whole meal…and Mother Rosaria began:

"O Sacred Banquet, in which Christ becomes our food…"

* * *

During the second psalm, I snapped back to the present, remembering I was meeting Gwendolyn again at 3:30. Whatever she "has on her plate" is going to be fine and an opportunity to turn things over to the Lord. Still thinking of my dream, I wondered why Eli the doorman was in it? I stayed in the chapel after None and sat quietly in His Presence till about 3:27…and then made my way to the parlor and waited for Gwendolyn to arrive.

Twenty

None: The "ninth hour" of the Divine Office.
The third "little hour" around 3:00 p.m.

It seemed rather strange sitting in the parlor alone. It is not a very attractive room, but very plain. There is nothing on our side of the grille but five wooden chairs. There's a table on the interior wall with a plain looking lamp that could be changed to something more attractive, something a little more colorful. The floors are bare hardwood. On the back wall is a wooden carved crucifix and on the wall behind the lamp a framed picture of the pope. That is actually the only thing that changes in the room. At that time, the Holy Father's picture showed a young and vigorous Pope John Paul II. He was my third pope, I think, since I entered: Pope Paul VI, Pope John Paul I, and now Pope John Paul II. I don't think we even had Pope John Paul I's picture on the wall.

The extern part of the parlor isn't much different. Chairs and a table with another nondescript lamp, a cabinet with dishes, glasses, napkins, silverware, and a small table which could be moved close to the grille if one wants to eat or drink with the nun or nuns one is visiting. We don't have one on our side except for a clunky folding table, which in the world we would call a TV table. We used to never eat or drink with guests, but somewhere along the way that got changed. We actually have three parlors. We have a large parlor which is even more austere than this, with only chairs, used when the whole community is gathered; and a smaller parlor, which we call the Prioress's Parlor, but is used by others, especially during retreat if you meet privately with the retreat master. It is the closest to the entrance hall, then the big parlor, and then this one, which also has a single window, too high to look out. It is the only parlor with sunlight, however, and one can open it with a window pole which stood in the corner. Most of us don't bother.

I remember it was the Prioress's Parlor where Mother John Dominic used to meet with my father. He first met her there on my entrance day, and unbeknownst to me, every month thereafter where Mother talked to him about Our Lord. Before his cancer incapacitated him, he was privately baptized and confirmed at St. Vincent's in Manhattan, and Mother John Dominic was his godmother. This became our secret known only to Fr. Meriwether who baptized him, Mother John Dominic, and me…and Gwendolyn and Fr. Matthew (Ezra) and Greta. No one in my family ever knew. I didn't even know, till after his death.

These parlors…if they could talk, they would have such wonderful stories to tell. They've been filled with laughter and tears, and probably every emotion in the book; they are our principal artery to the "world." Well, we do have a hidden away television, and we get newspapers, and mail, but human communication with the outside, face to face, is in these three rooms.

I think it's a bit of a shock for family members of our aspirants and postulants when they first see it. The Prioress's Parlor even has a curtain which can be drawn for even greater privacy but is never used these days. I think years ago, before my time, the parlors had double grilles which didn't match up so one's view of the person on the other side was always a little obstructed. Mother John Dominic once told me the double grille gave her a headache.

Mama got to be comfortable with the parlor and our grille; she always had a little something to nosh and usually a bottle of Mogen David wine; she got to know the setup and would rearrange things a little to suit her. She loved to sit up close to the grille. She never stayed overnight in the retreat section, but did stay a couple times for a meal. But the silence made her nervous. Sr. Paula told me she rearranged the furniture in the retreatants' sitting room, and Sr. Paula kept it that way. "It was nicer than the way we had it."

While I was lost in this sentimental journey, the extern door opened and in swept Lady Gwendolyn: "What a time I've had; I forgot how crowded New York can be, and the subways! I had to stand from Christopher Street all the way to 72nd Street. You'd think someone would give an old lady a seat, but then, maybe they didn't realize I am an old lady." She knew that would get a laugh from me.

"Did you go to Tea on Thames?" I asked sheepishly. "Tea on the Tiber, you mean. Yes, I did. It seemed so strange being a customer, you know."

"That's nice...and maybe some 'penguin-puff pastries?'"

Gwen shook her head and sweeping her hair back, everything clinked. "No, don't I wish! They've done away with the English tea menu and have Italian pastries or sandwiches."

"Okay, what's your bad news? I'm ready." I had my right hand fingers crossed under my scapular, and my left hand held tight to my side rosary.

"Well, I'll come right out with it." She took a deep breath. "Ruben was stolen." She paused to let this news sink in. Ruben, again, was her taxidermy penguin, which she named 'Ruben' in honor of my father. "It's my fault. I didn't have him chained and padlocked, all very discreetly, of course, as I did here, both at Tea on Thames and the Pub. Jacqueline didn't want him on a table at the entrance; something about fire regulations, but I don't believe her. I don't think she really liked Ruben. She had him in a wooden niche, like you'd put the statue of a saint, in a corner on the way to the loo."

"The loo?"

"You know, the rest room."

"And…?"

"And somebody walked off with him. You know he could easily fit into a large bag, or under somebody's overcoat. I didn't discover it till we were locking up at the end of the night. I felt wretched about it. When I got the news about your mother and brother, I decided to bring Ruben back with me and give him to you. If you're allowed to have Squeak in your cell, why couldn't you have a stuffed penguin? I thought it would bring you comfort."

I was very touched by Gwendolyn's intention, and I would have loved to have had Ruben in our cell, presuming

Mother would approve. Even if I couldn't have him in our cell, we would have found a place for him. But that was not going to be.

"I'm sorry Ruben has been stolen; or run off on his own." I smiled. "He's really the one consistent thing who has always been there, from Tea on Thames to Penguin Pub, to Ruthie's death, and your moving back to England. I guess God wants us to be detached." I couldn't say anymore as I was lost in my own thoughts.

Gwen sat silent. Funny how a stuffed penguin could be so…what? Symbolic? I had a flashback of walking into Tea on Thames and remember seeing Ruben for the first time. He wasn't named Ruben then, just "Penguin." Gwen named him Ruben after my father died. "Ruben," I said pensively, "more than my father, you know, Ruben is really an alter-ego for you. You are the stabilizing penguin who has always been there. I can't bring you in our cell, but you are here, here and now, and just that is very comforting for me. Maybe it's time we let Ruben the penguin go. He can't bring back your son; he can't bring back Papa or Ruthie, nor Mama or David. Sometimes we just have to let go."

Gwendolyn smiled, and I think there was a tear or two rolling down her cheek. Completely out of context she said, "It's sad how tragic moments mark the turning points in our lives, isn't it?" From Sr. Gertrude to Gwendolyn…the same meditation.

"I know. Death refocuses life every time."

"You're right, M.B., death and growing old. It's like one night I went to bed and when I woke up, I was old. The Dowager Lady Putterforth, O.P."

"O.P.? Have you become a Dominican?"

"No, that's Old Person."

"Or Order of Penguins." And we both giggled, which turned into a chuckle, and soon a comfortable old-fashioned laugh.

"Now, I have two things to show you if you sit tight; it'll only take me five minutes to get to our cell and back."

"Take your time, M.B., I'm going to visit the retreatants' loo, and make a visit to the chapel. I'll be back in fifteen minutes."

So that was our plan. I was able to speak to Sr. Paula and have a pot of Earl Grey brought into the parlor and a small plate of "biscuits." I dashed to our cell and back again.

Gwendolyn was already there when I returned. She was delighted with the tea and afternoon biscuits. We sat down like old girlfriends would do. It almost seemed strange, as I didn't have an old girlfriend to chat with, outside of the house. Maybe that's one reason I like visiting the infirmary.

"Okay…first thing. I told you Sally said Mama and David both had wills. Mama knew I couldn't inherit anything; it's part of our solemn vow of poverty, but she had written in a little gift. Remember me telling you about our family night at the theater, *Fiddler on the Roof*? And when we got home, David presented two gifts from my brother, Joshua, who was killed in Vietnam? Papa got a new Timex watch and Mama a beautiful brooch of old tarnished silver with five tiny flowers each with its own gem. These were sent to David from the Philippines. Mama loved it so much: she said right away that the five flowers were her five children. 'Five little flowers, so little and yet so beautiful.'"

Gwendolyn nodded. She remembered. “Yes, I remember, and it wasn’t a week after that that they got the telegram telling them that Joshua had been killed in action. And it was his death, really, that got you thinking about life and death…and faith…and God.”

“That’s right. You have a good a memory, for an O.P.” Gwendolyn scrunched up her face and looked at me cross eyed. “David has Papa’s Timex; Mama never wore the brooch again, but kept it in her highboy, next to a photo of Joshua in his uniform. And here it is.”

I took the silver box out of my pocket, opened it, and took out the brooch with the five delicately set flowers.

“Oh, M.B., it’s so beautiful. Those are real stones in there too.” I don’t know how Gwen could tell that at first glance, and through the grille, but she was the jewelry expert, not me.

“Mama left it for me. I told Sally she should take it, but she refused. She said she had lots of Mama’s things, and Mama wanted me to have this. I don’t ever wear it, of course, not even under my scapular, although I was tempted! I keep it on my ‘prayer shelf’ in our cell, and am praying what I should do with it. It might look very nice in the base of a chalice, but I’m not sure.”

I put it gently back in its box.

“And now—are you ready?” I reached under my scapular to my belt…

“Look it.” I held up a rather worn stuffed penguin with yellow feet. The day I entered the monastery, it was Papa, Greta, and Gwendolyn who came with me. Gwendolyn was very emotional about “goodbyes” and couldn’t stay for the opening of the enclosure door, she handed me this little stuffed penguin with yellow feet and told me to sneak her in with me, and dashed off. On her way out she called back, "Her name is Vicky. She always wanted to be a nun since her husband died!" It was Greta who guessed correctly that her husband's name was Albert.

"Oh my goodness, M.B., you still have her. Vicky. I'd forgotten all about her. Is she still in mourning for Prince Albert?" And we laughed like high school girls.

"Yes, I still have her, and she's been in my cell the whole time I've been here. She's lived on my bookshelf, in a drawer, on the window sill, and sometimes under my pillow."

Gwendolyn was duly moved, and I think quite comforted, even if Ruben had disappeared. We drank our tea and gabbed about old acquaintances and how much the Tea on Thames neighborhood had changed. And Vicky sat there silently taking it all in. She brought back years of memories.

Twenty-One

Give thanks to the Lord for He is good. His steadfast love endures forever. (Psalms 107:1)

The new year 2003 came in with a nice blanket of snow on the ground, which always brings a greater silence into the house and a peacefulness or warmth that other times of the year don't have. We welcomed it with our own regular little celebrations after a subdued but lovely Christmas Octave.

Sr. Agnes Mary spent most of the last week of Advent and the Octave of Christmas in the infirmary. The novices and postulants would visit her there several times a week, and she always welcomed them, but felt so weak and tired afterwards. And so it was the day after the Solemnity of the Mother of God, January 2, that Mother Rosaria called me into her office.

"*Shanah Tovah*, Sister Mary Baruch!" Mother was beaming with joy because she knew the Hebrew greeting for the new year, and could greet me with it.

"*Shanah Tovah* to you too, Mother. Such a blessing, the new year." And we both laughed.

"I suspect you know why I've called you in. I've had several good talks with Sister Agnes Mary over the past week, and I agreed with her that she should step down from being Novice Mistress. Her health is not up to the demands of the job, as she put it."

"I'm sorry to hear that; she always gives the novices such a wonderful example of being a happy nun!"

"And she can continue to do that, for all of us really. But it's time for you to become the official Novice Mistress. You have worked closely with the postulants and novices, and you are yourself, you know, a wonderful example of a happy nun."

"Oh, dear. Thank you, Mother, I'm very humbled by that. Most of the time I feel like such a 'schlepper', but I am a happy nun, although I don't say that very often to myself. I don't know if I've ever said it out loud! Maybe it sounds strange for us to talk like that. But, you know, there is no place in the whole world where I'd rather be than right here. I want to love the Lord more and more, and ...well, this may sound very strange, but there are times when I wish I were a novice again and was beginning all over."

"My dear Sister. We have been through it together, you know, and I'm with you. I think often about the effect of 9/11 on all of us. I am not a native New Yorker, as you know, but all my adult life has been here, as an *au pair*, or a nun—with lots of accidents in both lives. But in the end, it's the Lord who is our happiness, and He has poured out His mercy on both of us...us 'schleppers.'"

I laughed and shed tears at the same time. "We're quite a pair, Au Pair."

And that's how I became novice mistress in the new year of 2003. It was officially announced at our new year's chapter that evening. The night before, on New Year's night, recreation is without "business." But we all draw several items from a big velvet bag: our patron saint for the year; our individual prayer intention; and a Scripture passage to meditate on. I drew St. Teresa Benedicta of the Cross, Edith Stein. I was so moved by it, I couldn't say anything. In all my years, I never drew her, and always hoped I would. My prayer intention was for the Poor Souls, which I had drawn before; I think many of us get that intention, and I was happy to have it again. I think last year, which was the New Year's after 9/11 we all got it, which was *a propos*, as Sr. Anna Maria would say.

The next day, the first thing I did was visit Sr. Agnes Mary in the infirmary. She was all smiles and congratulations, which always amazes me—we congratulate others on getting a job wrought with many crosses.

Sr. Gertrude knocked on the door during our visit. "I hope I'm not intruding; is this a private conference?" She was already wheeling herself into the room.

"No, no, come in, Sister. I'm just congratulating Sr. Mary Baruch on her new position."

"I figured that's what it is—and I just want to add my own Mazel Tov."

"I hope you two know how much I'm depending on your prayers. If my mother were here we'd have a bottle of Mogen David to toast in the New Year." And they both laughed.

"Well, it won't be Mogen David, unless he's got sparkling apple juice, but I hope you'll be here this afternoon. We 're having a little 'Seton Séance.'"

"Sister Gertrude! You're not having a séance, please tell me you're not!" I exclaimed with sincere shock.

"Of course not. We pray *for* the dead, not invite them to our parties." And we all laughed. "In honor of St. Elizabeth Ann Seton, we have a dainty little tea party, like she may have had before she became a nun, and lived in Lower Manhattan. And we talk about the Sisters who have gone before us. We tell stories about them; we don't conjure them up."

"Well, that sounds like a delightful thing to do. What can I bring? Cookies?"

"Cookies? No we're sick to death of all the cookies; bring the novices!"

And so we did. It was a marvelous way of marking the transition to the new year. Our two postulants persevered, which was a real time of grace as they both were affected deeply by 9/11. Although there were several weeks between their entrance dates, we decided to let them enter into the novitiate at the same time. It was one double joy that we had inside that first year after 9/11.

Brenda Hubbard, our African-American registered nurse received the name Sr. Elijah Rose. I was happy that Mother included me in deciding what name each new novice would receive. Mother herself chooses the final name, but in most instances the prioress goes by the suggestion of the novice mistress who has lived with the Sister for a year. This name had special significance for both Sr. Brenda and me.

In the months that followed 9/11, I met individually with both Sr. Brenda and Sr. Grace mainly to let them talk it all out. Sr. Brenda actually had two friends and her grandfather die on 9/11. The two friends were police officers who were twin brothers and had been neighbors with the Hubbards all through elementary school. They went off to Catholic high school, and Brenda to the public school; but, being neighbors, they stayed friends. She told me their families were way ahead of the game when it came to Civil Rights; the twins were Irish Catholics and her family black Methodists, as she put it. Their families would often have the other family over for dinner and to play cards. They each had a grandfather living at home with them; Brenda's grandfather was named Elijah, which he said came from his parents who were Southern Baptists. He had many interesting jobs growing up in New York, including being a volunteer fireman. After Brenda and the McConway boys, Sean and Patrick, graduated from their different high schools, the Hubbards and the McConways had their own party to celebrate graduation. Brenda was going off to nursing school, and the twins to the Police Academy. A big hit at their parties were their grandfathers. Grandpa McConway played the Irish flute and the family sang.

"But my grandfather," Sr. Brenda boasted, "used to play the spoons. He could make those spoons rattle and roll like nobody's business. He'd be sitting down when he played them, hitting his knees and shoulders, and chest, and elbows, and ending with hitting himself on the forehead. We'd all laugh ourselves silly."

Sr. Brenda was very close to her grandfather, I learned over the year. He would take on extra jobs to help pay the rent and buy special food for special occasions. "But it was my grandfather who put me through nursing school. At graduation, it was a custom of the school to allow a parent to put your nursing pin on your uniform. I was the only one who had a grandfather pin mine on for me. He was so proud of me. He was a good man, Sister, let me tell you. He worked for a few years as a shoe salesman, then as a short-order cook in a greasy spoon in Hell's Kitchen, and for about twenty years as a doorman on the Upper West Side. He liked that job the best because he got fresh air and lots of gifts at Christmas and Chanukah."

And she put her head back and laughed; her dreadlocks shimmying in every which direction. "He was much too old to help at 9/11, but there he went. He died in the first tower."

I had heard this countless times in the past four months, and I guessed I would for months to come. She talked more about her grandfather than her parents. They were "Bible-believing Christians" and would go to a Methodist church on occasion. They sent Brenda to Sunday school and didn't go to the movies or eat out on Sundays. They didn't understand why she wanted to become a Catholic. They thought maybe she was dating a Catholic boy, and that's why she wanted to convert; but she wasn't. They went to the Easter Vigil at St. Paul's when she was confirmed and celebrated with her.

"Daddy said if I was in trouble, like with drugs and stuff, they would do everything to help me; but here I was wanting to do something good with my life, so they were happy for me in the end. I think it was Grandpa that helped them see it that way. He thought it was a 'precious gift from Our Lord and Savior.' And you know what he gave me?" And Sr. Brenda pulled out a beautiful silver rosary, the beads shaped like roses. "This was from Grandpa." She handed me her lovely rosary which was heavier than our usual wooden pocket rosaries, but so much more beautiful. "I'm just sad he won't be here now to see me as a Bride of Christ." Sr. Brenda had no idea all the bells she was setting off in my memory!

It took a few minutes, till it dawned on me. No, it couldn't be; but I asked, "You said his name was Elijah? And he was a doorman on the Upper West Side?"

"Uh-huh."

"Where on the Upper West Side, did you know?"

"Oh, I don't remember exactly; somewhere in the seventies, I think."

Could it possibly be? "Tell me, did people call him Elijah?"

"Oh no, everybody just called him 'Eli.'"

"Was Elijah, or Eli, a common name among…among your…your…"

"You mean among black people?" Sr. Brenda put on her southern black accent, "Yes'm, we done name the chillin from the Good Book."

I laughed. I knew she was being her "funny self" which we all enjoyed. It made me remember my early years too when I would put on an exaggerated New York Yiddish accent. It broke any unspoken prejudices others may have been harboring under their veils.

Sr. Brenda enjoyed a good laugh too, even at her own expense, or her own "puttin'on" for us.

"The present generation, so to speak, are giving their babies African names I can't even spell. My generation was given plain old American white-girl names like Brenda, Peggy Sue, Linda, Charlene…but in grandpa's day it was Hiram, Elijah, and Jeremiah. I have an Uncle Ebenezer, whom we just called Uncle Eben. When we were kids, we would call him Uncle Ebenezer the Sneezer." We both laughed. It was good therapy, as Sr. Brenda schlepped through her own post 9/11 depression when her grandfather Eli lost his life trying to save others. And the Irish twins who were both New York cops were among the first responders. They both had wives and children.

I couldn't imagine that our Eli and her grandfather were the same person. "Do you have any pictures of your grandfather? I would like to see one."

"Oh, I don't have any here with me, but my sister might still have one. She keeps scrap books with lots of family pictures. Grandpa was a handsome man, even when he got old. He had lots of hair, and bushy eyebrows. They would bounce up and down when he was playing the spoons. We have pictures of him somewhere in a big old Afro from back in the seventies, but he had the best smile; his big white teeth and one front tooth was like all gold."

That did it! I clapped my hands and got up from my chair, twirled three times around, and sat back down. "Sister Brenda, you aren't going to believe this, but I knew your grandfather. Hc was our doorman on W. 79th Street. I loved him…Mr. Eli, I called him, till I was about sixteen and he told me to call him Eli. And I said I would if he would call me just 'Rebecca', not Miss Rebecca. Everybody loved Eli. Would you believe, he still comes up in my dreams!"

Sr. Brenda was amazed. "What a small world we live in. I was just a kid when he retired. I think he did a few odd jobs after that, but it was his doorman job that put me through nursing school. And here we are!"

Sr. Brenda submitted her three names: first, Paul, because it was at St. Paul's where her conversion began; Rose, after Rose Hawthorne to whom she had a devotion, and it was at the Hawthorne home where she learned about us; and Conway, after the McConway boys.

I told her Conway was not a good choice. I didn't think Mother would ever approve it, if she wanted to change it. Or she could leave it up to Mother and me to choose a name for her.

"Better than Paul or Rose?"

"Yes, maybe better than Paul or Rose; we'll see." I already had in my head what name Sr. Brenda should have. I told Mother Rosaria the conversation we had, and that I think her grandfather was our doorman when I was growing up, and everyone loved old Eli. Mother was moved by that, but more by the real Biblical prophet Elijah. "I rather like that name," Mother said. "It was Elijah who appeared with Moses and the Lord on Mount Tabor; a very monastic feast and so a monastic name. Rose is a beautiful name too…close to Rosaria." And that's how Brenda Hubbard became Sr. Elijah Rose of the Transfiguration. Sr. Elijah Rose was thrilled with her name, and her feast day!

Grace White, former fashion designer—well, she never really worked as a designer, but identified herself as one—was also distraught over 9/11. She fell into a mild depression for several weeks. I was afraid we would have to ask her to leave and get some help outside. Mother was even willing for her to go see a grief counselor whom other Sisters had been to when loved ones died. Sr. Grace could also appear rather flighty at times, which came across as shallow or immature, but I knew underneath all that was a sensitive deep young woman wanting to come out. If I'm completely honest, I'm sure I also had a special place in my heart for her. She was introduced to us by Leah Levinson, her high school best friend. My high school friend was Grace Price and the Lord used her to eventually bring me into the Church and into the monastery.

Sr. Grace and I were walking in our garden shortly after All Saints, November 1. There was definitely a winter air making its way down from Canada, enough that we had to wear these over-sized parkas, which I knew Sr. Grace hated, but accepted without comment. I think she once said they had a "grunge" look, whatever that was. The garden had begun to look bare and settled down for its winter hibernation. There were still roses in bloom on the rose trestle near the garden swing where two could comfortably fit, and so we sat down there. It was a real "swing."

"The cold air feels good," Sr. Grace said breathing in a deep breath of it. "I hope it snows early this year; wouldn't that be nice for Thanksgiving?"

I also loved Sr. Grace because I love anyone who loves snow! "Oh, I do too. I was praying it would snow for All Saints." I really wasn't, but I knew it would get a laugh from Sr. Grace and she hadn't laughed very much recently.

We both were short, and needed to push off with one foot and then fall back into the seat. I let Sr. Grace do that; she was short, but also very thin, and more graceful.

"Have you heard from Leah?" I knew she had because I sorted the mail the day it came. We don't open the postulants' or novices' mail like years ago, but I saw the letter, especially the Israeli stamp with Hebrew letters.

"Oh, yes, I got a letter just a few days ago. She said after the terrible happenings on 9/11 it was not a joyous new year for them, that is Rosh Hashanah…"

"Yes, I know," I interjected.

"…But that after 9/11 the new year could only get better, so she wished me a happy new year, and said she would be praying for me and our friend Nick whom she somehow knew died on 9/11. He was a classmate of ours from high school who went to the International Culinary Center in Soho. This was really a big deal for him, and when he got out he worked in about three restaurants in New York, but landed the big one at Windows on the World. He was just a sous chef, but Windows on the World for him was the top. Leah and I went there for supper before she went to Israel. Nick came out to our table in his white chef's coat and a tall chef hat. We felt like celebrities. He whispered to us, 'I didn't actually cook your dinner; I'm in French cuisine, and neither of you ordered escargot.' I think I made a squealy sound and said, 'Yuck,' and Leah jokingly said, 'Escargot? I don't think that's kosher.' And we all laughed, and went back to our pasta."

"And Nick was working on the morning of 9/11?"

"Yeah. He was filling in for someone. They could do that to accumulate days off. It was just a routine breakfast menu, nothing really French…well, maybe French toast." And we both chuckled. "He normally wouldn't be there at that time."

"How did you find out he was there?" This was first time Sr. Grace opened up since 9/11.

"Nick had three roommates; two other guys and a girl. The girl, Bettina, was at the Fashion Institute with me. I think she was Nick's girlfriend, but I'm not sure. She had heard that I was a nun in Brooklyn, probably from Nick, whom I think Leah kept in touch with. It was Bettina who called here and asked for me. We weren't really friends at the Institute, but I remembered her; she wanted to design for full-figured women; she herself was one. I think she was a Catholic too, and so she called here and asked for me, and asked me to pray for Nick, and for them, the roommates; they were all pretty shook up. And to ask all the Sisters to pray."

"And you put a prayer note on the prayer-board; I remember reading it, but I don't think you signed your name."

"I didn't 'cause I didn't know if we were allowed to put prayer requests up there, like only the professed could do that, or something."

"It was okay for you to put a prayer request up there; especially after 9/11. You and Nick were good friends, huh?"

"He was my boyfriend for probably seven and a half months. I really had a bad crush on him, that's what Leah used to say."

"How come you broke up?" Here I was sounding like a lovelorn advice columnist, sitting on the swing with a broken-hearted debutante.

"I think he preferred full-figured girls, and I was a skinny-mini, like Twiggy."

I didn't know Twiggy had carried over into the next generation, but I was feeling more distracted by the full-figured image. Where were the Nicholases when I was in high school? I had to pray quickly to the Holy Spirit to bring me back to reality and this swing. Poor Sr. Grace. I figured she must've liked clothes more than food, and ole Nick, well, he was into French cuisine…lots of butter and escargot! And croissants with raspberry *confiture*.

"I couldn't watch the TV coverage showing the building collapsing, and all those people in it. Nick wasn't even supposed to be there…why did he have to fill in for someone that day? I couldn't pray. I think I was so angry with God. He blanked out of my mind; I couldn't even believe in Him. I'm sorry, Sister, I shouldn't be telling you this; you probably want me to leave now."

"O, Sister Grace, we don't want you to leave. Don't you know there were, still are, lots of people who 'blank out' on God, as you put it. How can God let this happen? I know what you are going through."

"You do?"

"Sister Grace, I haven't shared with you and the younger Sisters because I wanted you to get through your own grief, but my mother and brother were having breakfast at Windows on the World that morning. It was my mother's birthday."

Sr. Grace went ashen white for a moment, her face all crinkled as the tears welled up behind her eyes. "Oh, Sister, I'm so sorry. I had no idea."

"I didn't know till I listened to the answering machine, and there was a message from my mother telling me that she and my brother were having breakfast there the next morning. That was the night before 9/11. I put my head on the desk, and I think I blanked God out for a while, too."

"Are you sure? Maybe they didn't get there on time, or changed their mind. How can you be sure?"

"I know. I thought of that too. I called my brother's office; his secretary was all shook up from it too, and told me he had it on his calendar, and if they didn't go, she hasn't heard from him. My sister came in a few days later; no one ever showed up. If they had gone elsewhere, they would have called us, but nothing."

"It's been over two months now. I thought the same about Nick, maybe he didn't really go into work that day; maybe he was playing hooky or something. But I called Bettina a couple times since; I'm sorry I didn't ask permission, I was presuming on the general permission Mother gave that we could call people."

"Yes, that was for the day and a couple of days afterwards, but don't worry about it; you were dealing with your grief in your own way. Have you been able to pray? You've been very good about the Office and rosary; you never miss."

"Thank you, Sister, yes, I'm praying again. I know God doesn't do evil or cause it, and even if I can't understand it all, I needed to pray for Nick, and for all the others. I wanted to pray for Bettina too; she was his girlfriend."

"That's very thoughtful of you."

"I invited her to come visit me, when I'm allowed to have visitors. I told her I was just a postulant, and she didn't know what that was, but said she would love to come visit. She's gone back to church, she said, since 9/11. I guess she's letting God fill in the blank now, too."

We pushed back again; or rather Sr. Grace pushed back; and we sat in silence, thinking, enjoying the slow back and forth movement of the swing. The air seemed suddenly colder than before, and I got a slight chill.

"Why don't we go in and you can help me make tea for the Sisters in the infirmary." Sr. Grace was up and off the swing while I was skooching my full-figured body in a medieval habit off the seat. "Full-figured ain't all it's made out to be." And Sr. Grace got a fit of laughter, helping me get back my balance. (I put on a little imbalance just for her sake; it was so good to hear her full-bodied laughter!) We giggled our way to the side entrance of the monastery near the infirmary, hung up those grungy parkas and headed for the infirmary kitchenette.

Sr. Grace was boiling the water and getting the cups prepared while I scrounged around for something the Sisters would like to nosh on. "You know it's time for you to petition the chapter if you want to go on to the novitiate. If you and Sr. Brenda both petition now, the November Chapter will vote, and you would receive the habit in December during Advent. Wouldn't that be nice?" I was very nonchalant and informal about it on purpose. I wasn't sure if Sr. Grace herself was ready. Several weeks ago, I would have said definitely not. I wouldn't have been surprised if she had decided to leave.

"Oh, yes, I was hoping it would be before Christmas."

And so it happened. They both received the habit and their new names on the Third Sunday of Advent, which was unusual for us, but Mother Rosaria was wise. It lifted up the spirits of the whole community which was still hurting from 9/11, and brought us into the Christmas season with renewed joy.

Grace Darlene White became Sr. Leah Marie of the Immaculate Conception. Leah, of course, for her friend Leah Levinson who first brought her here, and Mary, the Immaculate Conception whose interior design was pure from the beginning.

Twenty-Two

What else have I in heaven but you? Apart from you I want nothing on earth...God is my possession forever. (Psalms 73)

It took two years for Sally and Mitzie to move. They had a business going which had to be closed or sold to others. It also took two years for all the legal red tape to be ironed out. David's duplex was secure with Olivia who sublet the place with a three-year contract, and when Sharbel would come of age, it would legally be his. Sally would come and go over the two years, always staying at our apartment on West 79th Street. She didn't want to sublet it at all. She couldn't abide the thought of a stranger living in "our apartment." The "our" meaning hers and mine. I would never see the place again, but I was supportive of her not wanting to sublet it. Between Mama and David, she had a sizeable inheritance. She could put down the dog clippers forever, but they both needed something to occupy their time. Travel would be a part of their lives once all the financial stuff got settled.

It wasn't till after the first anniversary of 9/11 that Sally called to tell me that she and Mitzie would be in town in October and would come together to see me. I don't know why I got nervous over the prospect of meeting Mitzie. I certainly heard enough about her for years and had no reason to be worried. Only with Mama did I express my concern for their relationship, and that was in the context of their eternal salvation; but I could only take baby steps in that direction with Mama. Gwendolyn was more of a free spirit and told me not to worry. "You don't have to condone the relationship; you don't have to even talk about it; and for all you know, M.B., they may be living a chaste life together." Those were Gwendolyn's exact words. I hoped she was right and made it one of my regular secret petitions at the rosary.

We had our prioress's election in March 2003, the week after Mother's first term was up. It almost seemed an imposition to have the bishop come to preside at the election as Mother Rosaria was reelected on the first ballot. But we did have an excellent recreation with His Excellency. He was very open, it seemed to many of us, about the burdens he's carrying and said he depended on our prayers. The sexual scandal fell on the Church in America like another 9/11. Again, he begged our prayers for both the victims of abuse, the priests who were involved, and for the priests who were very faithful to their vows and carried a new stigma of mistrust. And he asked us to pray really hard for the bishops who are shepherding a very dysfunctional flock at times. He spoke in general about the closing of parishes, the lack of vocations in the priesthood, and the crisis among women religious, not just in New York, but throughout the country.

He shared a little of his *ad limina* visit to Rome with his fellow bishops and their meeting with Pope John Paul II. They are all inspired and humbled by the example he gives in his old age and all the effects of his Parkinson disease. He told us that's what it was; it didn't come out officially in the news till May.

It's good to be reminded that our life, while hidden and enclosed, is part of the whole Mystical Body. We are, he reminded us, to be love in the heart of our mother, the Church. We all smiled at him, knowing that he was quoting St. Thérèse, the Little Flower.

I do hope the Communion of Saints are interceding for all of us. Our two white veiled novices are persevering and well into their second year. We had only one new postulant at the beginning of the year: Kim. She was Korean, but born and raised in New York. Her family ran a little Korean Deli in Queens. Kim was a concert pianist, having studied piano at Juilliard. She was very frail looking (to me), and I couldn't imagine her playing a grand piano. We don't have a grand piano, unfortunately, but we have several upright pianos which are probably all out of tune, but Kim sat down at the one in the novitiate common room, and—unbelievable! Her hands ran up and down those keys so fast I don't know how she could do it.

She would run up and down the cloister as well, which had to be curbed very quickly. It made me think of Sr. Catherine Agnes (SCAR). In my day, that would have given her a coronary right on the spot. Kim also had to be told not to hum or whistle in the cloister. Furthermore, our dish detergent was not going to do damage to her hands; she had insisted on being excused from washing dishes. Such problems I had to deal with as Novice Mistress? I thought I would be shepherding novices through the dark nights of the soul, not explaining that washing dishes was expected of all the novices. She could wear rubber gloves, but those Juilliard trained fingers were gonna meet the suds. I didn't quite put it like that to her; these were scenarios that would run through my head during the rosary.

She also wanted to practice the piano every evening after Compline and during the morning *Lectio* time. She didn't take correction well or refusals to her requests. There was a little stubborn streak in her which she hid with a pleasant little smile. She always said "yes" if I asked her to do something, but it never quite got done. Giving up something, like practice time, was a major difficulty.

She left before we asked her to leave, which is always so much better. The last I heard she was waiting to hear from different symphony orchestras, but in the meantime, she was working at her parents' deli. Hopefully with clean hands...

Several young women got as far as repeat visits. One, Evelyn, did a two-week aspirancy inside with us. It was her vacation time. She was very devout and a great hopeful, till we discovered she had been married and the marriage was never annulled. The sad thing was that she lied about it. Maybe she will come back in a few years if she can get all that straightened out—and if we don't hold that lie against her.

Stephanie was a young family attorney with a law firm in Manhattan and an office in Brooklyn Heights, which is how she discovered us. She was older than our age limit, but there are always exceptions. Canonically she was fine. But she couldn't quite make the adjustment from a law office to a monastery. She also wound up "monastery shopping" and found it difficult to settle on any one place. She had a "flow chart" of sorts with all her criteria necessary which she would check off and grade by percentages according to a scale of acceptable or nonacceptable. When I met with her in the parlor for the first time, I felt like I was being interviewed for a job, or as a witness for the prosecution. When the law firm wanted to move her to Atlanta, she went. And that was that.

The Sisters in the infirmary continued their weekly rosary for vocations. All of them were holding on quite well themselves. Sr. Gerard had calmed down after a year, when the chastisement didn't happen, although she "knew" it was coming. We were on high alert, usually around First Fridays.

Sr. Benedict was crippled with arthritis and couldn't really do jigsaw puzzles anymore. It was difficult to do lots of things when you didn't have use of your hands: like eat, brush your teeth, or put on your veil. She had lots of help, of course, and gave the younger Sisters a great example of humility and abandonment. She never complained, unlike Sr. Bertrand who couldn't find a lot of positive things to say about anything.

Sr. Bertrand, who was also rapidly losing her memory and would repeat herself half a dozen times in the same conversation. Sr. Amata—the queen of patience—would sit and listen to Sr. Bertrand and let her go on her various rampages. They were young Sisters together and could talk about the old days.

Sr. Bruna was confined to bed by the end of 2003. There was talk of sending her to a nursing home—which is something we've never done but were learning other monasteries have begun to do. She was an avid reader; I remember that even from my librarian days. She was content to sit up in bed and read all day. But she didn't retain anything she read, so she soon gave it up.

And Sr. Gertrude, who turned eighty-seven in the fall of 2003, was still sharp as a tack. Her hearing was beginning to go, which we all prayed would not get worse as she enjoyed listening to music more than any other recreation. She got indigestion a lot too, didn't eat much, and was losing weight. But not her voice!

Sr. Agnes Mary had several stays in the infirmary and would joke that pharmaceuticals were keeping her alive. This was probably true for more than a few of us.

The end of 2003 found me in the infirmary too for only four days. I passed out one morning in the refectory, of all places, and scared poor Sr. Leah Marie half to death. Sr. Leah could never be accused of running in the cloister, but she took off and flew down the cloister to Mother's office and banged on the door.

"Enter, enter…whatever is the matter?" Mother anxiously exclaimed.

"Sister Baruch fainted or something in the refectory; she's lying on the floor by her table."

When Mother arrived at the refectory, I was kind of sitting up and leaning onto Sr. Elijah Rose who was sitting on the floor next to me. She was taking my pulse and looking very concerned. My pulse was something like 35.

Sr. Elijah Rose was just coming into the refectory when she saw Sr. Leah Marie flying down the cloister and knew something was wrong. Mother and she exchanged words which I don't remember, and Mother left immediately, and the next thing I recall was being hoisted onto a gurney by two very able-bodied young men. Mother and Sr. Elijah Rose followed behind the ambulance to Brooklyn Hospital Center.

I think I got attended to more quickly because I came in by ambulance. They let the Sisters assist in moving my habit around to take blood pressure, and then, to help me undress behind one of those cubicle curtains, where I had an electrocardiogram. The whole thing felt very weird. After that, I was feeling much better and wanted to leave, but they insisted I wait till the ER doctor spoke to me. My pulse was back to the mid-fifties. Sr. Elijah Rose was very attentive and easily fell back into ER nurse mode till a real ER nurse told her to sit down.

"I'll sit down when I know you're takin' care of this one here; no one's been in here for over a half hour. How about a little water or something? Where's the cooler? I'll get it myself."

"Sit down, Sister. Someone will be with you shortly."

"Yeah, I know what that means…three hours later," Sr. Elijah Rose was spouting off to me, hoping I could get dressed and out of here.

"Calm down, Sister, I'm the one having the heart attack! In fact, you can forget the water and bring me a bagel with a smear." That was just what Sister needed to hear to make her laugh and calm her down. Mother sat silently on a folding chair in the cubicle, her eyes closed, fingering her rosary.

Well, I didn't have a heart attack. Probably anemia or just really low blood pressure. The electrocardiogram didn't show anything unusual. But I was told to take it easy for a few days, get plenty to drink, and check with my regular doctor if I got dizzy or passed out again.

I was so glad to get home after four hours in the Emergency Room. Mother insisted that I go to the infirmary for a few days. When I objected, she simply said, "I'm not suggesting this; Sister, I'm telling you."

"Yes, Mother, I'm sorry. I'm truly grateful to be home and not in the hospital. I'll go to the infirmary right away." And that's how it happened. I guess I really needed the rest, as I slept most of that day and the next day as well. I didn't lose my appetite, however, so I knew I was just fine. My pulse was good, but always a little low in the early mornings. By the third day, I was ready to go back to my cell, but Mother insisted on one more day. So I stayed, but the novices came in the morning, and we had our class there. After that the regular residents of the infirmary were in and out of my room like Grand Central Station. I joined them for their afternoon rosary, which was a first, actually; I always let them have that to themselves.

On the fourth day, I was able to leave and resume life as usual. Mother had already arranged for an appointment for me with Dr. Hirsch, who was kind of the community doctor, now called a primary care physician. He recommended a cardiologist, Dr. Whitman, whom I hoped was named Walt, but it was George. And he scheduled me for a nuclear stress test—the following week, no less! I told him I didn't need a stress test, let alone anything nuclear. But he assured me it was not painful, and I would not be radioactive; it was the first step to check for any blockages in the arteries around my heart.

"Do you experience any chest pains after exerting yourself?"

"No, Doctor, not at all." (I try not to exert myself. Of course, if I'm close to being late for the Office, I may walk faster than usual, and I may be a little out of breath, but I don't really exert myself. It's not our way!)

"Do you get pains in your legs at all? Or cramps? Or muscle spasms?"

"Well, I get cramps in the middle of the night sometimes, usually just in my right leg which is my genuflecting leg, you know."

"Your what?"

"My genuflecting leg; you know, when we go in and out of the chapel, we genuflect. But Sister Joseph, our infirmarian, says it's a lack of potassium, so I eat a banana, if we have them."

"Yes, ah, well, I don't think it's from your genera-flexing."

"Genuflecting." (Oy, he's got a doctorate in cardiology, and he doesn't know what genuflecting is.)

"Yes, genu-flecting. We'd like to have blood work done a couple days before. See the receptionist out front for an appointment. And I'll see you next week. In the meantime, take it easy—and any severe chest pains, get to the Emergency Room."

Dr. Whitman's bedside manner was not going to win him any awards. And his receptionist was a charming young woman who seemed new on the job and struggled with English, and very confused that my name was not Mary Baruch, but Rebecca Feinstein. Everyone calls me Mary Baruch except Blue Cross Blue Shield. I left the office with more stress then when I went in, but I offered it all up, especially when I read the instructions for the stress test.

Sr. Elijah Rose assured me I did not have to wear sweat pants or remove anything more than my scapular and long sleeves underneath my tunic. If I wanted to wear a night veil in place of the coiffure that would be permissible too. Sr. Paula would drive me to the doctor's office where the procedure would take place, and would stay with me, so nothing to worry about. That night at Vespers I realized that I had not been hospitalized since I had my tonsils removed over fifty years ago. I've been pretty healthy my whole life through, and so what's a little stress test? It will make me *schvitz* probably, but I've lived thirty-three summers in a full veil and haven't died of heat exhaustion…yet. Two years ago I lost my mother and brother on 9/11, and I live in a house with twenty-some other women—I shouldn't have a little stress once in a while?

I must've looked out of sorts, as I made my way to the refectory after our meditation time, as Sr. Elijah Rose came up beside me, took my arm and whispered, "Everything's gonna be just fine."

I couldn't reprimand her for speaking in the cloister as I was struck by her words. That's the expression Eli would give in my dreams.

D-Day arrived (Doctor-Day). I showed up twenty minutes early, having to show all the insurance information again, and assure them that my address and phone number hadn't changed since last week, and I still had the same birthday. A nurse (I presume) came to get me. Sr. Paula went with me. I changed into a night veil and removed my scapular and rolled my habit sleeves all the way up. I was given an IV in my arm which didn't hurt, too much. I realized I'm still a big baby when it comes to things like this. My blood pressure was a little high, and I was settled in a kind of lounge chair, while someone took "pictures" of my heart.

We went into another room where Dr. Whitman was waiting without a smile. I thought maybe I should genuflect to make him laugh, but he might not remember our discussion last week and he would think I was weak in the knees and schedule me for an immediate knee replacement.

"Good morning, Doctor, how nice to see you again." That probably sounded "lame" as Sr. Leah Marie would say. He responded with half a smile. "Good morning, Sister. Now, if at any time you experience chest pain let us know. We will inject you with nuclear dye during the test; you'll get a warm sensation, but that's normal, so keep on walking. Your blood pressure will be monitored as well. We'll also increase the speed and incline as we go. I'm glad to see you've worn sneakers."

"That was on the preparation sheet," I said. I didn't have the nerve to tell him I've been wearing sneakers for years. But I continued, "I like them; I think I'll ask 'Mother Superior' if I can keep them." (No smile.) So I hiked up my tunic, and climbed onto the treadmill. ("*Hail Mary, full of grace, the Lord is with thee.*") And we were off. It wasn't so bad; like a nice afternoon stroll around the outside garden, but then the speed got a little more rapid, and I felt a warmth flood me for an instant, and I was going uphill at an unsisterly clip. Thank goodness I had sneakers on; this thing was going faster all the time. I grabbed on for life and walked faster than I have in years…my legs were aching and my heart pounding, and the doctor announced, "Thirty seconds more." A deep breath, and I closed my eyes, and held tight. I must've looked quite a sight when I stepped off the treadmill, my poor night veil all askew, having dropped below my eyebrows, but I was happy it was over. I think Dr. Whitman was happy too. He said I passed with flying colors. I'm not sure what that means when I think about it, like exactly what colors fly?

Later reports showed my heart to be in good shape, but I would need to have a "vascular man" look at the legs. That they were aching near the end probably meant that circulation was poor. I told him I don't know about circulation, but those muscles haven't been pressed into action quite like this for many a year. But I relented and agreed to an appointment with a Dr. Rhonda Sparks. Fortunately she was all booked up till the first of the year. I would just stick to bananas for now.

So that ended my peaceful year 2003. No new postulants but three new doctors!

Twenty-Three

Hallel: The Fourth cup ending the Seder. The Psalms and their blessings are sung responsorially.

Fr. Matthew was home for a month before Lent 2004 began. The Passionist Fathers love him over in Lancashire and want him to return. He says it all depends on his provincial, but he thinks it can be worked out.

During the previous holiday I had a wonderful visit with Sharbel who came to see me during the Christmas Octave with a very attractive older woman, whom I never would have guessed was his mother, Olivia—that is Dr. Olivia Ghattas.

"You must be the legendary mystery nun, Aunt Mary. Sister, I'm so happy to finally meet you."

She was delightful, charming, and beautiful, in a humble, natural, Greta-way of beauty. While Greta looked like Princess Grace of Monaco, Dr. Ghattas looked like Ingrid Bergman with rich black hair. It made me remember Mama telling me about her, and Mama watching Ingrid Bergman playing Sr. Benedict in *The Bells of St. Mary's*.

"And I am so happy to meet Jack's, I mean, Sharbel's mother."

"I am sorry I never came to see you after that terrible day in September. I can't imagine what you went through losing both your mother and brother."

"It was a wrenching time for all of us here. I didn't know my mother and David were there till hours afterwards. Many of us lost loved ones that day. I would even say, it changed the…what? The mood? The atmosphere of the house? We immediately and automatically went into prayer-mode. And our prayer changed. The words of the Psalms had new meaning to them. The sudden and tragic realization of the shortness and sacredness of every life, of our lives, became almost tangible." Olivia and Sharbel didn't say anything; we just sat silent for a moment.

"I don't know how much you know of my relationship with my brother; he was opposed to my becoming a Catholic some forty years ago. He cut me out of his life entirely for thirty-five years. We had the last couple years before 9/11 to become reacquainted; and a blessing in it all has been to meet my nephew here." Sharbel smiled and blushed.

"And for me to meet my aunt, the cloistered nun! I brag about you at school; is that a sin?"

I laughed. "I don't know what there is to brag about, but I don't think it's a sin; it's the good kind of pride…I hope."

"Poor David," Olivia got in, "he was getting it from all sides, I suppose. He mellowed in his anti-Catholic stance over the years; his practice helped to change that. My faith was a huge enigma to him, and he came to know if he was going to have a relationship with his son, he'd have to be a part of that part of his life too." She paused for a moment, thinking back. "Sharbel never had a bar-mitzvah, but he made his First Holy Communion and Confirmation, and David was there for both of them."

"Well. I'll be." Thinking about things myself, I looked at Sharbel. "I'm sorry you didn't get to know your Aunt Ruthie better; she would have been there for you too. She used to come here and sit right where you are, and imitate Sister Paula, our extern Sister, or somebody she had sat across from on the subway. When we were kids, we would go to an afternoon matinee and then go to Horn and Hardarts' Automat for tea and a dessert, and Ruthie would put on a British accent like we were tourists visiting the city. She was a master of foreign accents."

"Oh, I know. I don't know how she could do it, but once she put on a Lebanese accent; even I can't do that." And we all laughed.

"David took us to an off-Broadway show she was starring in, and we met her afterwards in her dressing room. It's the only time I met her. David was very proud of her...David was a good man, I hope you know that," spake the mother of his son. "I couldn't marry him because he didn't share my Faith, and while we were both young physicians, our approach to our careers, and to our faiths, were different. It worked out better this way, but I always wanted David to know his son and vice versa."

"And his other grandmother," I added. "I cannot tell you how much joy you, Sharbel, brought into your grandmother's life." To them both, "She was a real Jewish Mother, you know. There's always something that rings true in a stereotype, and Hannah Feinstein fit the stereotype." Putting on Mama's accent, "I should have such a good-looking grandson? And his mother's a doctor." They both laughed.

"Well, I loved having such a great grandmamma…she was 'such a blessing,'" Sharbel responded. We all laughed.

We visited for a good hour and kept it pretty light-hearted. I was truly glad to finally meet Olivia, and she promised to come back and visit again. And Sharbel promised to be around to see me, and tell me all about Yale and St. Mary's where he went for Mass and served as an altar server. (I guess they weren't called altar boys after a certain age, but apparently St. Mary's had a whole group of young men from Yale who served at Mass.) I was happy to hear that; I certainly prayed he would find a home there.

Life in the monastery rolled along as usual. Sr. Agnes Mary became a full resident of the infirmary, her health was declining more and more. We would have two aspirants live inside the enclosure for a couple weeks during Lent, which was certainly different from my day.

One young woman was a native American, whom I mistakenly called an Indian, and was corrected by Sr. Anna Maria who seemed to know all the newly politically correct terminology. Her name was Pretty Flower, and she was a graduate of Rutgers University in New Brunswick, New Jersey.

When I told the Sisters in the infirmary that we have an aspirant coming named Pretty Flower, it was Sr. Bertrand who reacted the most, "Pretty Flower? What kind a name is that; sounds pretty egotistical to me; who would ever call themselves 'Pretty Flower'—maybe Daffodil, or Hyacinth, or Rose, but Pretty Flower?"

Sr. Gerard picked up the ball, "Or Lily, Lilac, Tulip..."

"Tulip?" It was Sr. Bertrand again. "What kind of name is Tulip? "

"I went to school with a girl named Tulip," contributed Sr. Benedict. "We called her 'Two-lips Open' because she was always talking and getting the rest of us in trouble."

"Pretty Flower is Native American..." but before I could complete the politically correct sentence, Sr. Bertrand interrupted, "Native American? I'm a native American; we're all native Americans, except for Maureen and the Sisters out back who were born in other countries, like Sr. Hildegard, and Sr. Boniface and maybe Sr. Jane Mary; wasn't she born in Canada?"

"Canada would still be American...just North American." Sr. Benedict let us know.

"Pretty Flower is an American Indian."

"Well, why didn't you say so in the first place?" an exasperated Sr. Bertrand responded. "I bet she does great beadwork." And everybody thought that was hysterical.

"I don't know about that, Sister, but she has a Master's Degree in Nuclear Engineering."

"Well, that and a dollar and a quarter will get her on the subway."

It was a good thing that Sr. Bertrand wasn't Postulant Mistress; she'd scare everyone away before they even really entered.

"So what are we supposed to call her, Sister Pretty?" This was Sr. Benedict asking quite sincerely.

"I hadn't thought about that yet. But I think Sister Flower or Sister Flora, perhaps."

"Or Fleur…Mother Rosaria would like that." Again, a sincere Sr. Benedict.

"Well, I'm gonna call her 'Pretty Flower' and she can call me 'Wilting Flower.'" Sr. Bertrand was back.

"And I'm Sister Drooping Flower," called out Sr. Agnes Mary from across the room.

"Now you all be kind to her. She's rather timid and nervous about it all."

"Of course we will, you know that, Sister. We'll be very kind to our new bloom." Sr. Benedict trying to settle everyone down. They all thought 'new bloom' was funnier than Two-lips-open and we all got laughing over it. I told myself I'm going to have to think of something serious when I bring her into the infirmary for the first time. Pretty Flower herself took care of it when she told me, "Everyone calls me 'Patty.'"

The second aspirant was actually a professed Sister from an active Order. She was already fifty, but a religious for nearly thirty years. She had been acquainted with the monastery for many years, and Mother wanted to give her a chance. Her name was Sr. Sheila. She said her original religious name was Sr. Joseph Michael. She taught elementary school for twenty years. Her community went through major changes and somewhere along the way she said, "We lost the religious life, at least the life I had entered years before. I loved teaching, but we were withdrawing from our schools and doing social justice things, and living in small communities in our own apartments without anyone really being the superior. We sat around in our living room chairs and recited the Office if we were all there. When I went back to the Motherhouse for a day of recollection, they had replaced the tabernacle with an earthen jug hanging in a macramé dreamcatcher."

Sr. Sheila stopped going to the motherhouse and would come to the monastery on her "day off." I remember her sitting in the chapel alone, sometimes quietly weeping. I asked Sr. Paula about her, but Sr. Paula said she just missed 'the life.' I'm surprised she didn't come to us sooner, but all in God's plan. I pray it works out for her. I think she and Pretty Flower will get along well.

* * *

Lent is a little different each year; we settle into the usual Lenten antiphons and readings. I think we all welcome the liturgical season with more spiritual motivation than we have at New Year's. Mother Rosaria had begun a new custom since Lent of 2001 of drawing for a special intention to be prayed for by each Sister. We did this at community recreation on Shrove Tuesday. The novices were invited to the recreation as well, and also drew an intention from the velvet bag used for such purposes. Some Sisters kept it secret, but it wasn't required, and the novices all wanted to know what the other novices drew. Many of the intentions were based on the General Intercessions on Good Friday, which made a nice liturgical connection.

Sr. Mary Kolbe: for the conversion of nonbelievers.

Sr. Diana: for the Sisters in the infirmary.

Sr. Maureen: for priests experiencing difficulties.

Sr. Mary Cecilia: for the poor souls in Purgatory.

Sr. Elijah Rose: for all who do not believe in Christ.

Sr. Leah Marie: for Pope John Paul in his illness.

I was to pray for protection from terrorism. I found it interesting that I was not to pray for the conversion of terrorists, although someone might have gotten that exact intention. And of course I could do both, which I did. Since 9/11 terrorism and our own safety had entered into our consciousness and prayers. We were locking the door to the public chapel immediately after Vespers, and anyone coming to the front door had to be buzzed in now. We had a new button by the main Turn, on the nuns' side, and in Mother's office, which sent an alarm alert throughout the whole house. Like old fashioned fire-drills, we had an emergency alert drill; if we were in choir, it simply meant getting on our hands and knees behind the form or kneeler in front of our seat. This was not an easy position to get into for the elderly Sisters or those who are more full-bodied, as Sr. Leah Marie would say.

We didn't know exactly how safe this would be; terrorists with machine guns could probably shoot right through the forms. Sr. Mark suggested that we stand straight up and link arms with each other, and be prepared to go to the Lord instead of hiding. She even suggested that the chantress should intone the *Te Deum*. This brought up a lively discussion in the Chapter. The debate was on whether we should get shot singing the *Te Deum*, or the *Salve,* or the Lord's Prayer. We had a good discussion drawing distinctions between the prayers. In the end, the *Salve* won out since we sing it every night at Compline after the hebdom prays: "*May the Lord grant us a quiet night and a peaceful death.*" And we sing it at every death bed and, in effect, this would be ours.

The conclusion, however, was that we would try the crouching behind the form first to see how it seemed. That was just for the chapel. In the refectory we would try to stand and link arms and sing the Salve, since getting under the tables wouldn't really hide us. In the cloister one should duck for cover wherever they could, and in our cell, get under the bed, which meant a little spring house cleaning for some Sisters.

We only had one drill after all this was discussed, and it was in the Lent of 2004. We were all in choir, at Vespers, and the Emergency Alert sounded. We hadn't taken into account that the kneelers were there, so that made getting into crouch position a little more difficult. One had to kind of straddle the kneeler which wasn't easy with a full skirt. But we did it. One Sister, not realizing it was a drill, cried out, "Lord have mercy on us." The chantress all confused by things, intoned the *Salve*, which defeated the purpose of hiding. And then, it only took two Sisters to get the giggles, and it spread across both choirs. Here we were on both sides, on our hands and knees, preparing to go to the Lord, and we got a fit of laughing.

After the "all clear" and we managed to get ourselves standing up again, with much huffing puffing and grunting by a few of us, and brushing ourselves off, and still laughing, Mother knocked quite loudly, and we all stopped and knelt to pray. Poor Sr. Dominic, who never said a word out of turn, hollered from behind her form: "I've got a cramp in my leg, and I can't get up." The two Sisters next to her grabbed her under both arms and lifted her up. "Are we safe?" And all Mother could do was to say, half laughing, "Yes, Sister, we are safe, blessed be God."

We were all very happy to process silently to the refectory for tomato soup, peanut butter and crackers, which never tasted so good. At the next Chapter, Mother announced that we would link arms in choir and go down together singing the *Salve*. We all thought that was the braver solution.

The infirmary Sisters, of course, revived the whole discussion on where our shrine would be as the Dominican Martyrs of Brooklyn Heights. There was always something just a little humorous beneath it all, which may just be our way of dealing with the reality of what we're living in these days.

I had no parlors to look forward to during the Easter Octave, but on Divine Mercy Sunday, Sr. Elijah Rose and Sr. Leah Marie would make first profession and receive the black veil.

It was Sr. Gertrude, on behalf of the "infirmary community," who invited the two novices to the infirmary for a little tea party. The rooftop was suggested, but it was still a bit chilly for most the infirmary Sisters and too much fuss getting everything organized. The infirmary was a much better place. They wanted just the white veils making profession, not Sr. Sheila or Pretty Flower. (Everyone else called her Patty, but the infirmary Sisters preferred 'Pretty Flower', led by Sr. Bertrand who still thought the name was a riot.)

Actually, the infirmarian and I did most of the work, as Sr. Benedict couldn't really use her hands, Sr. Gerard and Sr. Gertrude were in wheelchairs, Sr. Amata and Sr. Bertrand alone were able to help. Sr. Bruna had no idea what was going on.

"I thought this was going to be a graceful, Queen's garden-like tea party, with dainty cups and saucers—what are all these mugs doing out? It looks like a Hippie Café," Sr. Bertrand commented while rearranging all the mugs so their handles were in the same direction.

Sr. Gertrude was in charge of the music and Sr. Agnes Mary and Sr. Catherine Agnes (SCAR), who was now a part-time resident of the infirmary, made gingerbread nuns with black licorice veils.

"All these nuns are my 'Sisters of color,'" Sr. Elijah Rose announced when the gingerbread nuns were brought out. "And this one is built just like me." Then she broke one in half, "This one is more Sr. Leah Marie with a deep tan." And she turned to thank Sr. Catherine Agnes: "You done good, girl."

I had never ever seen SCAR blush before, but she was simply delighted with such an outrageous comment. "You better believe it, sweet pea, so eat up cuz these girls aren't gonna persevere on this plate, no way, no how." I couldn't believe my ears.

Sr. Elijah apparently loved it too: "Sho'nuf, Sista, and Mama's little baby loves shortnin', shortnin'."

That's all Sr. Gertrude needed, "Mama's little baby loves shortnin' bread." Everyone who knew the song broke into the chorus.

"Thank you, Sister Catherine Agnes, they're beautiful," Sr. Leah Marie quietly intruded into the conversation. "Did you design these yourselves?"

"Well, actually there's a mold for gingerbread girls, I just designed the veil."

With that, Sr. Bertrand decapitated one of them with one bite. We all laughed.

"Seriously," it was now Sr. Benedict talking, "we are so happy that the two of you are making profession. You've had a very interesting postulancy and novitiate, unlike any of us ever lived through. We've been praying for your perseverance and, well, here you are, on the eve of your first profession."

Sr. Amata: "And on Divine Mercy Sunday, how appropriate that is when you prostrate on the floor and Mother asks you what do you seek. And you both will answer together…"

Sisters Elijah Rose and Leah Marie: "God's mercy and yours."

The gingerbread nuns were eaten without much mercy, but a dozen were left for the infirmary cookie jar.

Their profession was indeed a joyous day. The liturgy was beautiful, and afterwards we met both families gathered in two separate parlors. The Hubbard family filled up the large parlor with parents, sisters, brothers, and nephews and nieces, plus a few friends—including Sister's godmother, who was a nurse at Roosevelt Hospital. Her parents who were okay with "Brenda's" conversion, but had been very opposed to her entering a cloistered monastery of nuns, seemed quite pleased to see how happy their Brenda was. I was really delighted to speak in a corner of the grille with Sister's father, who was Eli's son. They were all amazed that I knew Eli when I was a child, and that he was "my favorite of all doormen." His son had the same broad happy smile and laugh, without the gold tooth.

Sr. Leah Marie's family were just a few. Her mother, her aunt, and her cousin came. Her mother was separated from her father, who had remarried and lived in Tennessee. And Bettina came: the girl who had been at the Fashion Institute with her and later was the girlfriend of Nick, who died on 9/11. They had kept in touch with each other, which I think helped Sr. Leah Marie get through the trauma of it all. Bettina brought back memories of little Grace White visiting with her technicolor hair and display of earrings.

In the refectory there is a small bouquet of flowers at each of the newly professed Sisters' place. But at Sr. Leah Marie's place there was also a vase of white roses and a card which read, "Mazel tov, my dear friend. Love, Leah Levinson."

Twenty-Four

Let my prayer rise before You, O Lord, like incense in Your sight. The raising of my hands like an evening oblation. (Psalm 141)

Turning sixty is like Vespers. It's not the end of the day, but the day turns into evening. Some truly wonderful and remarkable things happened—and two very sad things which, like Vespers, are joined to the Magnificat of Our Lady. Our souls, even in sadness, rejoice in God our Savior because He never stops looking upon the lowliness of His servant. They are like Amen/Alleluia moments which are both happy and sad at the same time.

The first Amen/Alleluia came to us during Holy Week and in the splendid Alleluia of the Easter Octave, Divine Mercy Sunday, April 2, 2005, when our dear Holy Father John Paul II died at the age of eighty-four. The television Mother Rosaria had purchased when 9/11 happened was only brought out of seclusion for very special occasions. In addition, it was now possible to record things on the television and watch them at a different time. And so we were able to watch the funeral Mass celebrated in St. Peter's Square by Cardinal Ratzinger and all those cardinals, bishops, and priests, and a million of the faithful.

Our prayer for his health and a holy death had been rising like incense in our chapel for weeks before. It would, of course, continue for the repose of his soul, and for the Conclave and election of a new Holy Father.

I believe it was around 11:30 a.m. on April 19, 2005, when there was white smoke coming from the Sistine Chapel chimney. Fr. Ambrose called Mother, and after Sext, Mother announced that she arranged for us to have a pick-up lunch; we could get what we wanted on trays and go to the community room. I don't think this had ever happened in our hundred-year history. The television was on in the community room, and everyone was still abuzz, waiting for the new pope to appear on the balcony.

All week our refectory reading had been on the *papabili*, the Cardinals who were considered as possible popes. All week long, as well, there was much to read about Pope John Paul II, the first non-Italian pope in 600 years; would the new pope be Italian? Or perhaps African?

The news people suddenly became silent (thank God) as we went live to St. Peter's Square. There was movement behind the heavy drape in the back of the balcony, when a Cardinal came out and made the announcement we had all been waiting for:

> *Annuntio vobis gaudium magnum: HABEMUS PAPAM*! (I announce to you with great joy: WE HAVE A POPE!)

We all sat frozen to our seats: not a Sister chewed, clinked her silverware, or uttered a word.

> *Eminentissimum ac reverendissumum Dominum, Dominum Josephum Sanctae Romanae Ecclesiae Cardinalem*... (Everyone held her breath) *RATZINGER.*

Sr. Antonia, our quiet, reserved, never-say-anything librarian, literally leaped out of her chair: "Holy Moly—I don't believe it. Cardinal Ratzinger!" And we all clapped for three seconds, till Mother hushed us to catch his name: *Qui sibi nomen imposuit Benedicti decimi sexti.*

We were all Latin singers, but few Latin scholars; we caught the Benedict part, and waited for the English commentator to announce: Benedict XVI. We cheered at the words; at least most of us did. We all loved the writings of Cardinal Ratzinger and never believed he would be chosen as Holy Father—especially if you read all the negative voices in some of the papers.

Sr. Sheila was overjoyed but Sr. Patty (Pretty Flower) didn't know what to make of it. Sr. Elijah was twirling around and singing 'alleluia' and Sr. Leah Marie sat sedately and applauded with everyone else.

And there he was coming out on the balcony, waving with both hands. There was a flurry of activity on the balcony getting the microphone to him; the crowd which was screaming and applauding got silent, as the new Holy Father was getting ready to give his first blessing *Urbi et orbi.* We also got silent, and most of us got down on our knees, staring at the television, and blessed ourselves when he gave us his blessing.

With Mother's permission, the novices and I were able to move the TV into the infirmary, as we knew this would all be repeated on the Catholic channels, and the Sisters in the infirmary could see it all like it was live.

Sr. Benedict, of course, was thrilled at the name. Sr. Amata kept saying, "He's a holy man; he's a holy man."

Sr. Bertrand: "What kind of a name is Rats...singer?" Poor Sister got all hung up on people's names.

Sr. Gertrude was in a wheelchair, and at eighty-nine not as sharp as usual, but still joined in the festivities. "He was kind of like Pope John Paul's understudy. I hope he's ready for the role."

Sr. Benedict added, "Indeed...and the show must go on."

Sr. Gerard let us all know that this could be the last pope according to Nostradamus, to which Sr. Bertrand added, "What kind of a name is Noter-dame-us; did he teach at the University in Indiana?"

"No, I think it's for the cathedral in Paris," said Sr. Amata who knew very well it was neither, but loved to get Sr. Bertrand confused. "He was the vicar."

But all in all, they were very happy; they too had been praying every day since the death of Pope John Paul for the new pope.

The next Amen/Alleluia event, happy but marked with a twinge of sadness or concern, was that our chaplain, Fr. Ambrose, was being assigned to the Angelicum, the Dominican university in Rome. Their gain is certainly our loss. But it left us wondering when (and in whose name) we would celebrate our *own* "habemus papam"—when we would have a Father chaplain.

Fr. Ambrose was consulted on this by his provincial and the other friars in New York who make these appointments. We knew, as Sr. Assumption said at recreation, the "pickins were slim." (Sister was from Kentucky.)

There were so many "firsts" happening, and this was one of them. We have always had a Dominican Father as chaplain, except maybe ninety years ago when they had a Franciscan for a few years, and a couple diocesan priests. But Fr. Ambrose knew a priest from another Order whom he thought would be a wonderful chaplain; he knew the nuns very well; helped out a lot during busy holiday times, and if he heard right, his own provincial wanted him back…from England!

Both provincials came to an agreement; and Mother and her council also put in a positive word of approval, and so Fr. Matthew Goldman, CCSP, became our chaplain, and moved into the chaplain's quarters in early summer.

The chaplain and I met in the parlor in late May. "Well, Father Ezra Goldman, here you are back with us. Such a blessing the good Lord has showered upon us!"

"Rebecca Feinstein, I presume? Do you serve Earl Grey in this joint?" We both laughed.

He told me his health had improved for a while, but the cold and dampness of the UK brought lots of other problems. He loved his ministry there at the shrine, and didn't want to come home to the other assignments he might face in his province. When Fr. Ambrose contacted him and said he wanted to propose this to his provincial, he asked him if he was interested in it, and if his provincial would permit it.

"It was like an answer to a long-standing prayer. I know what St. Paul means when he says 'the spirit is willing, but the flesh is weak.' I need to be in an environment of holiness, at least where I can pray regularly, have silence in my life, and say Mass for people who believe and aren't in a hurry to get somewhere. The shrine in Lancashire was good in many ways, but I missed New York. Isn't it funny with all my years in Africa, I would still miss this crazy city. Or maybe it's just my age. I'm tired, Becky, of running from here to there and back again. You've helped me more than you'll ever know just by your being here and praying for me."

He continued, "So when the provincial called me and ran it by me, that he would be willing to let me serve as chaplain and live here, I couldn't believe my ears. Such a long-standing prayer should finally be answered?" (There was the old Ezra I remembered.) "So here I am, or will be, come June. Your Father Ambrose has been a great help in getting me settled, and he's the one going overseas!"

I just sat silent, smiling, trying not to cry. I've realized in my "old age" that I'm not going to get any more control over my emotions than I had when I was younger. The tear-bag can be very close. Maybe St. Paul would call it the gift of tears. And maybe so, when it overflowed from joy, and that was today.

"How did Gwendolyn take it?"

"Like the trooper she is. She was sad, but more happy than sad. She said she knew I wouldn't be in England forever, and now she had even more excuse for 'coming home' to visit. She's retired, you know, and living with her sister, who isn't retired, and doesn't think Gwen should be either. So,

I wouldn't be surprised if Ms. Putterforth putters forth on back to the U.S. of A. She'll make a decision after the new year."

I suppose I could say that was a third bit of joyful news in 2005, but I'd have to wait till after the New Year to see. I put it "on hold" along with another promise of good news, this time from Sharbel. In his infrequent visits he was hinting that he wasn't so sure he wanted to go on be a doctor, and wanted me to pray for him over all this. He didn't know how his mother would react to a change of career plans. He was also coming into his inheritance, or he already had, but hadn't moved in or moved back to New York, and didn't intend to immediately, at least.

I wondered if he was going to run off and get married or something. I had decided I was going to give his bride, if there is a bride, Mama's brooch. Till then it would stay in the corner of my small dresser.

It was a rainy Saturday morning when Sr. Paula came and got me. I was actually in the library with Sr. Antonia marveling at all the computerized cataloguing she has accomplished. Sr. Paula told me I had a surprise visitor in the small parlor. I couldn't imagine who it was.

There he sat all by himself, my nephew Sharbel.

"Aunt Mary, I'm sorry I didn't call ahead of time; I came home for the weekend and told Mother I was going into the city to see a film with friends, which isn't a lie, but that's not for a couple hours yet. I wanted to come to see you."

"I'm so happy you have; you've made my day! I've been praying for your special intention as you asked."

"Thank you, so much. That's why I'm here really. I need to let you in on my 'intention' as I'm not sure what to do, and I know you've been where I am."

"I have? That's very interesting…don't tell me you want to become Jewish and go to rabbinical school!"

Sharbel laughed, reminding me of David and Papa. Funny how little traits are passed on from one generation to the next.

"Not really, Aunt Mary, but you're kind of close. I don't want to be Jewish and become a rabbi…I want to become a Dominican and a priest."

I almost fell off my chair, not with shock, but with unexpected delight. Leave it to me, but the water-works rose up and ran down my cheeks.

"Oh, Jack, I am so happy; I don't know what to say."

Sharbel (Jack) relaxed his face and smiled. "I'm so happy you are happy; although I never thought you wouldn't be. My problem is my family—well, my mother! She doesn't know this yet, and she thinks I'm applying to med schools, and is already bragging to her doctor-friends that I'm following in her footsteps. I don't think she will accept that I want to be a priest. She is a good Catholic in her own way, you know, but I am her only son…and…"

"And she wants grandchildren as well as a doctor in the house."

"I think so."

"Well, you'll never know unless you let her know. You may be surprised at her reaction, and then again, you may be right; but either way, you need to follow your heart. My first and dearest spiritual father, Father Meriwether, once told me you have to listen to the deepest desires of your heart, for that is where the Holy Spirit is speaking to you."

"I hope I can do that. I'm not sure. How does one know what God's Will is?"

"It's not a common desire, an ordinary desire, even a natural desire, to want to give oneself to Our Lord completely as a priest. For most young men your age, it never crosses their mind, let alone their heart. Such thoughts you should have?"

His smile broadened. "Such thoughts I have, especially the last year. It's like I want to take care of sick souls, more than sick bodies."

"I think we only come to know God's Will in prayer, and in listening to the deep desires of your heart. If that is God calling you, surrender to it and see if you are at peace with it. You're coming to share this with me is a little surrender, you know."

"That's true. I thought I could keep it all secret. Nobody would understand. But I knew you would. If this is God's Will, please pray for me and with me, that I will know that and have the grace to say 'yes' and to know how to let my mother know. She thinks I'll be moving into my father's duplex once I get out of school and start my practice."

"Well, duplexes are just duplexes. They're not the be-all and end-all of life. Who knows anything of one's future? You could land a job in Seattle for heaven's sake!"

He laughed. "You're right. Let this be our secret for now, okay. And I'll be back at Christmas time and let you know how it all goes. Thank you for being here." And he couldn't say anything more…he squeezed my fingers, and blew me a kiss as he ducked out the door.

And I took him with me to Vespers each night entrusting it all to Mary's Immaculate Heart, and his mother to Our Mother. Indeed, I had so much to pray for especially at Vespers. It was really like the "paschal hour" for me each evening…passing over from the noise and activity of the busy day, to a more silent, peaceful eventide.

Twenty-Five

Compline: The Church's Night Prayer, ending with a blessing and chanting the Salve Regina with a procession led by Sisters with lighted candles.

"May the all powerful Lord grant us a restful night and a peaceful death." (Blessing at the end of Compline)

COMPLINE, LIKE VESPERS, is also very conducive to meditating or remembering times past. I think that is especially true in the fall. October is such a prayerful month when the leaves display their grand array of autumn colors. There's a chill in the air, and it just seems easier to pray and think than in the heat and humidity of summer. I suppose early September will always be a sad moment of remembering when September 11 rounds around, but time will heal that too.

We enjoyed the weather on our rooftop garden…autumn in New York stretched out in front of our eyes. In mid-September there appeared a large bowl of apples on every table in the refectory. Someone must've made a great donation of apples for us; and, of course, at Vespers I kept thinking of Mama making the *charoset* for Rosh Hashanah. The Jewish New Year was late in 2005, not until October 4. It really came and went without my thinking much about it. Maybe because I didn't have anyone sending me Rosh Hashanah cards anymore. My mind was travelling ahead this year instead. November 1 would be the thirty-fifth anniversary of my receiving the habit and becoming Sr. Mary Baruch of the Advent Heart. Papa and Ruthie were there for that. And it was the last time I saw Papa. He was so proud of me, acting very much like the "father of the bride."

Ruthie, of course, was swept up in the drama of it all, especially when I disappeared from view carrying my habit, and returned a few minutes later fully clothed. I'm not sure if I thought these thoughts thirty-five years ago, but it must've crossed my mind, that these would be my clothes for the rest of my life.

There's a little paschal mystery going on when we pass over the threshold of the enclosure door, from the world into the monastery. I decided I would not observe my thirty-fifth anniversary in any big way; I'd save that for fifteen years down the road. But I would ask Ezra to remember me at Mass in a special way. It would be All Saints' Day, and he would have the community Mass intention. My meditations after Compline the week before were filled with gratitude and sorrow: sorrow for the thousand ways I was unfaithful or ungrateful in little things. My self-centeredness can still run amuck, and I can be lazy about everything, and have all kinds of unkind thoughts run through my mind over this Sister or that Sister.

I know the Lord has blessed me tremendously from my earliest youth. Like Him, I knew the love of a Jewish family and the joy of our holidays, even if we weren't the most observant Jews on the block, as Ruthie once put it. There have been many little paschal moments in my life. I am grateful for them all, even if I have come crashing down on the floor like Mama's Seder plate. The Lord is with us all the time, and puts us back together.

It struck me again how moments of death can seem like the crashing of the plate; they are moments of surrender and trust in God's infinite love and care for us. My brother Josh's death was just the beginning of a whole new way of life for me. Gracie Price, my best friend whom the Lord used to bring me to St. Vincent's on Lexington Avenue where He showed me His Sacred Heart and drew me into His presence in the Eucharist before I even knew who He was.

There was Papa's death early on in my life here, and Fr. Meriwether's sudden death, and then Mother John Dominic. When she died, I didn't know if I could go on. All along the way, Lord, you brought me through. Then there was Ruthie's sudden death and all that came from it. What joy You, O Lord, brought to my poor soul. Finally there were Mama and David and all the others whom we have carried in our prayers since 9/11.

Such was my meditation two nights before All Saints. After supper, I grabbed a grungy parka and made my way alone to the cemetery. I had been thinking about all those Sisters after Vespers, and it felt like a good night to "visit." There was just a hint of snow in the air, which would be wonderful for All Saints. At the far end of the building I could see a light on in the chaplain's quarters. Ezra was happily settled in, and everyone seemed so happy to have him as our chaplain.

I sat for just a moment on the bench on the edge of the cemetery, distracted by the movement of another Sister in a parka heading my way. I guess I wasn't the only one getting ready for All Saints' and All Souls' Days. But it wasn't a Sister, it was Mother Rosaria. She very quietly came and, sitting next to me, reached over and took my hand.

"Sister....It's Sister Gertrude. She's had a heart attack. I came to get you."

I caught my breath and squeezed Mother's hand. "Oh, Mother...is she...is she?"

"She's still with us. Father Matthew is on his way to anoint her, and we're gathering as many as we can. Sr. Bertrand was sitting in the picture window praying her rosary, and she grabbed me and said, 'Get Baruch; she's out in the cemetery.'"

We rushed off together, hanging up the parkas and making our way to the infirmary. Ezra arrived shortly after us but before the doctor. He spoke in a clear but soft voice, and prayed the prayers for the dying. Then he anointed her head and hands with the oil of the sick and prayed the beautiful prayer bestowing on her the Apostolic Blessing.

Mother arrived with Dr. Hirsch, who felt Sr. Gertrude's pulse and listened to her heart. Her breathing was very shallow. She was not perspiring, nor did she appear at all agitated. The doctor said she should not be moved from here. She was comfortable and not in pain. He left a sedative and a heart pill in case she should become agitated or experience chest pains; he was not sure if she would make it through the night.

Sr. Elijah Rose asked permission to stay the night with her. "Perhaps not the entire night, Sister, that's very kind of you. Stay till midnight, and we'll see how she is then. I'll be here with you too." I looked over at Mother to presume permission, and she whispered, "Of course."

There were perhaps twelve Sisters gatheredaround her bed and out the door. Sr. Lucy quietly, but with perfect pitch, intoned the *Salve*, and we all sang without perfect pitch, but with much fervor. One by one, the Sisters quietly left; the infirmary Sisters were last to leave.

Sr. Amata put a framed picture of the Sacred Heart on the bed table and placed a single vigil light in a red glass held in a golden vigil candle holder with ruby-like stones around it. Each Sister then came to her bedside and kissed her hand. Sr. Gertrude didn't stir, but slightly moaned and changed the position of her head. Sr. Elijah Rose and I sat on the opposite sides of the bed and quietly prayed the rosary together. I took my old pocket rosary and put it in Sr. Gertrude's hand, and used my side rosary to pray.

We could hear the Sisters singing Compline over a distant P.A. in one of the infirmary rooms:

> *. . . Upon you no evil shall fall,*
> *no plague approach where you dwell. For you has he commanded his angels, to keep you in all your ways. . .* (Ps. 91)

The reading at Compline we knew by heart: *They shall see the Lord face to face and bear his name on their foreheads. The night shall be no more. They will need no light from lamps or the sun, for the Lord God shall give them light, and they shall reign forever* (Rev. 22:4-5).

Sr. Elijah Rose and I sang very quietly along with the Sisters over the P.A.: *Into your hands, Lord, I commend my spirit. You have redeemed us, Lord God of truth.*

We sing these words every single night, and yet how full of meaning they become when sitting at the deathbed of one you love. *Lord God of truth.* In the end, it's the truth that matters; and we have given up our whole lives to live by that truth, who is not a thing but a person—God.

Lord, now you let your servant go in peace; your word has been fulfilled: my own eyes have seen the salvation which you have prepared in the sight of every people: a light to reveal you to the nations and the glory of your people Israel.

I thought of Sr. Gertrude's little Tony Award acceptance speech when she told us about the single light left shining on the empty stage. From there she found the light of the tabernacle burning in the sanctuary of St. Malachy's Church. Here, there was one before the Sacred Heart of Jesus whom she loved with all her own heart. The vigil light by her bedside flickered and seemed to make the image of the Sacred Heart breathe.

And then it got very silent. Mother stopped in around 10:30 to see how things were, and asked if we needed anything. Without our answering, she said she'd bring us each a cup of chamomile tea, which she did. I thought, it's the little things people do that count so much. I could remember Sr. Gertrude saying to me once, "It's the little scenes that matter; not the show stoppers." That's our life. It's little scenes, one after another, day after day.

I could see Sr. Elijah Rose beginning to nod during the third decade of a second rosary, so I told her she should go to bed; she could stop by here in the morning on her way to Matins. Sr. Maureen, who was assistant infirmarian now and would be here all night, looked in and then made her way to the infirmarian's cell.

It was a little after midnight, and Sr. Gertrude turned her head slightly towards me and opened her eyes. She smiled and whispered, "Sister Mary Baruch?"

"Yes, Sister, I'm here. Do you want some water?" And she nodded her head, so I held the glass down by her mouth, and she drank through a straw. "Are you warm enough, Sister?" I was fussing with her blanket, but she waved "no" with her right hand.

She turned her face to the picture on her bed table with the single candle burning. Only a table lamp was lit in the corner. Sister again turned towards me and had the most serene face I ever saw and such a lovely smile. She said, "Why is this night different from all other nights?"

I couldn't say a word, but recognized the question instantly. And so I kind of muttered, "It's the Passover question…" I don't think Sister even heard me, and a little louder I simply said, "Tonight is your night, Sister Gertrude."

"Tonight is my night," she repeated. "I think this is the final curtain."

I took her hand in mine and said, "I think it is…are you ready to make your curtain call?" She smiled again.

"I've been ready for a long time." And she closed her eyes for a moment then looked at me again. "What time is it, dear?"

"It's almost one o'clock in the morning."

"Oh my, we're late for the midnight office."

"That's right, but we'll make it up a little later. Try to rest now, Sister."

Only a couple minutes went by. She opened her eyes again and looked at me. "Sister Mary Baruch?"

"Yes, Sister, I'm right here."

"Tell the other Sisters I will get a place ready for them; we've got an opening night to get ready for…" and her voice faded, but she squeezed my hand.

"I'll tell them, Sister; but they'll all be by in the morning. You can tell them then." I could feel the silent warm tears roll down my cheek. Sister opened her eyes again and looked at me. "Everything will be just fine…tell them everything will be just fine…" and her voice faded off.

I sat in silence. The words of Compline came back to me: *For you has he commanded his angels, to keep you in all your ways.* And I realized Sr. Gertrude had spoken the words of Eli in my dream: *Everything will be just fine.* Eli our doorman was like our guardian angel, letting us into our home and keeping us safe.

Lost in my thoughts, I think I dozed off for a moment, but woke up quickly when Sr. Gertrude became a little agitated. She was having a difficult time breathing, or so it seemed. I quickly took her hand again. She became very calm and opened her eyes, but this time she wasn't looking at me. She had a beautiful smile, and spoke in a whisper, what sounded to me like "*Mama*". Her eyes opened wide with amazement; she sighed heavily and took her last breath. Her eyes were fixed on something…or Someone. Then she was gone.

I sat and just stared at her. "*Mama*," she said. *Mama*. I knew Our Lady had come for her, to take her to the Lord. She is the *Porta Caeli*, the Gate of Heaven, the "doorman" to Eternal Life.

I looked at my watch…3:33 a.m. I sat there for maybe fifteen minutes, praying, and I kissed her on the forehead and closed her eyes, and made my way to the infirmarian's cell.

Sr. Maureen called Mother who came within a few minutes. The Sisters would be making their way to the chapel for Matins. Before Mother prayed the *O Sacred Banquet,* she announced that "Sister Gertrude of the Sacred Heart has gone home to the Lord."

Without a pause to reflect much, the Office became the Office of the Dead with the beautiful First Antiphon: *From the earth you formed me, with flesh you clothed me; Lord, my Redeemer, raise me up again at the last day.*

There was a stillness in the house all day. It reminded me of the stillness of Holy Saturday. The infirmary Sisters were quiet; there were no cards being played or jigsaw puzzles being worked on; everyone seemed enclosed in their own thoughts.

Sr. Gertrude's final scene was without drama, and it was "played out" here, not in a hospital or nursing home. It was sudden, but not surprising. It was just the way she would have wanted it to be.

And, Lord, I was with her. You gave me that great privilege to be holding her hand and as she would say, to be on stage when the curtain came down. It is a moment I will always cherish.

Twenty-Six

Out of the depths I cry to you, O Lord, Lord, hear my voice!
O let your ears be attentive to the voice of my pleading. (Psalm 130)

IT HAS BEEN quite a time the last few days. We received the body of Sr. Gertrude before Vespers on All Saints' Day, and our Evening Prayer was full of joyous Alleluias. It was hard to believe that this body was eighty-nine years old; her face was smooth without the usual wrinkles. Her rimless glasses were on and her expression wasn't quite real looking, but it was Sr. Gertrude. Last evening before Compline was the public wake and a number of people came to pay their respects. These were mostly lifetime friends of the monastery. Mr. Feldman of Solomon's Deli down the street came with his wife and two daughters. And there was a young mystery woman who came swathed in black, reminding me of Gwendolyn from years ago. She met with Mother in the Prioress's parlor briefly afterward. All we learned about her was that she was an actress and a friend of Sr. Gertrude's. Perhaps she was Mother's connection with getting a Tony Award statuette. Sister's great-nieces and their husbands came briefly last night, but were not here for the funeral this morning.

Her body lay in the middle of choir for Matins and Lauds today, All Souls' Day. The funeral Mass was at three o'clock this afternoon as our dear bishop said he wanted to offer the Mass, but could not come till the afternoon. We sang the Gregorian Requiem Mass, which is really filled with inexpressible beauty and joy. Fr. Matthew preached a moving homily on the single line in the first Preface for the Dead: "Life is not ended, just changed."

The bishop gave a spontaneous eulogy before the final commendation. He told us Sr. Gertrude corresponded with him since he was a young seminarian and was like a spiritual mother to him. He called her "Sister Gert," and had us all near tears when he put his hand on the coffin and spoke to her. "Sister Gert, I shall miss you and pray for you every day, and can only imagine the glory of Eternal Life, as your 'opening night' unlike no other."

Wrapped in our black cappas, we formed the final procession from the chapel to the cemetery out back. I thought of all the times Sr. Gertrude and I and countless other Sisters had sat with her by the picture window looking out on this scene. We have the custom now to chant the Litany of the Saints in Latin as we make our way to the graveside. It's our way of calling on all the Court of Heaven to come and welcome her. There must be so much joy in the crowd there to welcome her, and our own small Communion of Saints along with the big one.

It was a clear crisp afternoon. The sun was low in the sky casting long shadows across the cemetery lawn. The graveside prayers of commendation were prayed by Fr. Matthew who wore our old black cope which I think he brought out of storage…he knew the vestment had to be just right. Sr. Gertrude's plain wooden coffin was lowered into the ground. The bishop, Fr. Matthew, and Mother sprinkled the grave with holy water as we all sang our final *Salve Regina*, as is our Dominican custom.

We would normally process back together into the monastery, but Mother had given the Sisters in the infirmary permission, at their request, to remain graveside while the funeral men filled in the grave, gathered their equipment, and left us alone. I had planned to process in with the novices, but waited and stood with Sr. Gerard and Sr. Bertrand. I knew the Sisters in wheelchairs would appreciate a push back as well. Sr. Anna Maria also stayed back, as did Sr. Maureen. We just wrapped our cappas tighter around us as the sun slowly set behind the clouds. After the grave was completely filled in and the men had left, Sisters Elijah Rose, Leah Marie, Mary Cecilia, Sheila and Pretty Flower made their way back to it, so we were a good little group there gathered. Sr. Mary Cecilia brought back a funeral bouquet of red roses from the chapel and laid it on the grave.

We were standing (and sitting) there in the silence of the graves—each, no doubt, lost in her thoughts remembering Sr. Gertrude. Then Sr. Benedict called us to gather close together as she pulled out a round pitch pipe from under her cappa. "Sister Gertrude, our dear Sister, our dear friend, we shall miss you more than words can say— so, Sister Honeybunch, this is for you." And in lovely soft harmony we sang

Sister's favorite song by Edward Kleban from *A Chorus Line*. My tears flowed silently as we concluded:

> *. . . Won't forget, can't regret*
> *What I did for Love,*
> *What I did for Love,*

The cold November air was still. Only the creak from the old apple tree could be heard. Silence. Then the monastery bell tolled…calling us to Vespers.

